THE ONES WE PROTECT

A Post-Apocalyptic Novel

Kevin Hawkinson

Paperback ISBN: 979-8-234-10482-3

Published by Kevin Hawkinson

First edition 2026

Dedication

For my wife and sweet boys —
the reason to prepare and be ready.

For those who love survival and grid-down stories like me.

And for those who train and prepare quietly.

If the world ever stops, may you be the decent one. The one who stands up when others step back, protects those who cannot protect themselves, and keeps civility alive when the darkness comes.

Dedication

To my wife and sweet [illegible]
the reason to [illegible]

For those who [illegible]

And for those who [illegible]

If the world ever [illegible]

Acknowledgements

First and foremost, thank you to my wife and our boys. You are the reason behind the late nights, early mornings, and more "what if" conversations than most families probably have. Thank you for putting up with my endless lists, storage-room projects, gear experiments, and hobbies that somehow always seem to involve guns, gear, radios, or contingency plans. Your patience, support, and steady presence made this book possible.

To my dad, thank you for everything and for always having my back. Thank you for teaching me how to do things, then letting me learn by doing them myself. You gave me responsibility before I felt ready for it, and more of that found its way into this story than you probably know.

Special thanks to my editor, Maryssa, whose insight and guidance helped strengthen this story.

I'm grateful to God for the discipline to finish what I started and for the family and opportunities He has entrusted to me. I'm truly blessed.

To the early readers who gave honest feedback and weren't afraid to tell me what wasn't working, thank you. Every story gets stronger through refinement, and I'm grateful for your time and candor.

And to those who quietly prepare, think ahead, and take responsibility seriously, this story is for you.

CHAPTER 1
THE SKY

The colors were wrong.

Logan stood on the cold driveway and couldn't look away. Red, orange, and purple smeared together across the sky like sunset, except it was after nine at night.

It was a chilly Friday evening in April, which was already weird enough for Middle Tennessee. But the sky was stranger.

He had heard of the northern lights. Everybody had. But he'd never actually seen them, not this far south, and whatever this was didn't look like the pictures or videos online.

This was different.

Logan tried to make sense of it. He ran through every news story, science lesson, and half-remembered thing his dad had ever said that might explain why the night sky suddenly looked broken.

Behind him, the front door burst open.

Fast little footsteps slapped across the entryway. Logan didn't even have to turn around.

It was Charlie, his little sidekick. The youngest of the three brothers and every bit of four years old.

"What are you doing, Lo Lo?" Charlie yelled. "You've been out here for like ever!"

Logan glanced back at him, standing on the porch in pajamas, bare feet, and absolutely no concern for the cold.

"Just looking at this crazy sky," Logan said.

Then, in his sweetest little brother voice, the one he had somehow mastered before kindergarten, he asked, "Why is it all different colors like that?"

Logan looked back up.

"Well, bud, I was just trying to figure that out."

Charlie looked serious for a second, then nodded.

"Well, when you do, let me know. I'll be playing checkers with Tripp," Charlie yelled, then spun around and ran back inside, leaving the front door wide open behind him.

Logan laughed under his breath.

Yep. Definitely didn't shut the door.

Because—Charlie.

He pulled the door closed and looked back at the sky one more time.

The only thing that made any sense was the solar flare stuff everyone had been talking about all week. The news wouldn't shut up about it. His dad had mentioned it too, though in that calm, trying-not-to-sound-too-interested way he used whenever Mom was close enough to hear him.

They kept calling it a coronal mass something. Logan remembered the acronym, though.

"CME," he said quietly.

From inside the house came the sound of Tripp yelling about an illegal double jump, followed by Charlie yelling back that it was not illegal because he made the rules.

Then Tripp yelled something about a backward move.

Nope. Apparently, it was both.

Logan smiled and went back inside.

His parents were standing between the sink and dishwasher, finishing up the cleanup from dinner. It had been another healthy meal with a bunch of vegetables and other stuff Logan hated.

He always seemed to find a way to disappear around cleanup time to avoid kid duties, which was how he found himself outside staring into the sky.

Conveniently disappearing was probably one of his superpowers, along with building block mansions, video game battles, and procrastination.

Standing there watching his parents laugh and flirt gave Logan the icks. He loved them fiercely, but they were lovey-dovey all the dang time. Still, he figured at least they were happy together. Several of his friends couldn't say the same about their parents, so he found ways to overlook the all-too-often PDA.

He had always looked up to his dad. They had been inseparable for as long as Logan could remember. Even when Tripp came along, and most recently Charlie, Dad had always found time for him.

His dad had grown up in Mississippi — some small town three hours south — and his mom had gone to the same school. High school sweethearts together for twenty-five years, three kids, and a mortgage. The walking cliché. Annoying in the best way.

As David placed the last plate in the dishwasher, he told the boys to get ready for bed.

"It's late, guys, and you know Mom and Dad have to go to Dallas tomorrow, right?"

Tripp piped up, asking, "Why are you guys going again?"

Nicole grabbed up Tripp, the middle child, and pulled him against her. "Well, tater tot, it's a parents' trip for the weekend, and we're going to see this huge boy band from the late nineties and early 2000s."

This prompted a quick look from Dad to Logan, accompanied by an eye roll.

Charlie, even at four, had laser-like observation skills.

"Dad, why did you look like that at Logan and move your eyes up?"

Nicole snapped around. "Yeah, why did your eyes do that, Dad?"

"I plead the Fifth," Dad said, quickly changing the subject. "Alright, hop to it, guys. Wash your faces, brush your teeth, and get into bed."

The three boys raced upstairs, knocking and pushing each other the whole way. Somehow, it always seemed to be Logan and Charlie versus Tripp in these mini competitions.

Behind them, Mom called out, "Why is everything a race with these boys?"

"Well, they're boys, that's how we roll," Dad said.

Logan was halfway down the hall when he heard Dad add, "Come on, I'll race you packing our bags. First one finished doesn't have to fold the laundry in the dryer."

Logan smiled to himself. Of course Dad would turn that into a race too.

A little while later, their parents came upstairs for the official tuck-in routine. Charlie was first, mostly because if he wasn't, he'd yell questions from his room until somebody came in.

From his own room, Logan could hear pieces of it down the hall. Charlie's room was really more of a locker room, at least according to Charlie. Sports stuff covered almost everything. Balls, jerseys, helmets, random plastic bats—whatever he had collected or refused to throw away. NFL jerseys were his favorite.

Usually, turning off Charlie's TV involved at least one argument, some crying, and some form of negotiation. Tonight, there was barely anything. That surprised Logan.

Tripp was next.

From his room, Logan heard his parents move down the hall and stop at Tripp's door. Tripp was the easygoing, carefree kid of the house. Somehow, being stuck right between Logan and Charlie had not ruined him yet. Eight years old meant he was too old for Charlie's little-kid stuff and too young for most of the things Logan got to do, but Tripp didn't seem to care much.

Logan heard Tripp laugh, probably flashing that big Cheshire-cat smile with the missing bottom tooth.

"When we get back, we need to cut this mop, boy," Dad said.

Logan could picture him rubbing Tripp's messy blond hair, the way he always did when it got long enough to hang over his ears.

"We most certainly will not be cutting it," Mom said.

Logan smiled. He didn't have to see her face to know Dad had just gotten one of those looks.

"Well," Dad said, backing down, "it needs it."

Tripp said something about liking it long and how it was his style.

"Fair enough, my man," Dad said.

A few seconds later, Mom's voice softened. "Night-night, bud."

Then their footsteps moved toward Logan's room.

As his parents came into his room, he turned off whatever online gaming streamer was popular that day.

"Becca getting here early?" Logan asked.

"After breakfast," Mom said. "So don't act like you're in charge just because we're gone."

Logan gave her a look. "I wasn't going to."

Dad laughed. "That means he definitely was."

Looking up, Logan asked, "Did you guys see the lights and colors in the sky tonight?"

"No," they answered in unison.

"We were getting ready for the trip, making dinner, and trying to keep your brothers from beating each other up all night," Mom said.

"What about it?" Dad asked.

"Well, I've never seen anything like it," Logan responded. "It was the craziest colors I've ever seen in the sky, especially at night. I don't know what it is, but I'm afraid it has something to do with that solar flare stuff everyone keeps talking about. Do you think that's a real thing we should be worried about?"

His mom quickly responded, "It's certainly not anything you need to worry about, baby boy. Get some rest and let us worry about the grown-up stuff."

"I don't think it's anything to worry about, man," Dad added. "They've been talking about these things more and more lately. You know what, if it is something bad, you know we have a plan for that, right?"

"Oh, Dad, stop with the prepper stuff," Nicole said. "You sound like one of those tin-foil-hat-wearing conspiracy people."

As Nicole kissed Logan goodnight, David muttered to nobody in particular, "It's better to be prepared and not need it than to need it and not be prepared."

David gave Logan one of those tough-guy hugs and followed Nicole out, mentioning something about her folding laundry.

Logan wasn't sure why, but the way his parents answered felt a little too quick.

Like they were trying to make him feel better.

He stared at the ceiling for a while after they left, listening to the house settle around him. Tripp laughed once from down the hall. Charlie called out for someone to bring him water.

The normal bedtime sounds.

Logan told himself his parents were probably right. It was probably nothing. Some science thing adults would explain on the news tomorrow and then forget about by Monday.

Still, when he closed his eyes, he could see the colors again.

Red. Orange. Purple and blue.

Glowing quietly over everything.

CHAPTER 2
SEE YOU SOON

Saturday morning, Logan awoke from a dream where he was leading his squad to a victory. It was the final circle, with buildings everywhere. An intense battle—but apparently the parentals had other plans. They were banging pans, setting the oven timer, which had the most obnoxious beep with every button push, along with stomping around downstairs.

He sleepily made his way downstairs, subsequently smelling the early hint of cinnamon rolls. Cinnamon rolls were a huge hit in the Hopkins household. At least they didn't wake him up for nothing...

Nicole smiled. "Hey, kiddo, good morning."

"Hey, dude," David added. "How was your sleep?"

Logan responded, "Well, it was great until I was rudely woken up from my battle, which I was most certainly going to win."

"Well, I would hate for you to miss game time even when you're sleeping, my guy," David rebutted sarcastically.

To Logan, game and screen time were always a hot topic in the Hopkins household. His parents were a bit old school in that sense. It must have had something to do with them growing up in the middle of nowhere, probably chasing goats and chickens for fun. They always wanted him outside "doing something productive," which, to him, meant anything without a screen. It was a balancing act. After all, how would he become a professional streamer without putting in the hours?

Right on cue, Tripp and Charlie came wobbling down the stairs. Midway down, they realized they were even, so naturally, the race was on.

Mom yelled, "No racing on the stairs, guys!" Then, looking at David, she added, "See? This is what I was talking about."

"Don't look at me, they're yours too," David rebuked.

Charlie jumped into Logan's lap and gave him a giant brotherly hug.

"I smell cinnamon rolls!" Tripp announced, hugging both parents long and hard.

"Good morning, all my munchkins," Mom gushed. "Great having my boys up to spend some time together before Dad and I leave for Dallas."

For a moment, nothing felt urgent. Mom was smiling, Dad was joking, and the kitchen smelled like cinnamon. It felt familiar. Reassuring.

The calm broke with a soft chirp from the alarm system as a door sensor opened and closed. Logan glanced toward the hallway, reminded, again, that his dad seemed to have a sensor or camera on just about everything.

Tripp immediately ran at full speed toward the side door of the house. Hot on his heels, Charlie was already yelling, "Ms. Bee! Ms. Bee!"

Logan saw Ms. Becca round the corner from the mudroom. Hilariously, she was carrying Charlie upside down, with Tripp on her back.

David turned to Nicole. "I wish they loved us as much as Becca, geez."

"I know, right?" Nicole shot back.

Smiling at Becca, he said, "Good morning!"

Repeatedly, he'd heard from his parents that Becca was a Hopkins family staple, sort of like the cinnamon rolls. Probably just as sweet, too. Four years ago, Mom and Dad had told Logan that three kids were too much for two full-time working parents without a bit of help. They got lucky with Ms. Becca on the first try. She had been with Charlie since he was an infant. Logan bet that Charlie didn't know that every family didn't have a Ms. Becca. Tripp was essentially in the same boat. Logan loved and respected her, but at the end of the day, she was another authority figure telling him what to do, which was annoying. After all, she was only like sixteen years older than him.

It was hard not to laugh at how easily Becca carried his brothers. She was nearly six feet tall, almost as tall as Dad, and surprisingly capable given her wiry frame. Making a quick mental connection, it seemed as though the Hopkins household had a requirement that everyone be blond, except Dad. Ms. Becca was no different, although Logan wondered if it was real blond or not.

Becca came in, saying hello to everyone.

David and Nicole smiled and exclaimed almost in unison, "Good morning, Becca."

Logan grimaced. They said the same things at almost the same time way too often. It was honestly annoying. The icks started to creep in again.

"Hopefully the traffic wasn't too awful this morning," Nicole said.

"Luckily not," Becca said, smiling back. "After all, it is early on a Saturday morning, though Nashville seems to get worse by the day."

Dad took his chance to expand on an earlier conversation where he kept advising that Becca should get out of Nashville sooner rather than later. "It's crazy up there, and it would be more dangerous, especially if there was ever a serious emergency."

Between Mom and Becca, a look passed. He'd seen it before.

"Dad, that tin-foil hat is showing again," Logan said, smirking.

David bristled. "Well, fine then. Nobody wants to listen to the one who's read like fifty books on that stuff or studied how scary disasters could impact us. No, I'm just crazy, I suppose." He gave a thin smile as he walked past the family, saying, "If you need me, I'll be finishing up our packing."

Trying to earn some brownie points, he yelled down the hall in support. "Well, I appreciate all the things you've tried to teach me over the years, Dad. Even if I can't remember most of it and we won't need it."

Still, he thought about the time Dad had tried to explain CMEs and this kind of stuff before. He hadn't paid much attention then.

Mom looked at Becca. "He gets sensitive about his hobbies. He's not crazy... I think." They both giggled.

Nicole asked Becca to take over breakfast for the boys and headed off to help with the final packing and logistics for the trip.

Looking at Becca, Charlie asked, "Ms. Bee, did you see the sky last night? It was super cool. It was all different colors. Lo Lo and me saw it when we were out there."

"No, I didn't, little man," Becca said. "But I did see some pictures on the news this morning, and they were reporting all about it. They mentioned that solar flare thing again."

Tripp curiously asked, "What's a solar flare, Ms. Bee?"

Never one to resist showing off a bit, Logan drew on some of Dad's shared knowledge. "It's a quick burst of energy from the sun that travels toward Earth. Generally, they don't cause issues, but if they were big enough, they could mess up our electronics, and most importantly, our Wi-Fi!"

Charlie interjected in his still-sleepy voice, "WE live on Earth, don't we?"

Tripp's second-grade education came to the rescue. "Yep, we sure do. It's our planet, and we're the third closest to the sun," he said, proud of himself.

"Great job, boys," Becca encouraged, adding, "The news people also mentioned something about a CME, which apparently stands for coronal mass ejection. They said that was a different thing altogether, so who knows. I'm kind of tired of hearing about these things, though."

Logan looked back at the TV. He didn't say anything.

Logan grabbed the remote, something he was an expert at manipulating. He flipped to the local Nashville news station, turning the volume up in hopes of hearing something reassuring. Meanwhile, Becca and Tripp returned from the food storage room with Goldfish and Cheez-Its to supplement the "two cinnamon rolls only" rule enforced by Mom. Allegedly, they had way too much sugar and weren't actually healthy for you.

Charlie was at the table, hard at work scribbling his letters and numbers, which he was particularly proud of.

Seeing the news station on TV, Becca asked, "Oh, you have it on. What are they saying now?"

Just then, the lead anchor said in the background, "What we do know is last night's rare lighting event was the result of what scientists at the Space Weather Prediction Center are calling a large coronal mass ejection, commonly abbreviated as a CME."

The anchor continued in a formal, professional tone. "Per the SWPC, it's not exactly known just how big the CME actually was, or what that means, if anything, for our viewing area and beyond. The SWPC shared that, frequently, these happen with no impact to Earth, as we've seen over the last few months with increased solar activity."

"Our team here at WNAH Nashville reached out to officials at NASA and the National Solar Observatory for further clarification. Responses from both institutions were similar. They advised that there was a measurable event that occurred late Friday. What we were seeing last night was Earth's atmosphere glowing as a massive cloud of charged particles and magnetic fields from the sun interacted with our planet's magnetic shield, called the magnetosphere."

Tripp interrupted the broadcast. "What in the world does all of that mean, Bee?"

"Well, I don't really know, bud," Becca responded, "but it doesn't sound too scary, besides all the science-y talk. They said this should be sort of like the last few, when nothing really happened."

The broadcast concluded with the anchor advising, "Per the various agencies and institutions we've been in contact with, there is no immediate concern, and we won't know just how intense the

CME is for a couple of days, as it's slow-moving, unlike a true solar flare."

Logan turned the volume down and set the remote on the couch. Why did Mom and Dad have to be leaving at the exact same time as this CME thing?

Searching for reassurance, Logan slinked to his parents' room. He passed Mom folding the final pieces of clothing and headed toward Dad, who was in the closet organizing a bag for the trip.

"What's that, Dad?"

"One of my go-bags, actually," David said. "I'm cleaning out a bit of stuff and organizing it for our flight. Unfortunately, I can't bring along some of the key items I'd love to have for the trip."

"Like what?" Logan asked.

"Well, when you fly on a plane, you definitely can't carry a gun or ammo, it's illegal, so those have to go," Dad said, showing Logan his Walther 9mm. "I also have to pull my extra magazines, multi-tool, and this super-sweet Benchmade Bugout knife." Dad lifted it into the light, letting Logan feel its heft and flip the blade out. "Careful, dude, that blade will shave your arm and take your pinky off," he joked.

"This stuff is cool. What else do you have in there, and what exactly is a bug-out bag again?" Logan asked.

Zipping everything back up, David took a second to explain. "This is a bag from a company called Eberlestock. It's meant to be super organized and carry essential gear in an emergency. You've seen similar bags in my truck and Mom's SUV, right?"

Logan nodded.

"The point of a bug-out bag is to put the absolute minimum key equipment in an easy-to-grab space for quick reactions to emergencies," Dad added.

"What kind of stuff?" Logan asked, feeling the bag.

"Generally, most folks include basic medical supplies, fire-starting materials, food, water, and water-purification systems," Dad said. "That covers basic life needs. Then you get into safety and convenience items. Things like a pop-up tent, lighting, a compass, and some form of communication. Usually a walkie-talkie, or in our case, a handheld ham radio. And last but not least, protection!"

Logan decided now was not the time to ask about the ham radio. He didn't want to send Dad down another rabbit hole, especially with a flight to catch.

Looking around the large closet, Logan said, "That's a lot of stuff, Dad." He talked about it all the time and frequently showed Logan some of the cooler items. Like most teens, Logan usually wasn't paying attention and dismissed it. Now, though, he found himself intrigued.

In the corner stood a large gray safe with a digital number lock.

"What's all in there, Dad?" Logan asked, pointing.

"That's where I keep all our guns, ammo, and some other cool gear. I'll have to show you when I get back, if you're interested. Maybe you'll take me up on those range days I've been begging you to come out for," David added inquisitively.

"Sounds like a plan," Logan replied with a bit more interest than usual.

David grabbed his slimmed-down bag, and they both headed back toward Nicole, who was zipping up the carry-on.

She exhaled quickly. "Good to know we're giving up carry-on space for that junk, Mr. Boy Scout."

"At least this stuff can help us, unlike four more pairs of shoes for a weekend trip, MOM," David shot back, emphasizing the last word.

Remembering why he'd come in, Logan said, "So we were all watching the news. They're saying the weird sky last night was because of something called a CME."

A quick glance shot between Mom and Dad. He caught it. "Is this something we should be worried about? And should you guys really be going on a trip right now?"

"Well," David said softly, "your mom and I just had this same conversation. We saw the same information earlier this morning. Right now, they don't think it's anything too crazy, and it should have minimal impact, if any. It could even take a few days to get here. So, we decided it should be safe to go."

Mom nodded, though her smile came a second late.

"It's such an important trip for your mom," Dad continued. "I'd hate to cancel on a big what-if, even if it goes against my 'safe rather than sorry' rule this time. She's been wanting to see this band since she was, like, fourteen."

Mom took a breath, deeper than usual. "Lo, you guys will be safe here. You have Becca, TV, internet, and, God forbid, enough food to feed the town for a month, thanks to your paranoid father. We'll only be gone for two nights and back on Monday around lunch."

Logan offered a smile and pulled them both into a hug.

The trio grabbed their bags and headed toward what sounded like Ms. Becca actively refereeing yet another sibling argument over who got to watch TV first.

Becca had come up with a solution: rock-paper-scissors, best of three. Unfortunately for Charlie, Tripp had learned his move. Nine times out of ten, Charlie went with rock, because why not? Rock was big and tough and should always win, right? Tripp won handily, with Charlie never being the wiser.

Predictably, Tripp teased his younger brother and snatched the remote, claiming the spoils of battle.

Of course, it was predictable and annoying that his middle brother immediately turned on his favorite show. Some show about a kid Tripp's age opening toys, cars, and monster trucks and racing them around. The kid's voice grated on Logan almost immediately. He gave it a minute, maybe two, before deciding he'd retreat to his room the second the parentals pulled out of the driveway.

"Becca, it looks like you've got everything handled here," Nicole said confidently.

"Yes, ma'am," Becca replied. "Anything special I should know for this weekend?"

"Nothing too special," Nicole said. "We just want you guys to have fun." She shot a hard glance at the younger boys. "And you boys better be good for Becca or no screen time or games for a week!"

"Oh no," Dad added sarcastically. "You mean they'd have to go outside and entertain themselves? A real travesty."

Logan rubbed his forehead. It was cringe how predictable Dad was at this point.

Simultaneously, the two younger Hopkins boys replied with long, slightly annoyed, "Yes, ma'am..."

"Well, Becca, there's plenty of food in the fridge, pantry, and storage room," Nicole added. "Feel free to order in if you want."

David hugged Logan goodbye. Logan squeezed him a little tighter and whispered, "Keep us updated on the sun stuff, please."

"Will do, bud," Dad said, squeezing back. He lowered his voice to match Logan's whisper, "You're the man of the house while I'm gone. Take care of your brothers."

"Just in case, you remember the plan, right?"

"I do, Dad...I think," Logan nervously replied. "Let's not talk about that, though."

"Well, you know what I always say—"

"It's better to be prepared and not need it than to need it and not be prepared," Logan recited flatly. "Got it."

Dad smiled proudly. Maybe some things had stuck.

The other boys rushed over, hugging Mom and then Dad. Tripp grew teary-eyed at the thought of them being gone. He was the sensitive one.

After lingering hugs all around, Mom headed out first, followed by Dad. Logan heard David ask Becca to keep an eye on the news and weather, just in case. If there was a problem, they'd fly back from Dallas immediately.

Through the side garage door, his old man walked out and hopped into the gray SUV with Mom.

As they backed down the driveway, the three Hopkins boys raced to the front door with its rectangular windows, waving and blowing kisses as the SUV turned and drove away. At the door, he stayed a moment longer than his brothers.

CHAPTER 3

ALL GOOD ON THE HOMEFRONT

This particular Saturday didn't feel special.

After the departure of Mom and Dad, the squad pushed down the lingering anxiety and settled into the usual rhythm of a lazy Saturday.

By midday, the house was organized chaos. There were doors opening and mostly slamming, someone running around upstairs, Becca moving between rooms calling out reminders. Shoes. Sunscreen. Water bottles. Breaking up squabbles. The same stuff she always did, just without Mom or Dad in the background.

Logan joked with the younger Hopkins duo, "I bet Dad is watching you guys on the cameras right now." The boys looked at each other. They backed down.

Becca flashed a smile his way, slowly mouthing, *Well played.*

Logan stayed close, grabbing what she asked for and stepping in when one of his brothers started pushing limits. He made himself useful.

They drifted toward half-plans for the afternoon, nothing locked in yet. Logan checked the time out of habit and did a quick headcount before heading outside.

They set out on an easy suburban trek through the neighborhood toward the park just across the street. It was about half a mile or so. "Enough time to get the juices flowing," Becca joked.

Logan glanced around at the houses, all of them packed together. Nothing like his family's place back in Mississippi.

He recalled several conversations over the years between his mom and dad. They always said things used to be slower. Simpler. Friendlier.

Glancing around a second time. It's not so bad here.

After passing four or five houses, the foursome bumped into Mr. Ira and Mrs. Rose. Newer to the neighborhood and recently retired, they were always outside working on something. Logan wasn't sure how old they were, but they were definitely older than most of the other adults nearby. He guessed late sixties.

Thinking back, Dad and Ira had hit it off instantly. Logan couldn't remember exactly which, but Ira had been in the military or government or something. He looked it, too—sharp jawline, focused eyes, and an aura of unexplained confidence.

Frustratingly, he and Dad would talk forever about guns, gear, supplies, and the happenings around the world.

Mrs. Rose was a short but sturdy soul and was the first to acknowledge the Hopkins crew...plus one.

"Hi, boys! How are you young gentlemen today?"

"Hey, Mrs. Rose and Mr. Ira," Charlie said sweetly, smiling. "We're going to the park to play on the slides and swings."

"That sounds fun," Ira replied, looking over to Tripp. "How about you, monkey man? You going to hit the monkey bars?"

Tripp laughed at the nickname. "You know it, dude!"

"Great seeing everyone," Ira added. "You guys and gal have fun." He looked at Logan. "Your dad mentioned they'd be out of town for the weekend. If you need anything at all, you know we're a few doors down, okay?"

Logan nodded. "Thanks. Will do."

"Thank you, sir," Becca added.

Before they made it to the park, the sidewalks were dotted with people out enjoying the weather. It was another nice April day, and the neighborhood seemed awash with activity, like everyone had been stuck inside for too long and finally got loose.

At the park, Logan had fun with his brothers. Even with the age gaps, he enjoyed the healthy sibling rivalries. The younger two could be annoying at times, but they could also be fun.

After exhausting the playground, the boys looked for new ways to burn off energy. The big green space at the park did the rest. They played two-hand-touch football that nobody enforced, tackle that nobody actually agreed to, and somehow a lawless soccer game at the end of it all.

"Lo, can you watch your brothers while I go check in with your parents, please?" Becca asked.

"Sure thing, Bee," Logan replied nonchalantly.

Becca walked over to the bleachers by the baseball field. Just within earshot, Logan half-listened to her conversation while keeping an eye on the boys.

Oddly, the conversation sounded disjointed. Becca talked for a bit, redialed, and then talked some more.

Logan noticed the way she scowled at her phone. This happened a few times before she returned. "Well, I gather they landed and made it to the hotel. They must not have good cell service or something—the call kept dropping. At least we know they made it safely. They asked about you guys and told us to have fun."

With a dismissive wave of thought, Becca added, "Let's get you guys home and figure out dinner plans."

Logan nodded. "Sounds good to me. Let's roll."

Gathering everyone and everything up, they headed back toward the house. The neighborhood was still alive with people squeezing the last bit of daylight out of the day. It was later in the evening by the time they got home.

As they crossed the little neighborhood creek bridge, Logan smiled at nothing in particular. It had been one of those days that felt easy, like something had forgotten to go wrong.

A small emptiness tugged at him. Mom and Dad should be here. He glanced back at his brothers, and just like that, the moment passed. The house came into view at the end of the street.

Arriving back home, Becca said, "Hey, let's turn the news on. Just to check what's happening."

She was overruled by Charlie. With as much authority as a four-year-old could muster, he declared, "It's my turn to watch TV, Bee! Remember?"

With a smirk, Becca let Charlie pick the show. He landed on one of his heavy-rotation favorites. Logan recognized it immediately and giggled. It was a sneaky-good show about a cute dog family navigating life with two young kids. Logan wouldn't admit it, but he liked it—and the irony of the show wasn't lost on him. The humor also punched above its weight. It was bearable.

Becca clanged pots and pans in the background. "Want to help with dinner, Lo?"

Logan paused. "Umm...sure, I guess. I really need to get some game time in, though."

"Come on!" Becca laughed. "I could use the help, and you could definitely work on your cooking skills."

Logan glanced upstairs toward his computer. Defeated, he replied, "Fiiine."

Becca and Logan worked well together. Logan cooked hot dogs on the kitchen griddle while Becca boiled water for mac and cheese. She slid a long rectangular pan into the oven, neatly arranged with dino nuggets.

Logan joked, "What a feast we have here. This should fix us kids up, but what are you going to eat, Bee?"

Becca looked confused. "What do you mean?"

"Like...what are you going to eat? I figured you'd eat something healthy. Salad or vegetables or something," Logan shot back.

Looking very serious, Becca threw up a peace sign. "Nope. I'm down with dino nuggets and mac and cheese, bro. Who needs all that color in their diet, anyway?"

They both burst into belly laughter. Logan grabbed the counter to keep from falling over. "Okay, IceBee..." Between the two of them, somehow, dinner actually got finished.

Dinner went well, and all three boys were happy. Logan noticed the two younger ones completely finished their plates. Even Tripp had seconds—and he never ate much to begin with. Logan figured it had something to do with not being pressured to eat vegetables and organic crap. Maybe there were some benefits to the parentals being gone for a couple days.

Settling onto the couch, Logan finally got a chance to watch his favorite streamer playing his favorite battle royale. He watched intently, trying to pick up new skills to apply to his own gaming prowess.

Glancing over, Tripp was right beside Becca at the sink, handing her plates with a big smile. Logan left them to it. Charlie had already passed out on Mom's giant fleece blanket near the end of the couch.

A few minutes into his streaming bliss, the TV flashed an error. A circle spun in the middle of the screen. Buffering.

"No. No. No. No. Seriously? I just sat down. Come on, man!"

Becca looked over from the cabinet where she was putting plates away. "What's wrong, Lo?"

Not looking back, Logan snapped, "The dumb TV isn't working. Or the app. Or the internet. Or something."

"Did you try restarting the app and the streaming box?" Becca asked.

Annoyed now, Logan clapped back. "Yes and yes. Nothing seems to work. It's like the internet is just down."

Trying to help, Tripp ran into the laundry room to check the modem and router lights, yelling back, "Everything's lit up like it always is. The green light's on."

Defeated, Logan sighed. "I guess the connection's just down or something. I'll call Dad and see if he has any ideas."

It was getting late, and frustration was building. He didn't want to wait until morning to solve this. He picked up his phone, tapped Favorites, and dialed Dad.

To his relief, Dad answered on the second ring.

Logan jumped straight into explaining the problem and the troubleshooting steps they'd already tried.

On the other end, Dad suggested unplugging the modem and router for thirty seconds, then plugging them back in.

He gave Logan a quick update on the trip and asked about the park and dinner. Logan switched to speaker so Mom and Dad could both say goodnight.

"Night-night," Tripp added.

"Good night, guys," Logan said.

The boys blew air kisses toward the phone, then Logan hit the red end button.

"It's late, and it's time for bed," Becca said. "We can fix the router in the morning. Deal?"

Logan reluctantly agreed. It had been a long day. They collectively decided to let Charlie sleep on the couch. Nobody was waking that kid. Becca did one last check on everyone, checked the doors, and headed toward the guest room.

Just before drifting off, Logan stared at the ceiling longer than he meant to, replaying the router problem in his head, trying to solve it. The dots weren't connecting as he faded to sleep.

Blinking a few times, Logan had to regain his bearings. Rubbing his eyes, he realized it was daylight. For a moment, he didn't know where he was. That almost never happened.

He could hear the crew downstairs already.

Swinging his legs over the side of the bed, the first few steps were shaky. Still impressed. Why can't I sleep like that all the time?

He found an empty spot at the table and pulled up a chair next to Tripp, who was engrossed in his Pokémon cards.

With a dry voice, Logan croaked, "Bee, did the internet come back on?"

Scrambling eggs and loading slices of bread into the toaster, she glanced over her shoulder. "Unfortunately not. It's still o—"

EVERYTHING stopped.

The house went quiet, except for the faint sizzle of eggs in the pan.

Nobody moved. Nobody spoke. Becca slowly set down the spatula.

CHAPTER 4
THE QUIET AFTER

Logan's first thought was Dad. His second was the CME. There was a growing unease in his belly.

Sunlight spilled through the windows like nothing had changed, striping the kitchen floor. Logan noticed it first because the house felt wrong. No low hum from the refrigerator. No click from the thermostat. No TV blaring in the family room.

Becca stood at the counter, an overly concerned look growing on her face. "Okay," she said, nodding to herself. "Probably the whole neighborhood." She said it matter-of-factly.

Logan just started moving, doing the things Dad always did first. At the breaker panel, he flipped the main off, counted silently, then flipped it back on.

Nothing.

"That's weird," Becca said, not alarmed, just puzzled. She walked to the fridge and opened it, then closed it again, as if it might yield a different result. "Power's out, but...like, everything is out."

Logan knew what she meant. Usually, something still worked. A porch light. Blinking clocks. Nothing worked, not even some of the battery-powered stuff.

Becca found her phone on the kitchen table, tapping it repeatedly. Nothing happened. "Normally the screen comes on when I tap it or hit the unlock button," she said to the room. Then she frowned at Logan. "Check yours."

Logan ran upstairs to his bedroom. His phone was still plugged in on the nightstand. He tugged the cord free and tried every button. "I've got nothing," he yelled down.

When he came back downstairs, he joined the rest of the household. The concern had settled in on everyone now. Mom and Dad were six hundred miles away, with no way to communicate. The boys were already growing restless. No TV. No tablets. No arguing over what to watch, just a quiet that quickly turned into boredom.

Outside, the neighborhood felt muted. No garage doors lifting. No cars starting. No distant hum of traffic. Even the air felt different, heavy and still, like the world was holding its breath. The sky was full of color again. Reds, oranges, and purples streaked across it.

"It'll be back," Becca said, more to herself than anyone else. "This happens." It did happen. Storms knocked lines down. Transformers blew. Sometimes there was a disconnect because of construction or repairs. There was always an explanation.

Logan stepped onto the porch. A few doors down, Mr. Ira stood in his driveway, arms crossed, jaw set, staring at his truck with the hood up.

"You guys out too?" Logan shouted.

Mr. Ira looked up and shook his head once. "Yeah, and the truck's dead. Rose says the radio in the kitchen's the only thing making noise."

That should've helped. For some reason, it only added to the confusion. Why did it work?

When Logan came back inside, he relayed what Ira had said. Becca kneeled by the pantry and pulled out the emergency weather radio, the bulky, old-looking one Dad had insisted on. It was battery-powered, with a hand crank for backup. Old-school. No screen. Just a speaker and a dial. She cranked it a few times, then turned it on.

Static filled the kitchen. An announcement blurted out, loud and sudden enough that everyone jumped. Cutting through the static was that semi-familiar, official, robotic voice.

"--repeat--widespread grid failure--remain calm--do not attempt travel--"

The signal dissolved back into static, coming and going like a wave, almost like a pulse. Becca froze, one hand still on the dial.

"Grid failure?" Logan said quietly.

"That doesn't make sense," she replied too quickly. "That's...that's just power."

The radio crackled again. "--communications disrupted--unknown duration--this is a civil emergency--" It ended with that eerie Berrrrrrrp--Berrrrrrrp--Berrrrrrrp--Berrp, then silence again.

No hum. No power. No electronics. The house felt unplugged from the world.

As a final test, Logan suggested they try starting Dad's truck. Becca agreed, grabbing the key fob from the hook by the garage door. With the Hopkins crew in tow, everyone waited nervously.

Becca stepped on the brake of the silver pickup, whispered a quick prayer, and pressed the red start button.

There was Nothing. No click. No lights and no movement.

Becca dropped her head to the steering wheel.

That was the moment the rules changed.

Power could fail. Phones could die. But cars and engines didn't just stop. Dad had always talked about systems, how everything leaned on everything else.

Back in the dining area, Logan stared at the dark kitchen, the quiet street beyond the windows, the radio sitting uselessly between them.

This didn't feel like something that was coming back.

By early afternoon, hours had passed. The younger boys kept asking for screens. For TV. They tried Monopoly. No one finished setting it up. The dice sat untouched. Cards and money lay scattered across the table. No one cared enough to organize it.

Logan couldn't do it. He needed to move. "I'm going to explore a bit, see what everyone's saying," he told them.

When he stepped outside again, his nose caught something unusual, the smell of barbecue grills. It lingered through the neighborhood. He found it strange, given it was still early afternoon. Connecting the dots, Logan figured neighbors were cooking food before it spoiled. Especially those without gas stoves. That's why Dad always insisted on gas, he thought.

Another thing struck him, the steady hum of small gas engines nearby. As he walked toward Mr. Ira's house, one of the sounds grew louder. Rounding into the driveway, he saw it: a large gas generator running beside the garage. Ira was tinkering with something inside. When he noticed Logan, he walked over, escaping the generator's roar. The exhaust hit Logan's nose as Ira got closer.

"Mr. Ira, do you know what's going on?" Logan asked. "Have you heard anything? We're kind of freaking out."

"Hey, son," Ira said, forcing a smile. "You guys doing alright?"

"We're okay," Logan said. "Just nervous."

"I'm sorry you kids are dealing with this, especially with your parents out of town," Ira said. "I don't know exactly what's going on. I heard the announcement from the National Emergency Service earlier. Did you guys hear it?"

Logan nodded.

"Other than that, it's speculation," Ira continued. "There was solar activity. Maybe something to do with that CME they'd been tracking. Slim chance, but a chance." Shaking his head, Ira added, "I'm trying to get my ham radio up and running. See if I can reach some old friends around the country. Maybe they've heard something."

"Will you let us know if you hear anything?" Logan asked. "Please."

"Absolutely," Ira said, patting him hard on the shoulder.

On the walk home, Logan made another unsettling realization. He hadn't seen or heard a single airplane all day. Planes were constant here. The neighborhood sat right under the approach path to Nashville International.

When he got home, Logan went straight to the garage. Under one of the storage racks sat Dad's generator, right where it was supposed to be. Big red and black. A bold 5000 stenciled on the side. It had wheels, thankfully. Dragging it into the driveway took effort. It was heavy. Logan went back for a gas jug. Dad never left fuel sitting in engines. Something about gumming things up. The instructions were still taped to the side.

A few pulls later, the generator coughed, then came to life in a puff of dark smoke. For a moment, it felt like a win.

Why do generators work? Logan wondered.

The younger boys ran outside, drawn by the noise. Holding up a bright orange extension cord, Logan yelled, "At least we have power now!"

Becca grinned and bumped his fist. "Good thinking. Finally some good news."

"Wow, that thing's loud!" Charlie yelled.

With spirits lifted, Becca said, "Let's go inside, boys. We'll plug a few things in and try to get some normal back." They ran the cord through the side window. First priority was the refrigerator. It had been without power for hours, but Becca hoped most of the food was still okay. Next came the freezer, packed with ground beef, roasts, and the steaks Dad had been saving for Tripp's birthday. Finally, Logan plugged in a lamp from his nightstand.

Light filled the room. The boys gathered around it like moths.

The house wasn't normal again. It was pretending.

As the afternoon wore on, Charlie and Tripp kept asking about Mom and Dad. When they could talk to them. When they'd be home. Becca and Logan deflected, redirected, reassured, trying not to scare them. But the questions stuck with Logan, too. Each one made the weight heavier. He pushed it down and kept moving.

As they started talking about dinner, the forgotten emergency radio chirped to life.

Berrrrrrrp--Berrrrrrrp--Berrrrrrrp--Berrp.

The sound alone unsettled the house. Static faded into a calm, practiced, unmistakably official voice.

"This is an emergency announcement from state and federal authorities."

A pause.

"We are aware of widespread disruptions affecting power, transportation, and communications across multiple regions. At this time, restoration timelines are unknown."

Becca's hand tightened on the radio. She locked eyes with Logan.

"Citizens are advised to remain where they are, avoid unnecessary travel, and conserve all available resources. Emergency services may be delayed or unavailable."

Another pause. Longer.

"This situation is ongoing. Further updates will be provided when possible."

The transmission ended. No sign-off. No reassurance. No timeline. No help coming. Just static.

CHAPTER 5
THE DARK

Night fell differently now. It wasn't just darker. It came faster. The streetlights never turned on. No porch lights or shining windows. The neighborhood disappeared as soon as the sun dropped behind the trees, leaving a loneliness Logan hadn't felt before. He stood at the front window for a moment, staring out at the black where familiar shapes should be.

Inside the house, every sound carried too loud. Clapping of feet. Clearing of a throat. A flashlight being dropped. All unsettling. Becca moved through the kitchen with a flashlight, the beam hopping across counters and walls. The younger boys tried to make shadow puppets on the wall, with little success and much-needed comedy.

Dinner came from Dad's storage room, the one he'd put together over time. Everything was stacked and labeled, cans by type and date, boxes of goods organized neatly on every shelf. Logan thought about how Dad was always reorganizing this room, always adding something small with purpose. At the time, it had felt excessive. Now it didn't.

They ate cold food at the table. Simple meals. They could have cooked on the gas stove, but nobody had it in them. Becca talked through it softly, repeating numbers under her breath. Rations.

Days. They still had water, at least. She turned the sink on and let it run, the sound steady and normal with good pressure.

Candles came next. A large box pulled from the same room, the cardboard worn like it had been waiting a while. The flames softened the rooms and filled the dark corners. Becca lit the gas fireplace before the house cooled too much. The heat helped. The glow helped. For a little while, it almost worked, reducing the gravity of the situation.

They settled into the living room, lights gathered close. Logan checked his phone mostly out of habit. Still dead. He turned it face down and watched the candle flames instead, listening to the steady hiss of the fireplace. Somehow, without saying it out loud, they just ended up together. Camp-out style, they made pallets, scavenged pillows, and lay down side by side.

Just as everyone got comfortable, Charlie looked up with innocent eyes, curious. "Ms. Bee, what about your family?"

"They're still in North Carolina, bud," she said after a pause. "Remember? I live here in Tennessee by myself. I just have you guys."

Logan looked at Becca, then at his brothers, and didn't say anything.

Charlie followed quickly in a sweet voice. "But you're not old enough to live by yourself, are you?"

"Ha, I'm twenty-nine," she said with a soft smile. "Let's get some sleep, guys." Her voice faded at the end.

Tripp whispered toward the back door, "Goodnight, Mom and Dad."

Logan lay on his pallet, staring at the ceiling and the flickering shadows. Any other time, it would have been peaceful. Right now, he wanted to know what the future held.

Logan woke once in the night to the sound of the house creaking. For a moment, he thought the power had come back. Looking around, the room almost felt normal. Then he saw the candle beside the fireplace and remembered. He didn't wake anyone. He just lay there listening until he drifted back off.

Morning started to break through the windows and the other open cracks. In such close quarters, when someone stirred, they all did. Soon everyone was up and moving. Naturally, the first discussion was about food. The one thing that was consistent was the boys' appetites.

Logan ventured back to the food storage room, this time really taking stock. He noticed how large it was and the amount of time it must have taken for Dad to put it together. Food and necessities were stacked neatly on shelves, top to bottom. Grabbing some Pop-Tarts, he returned and spread them out on the table. "Breakfast is served." He grinned.

Becca grabbed some fruit from the counter to add. "We need a little nutritional value, don't we?"

As everyone finished up, Tripp panicked. "We have school today. What time is it? We're going to miss the bus!"

"I don't think we're going to have school today, man," Logan said. "There's no power or anything. We haven't seen a car run, and nobody's coming in or out right now."

"But we don't know if it's happening at our school!" Tripp shot back.

Becca jumped in. "Let's just wait and see. If the bus runs, we'll know."

They sat around trying to occupy themselves, trying to figure out what they might do today. Suddenly, a knock at the door broke the silence. To everyone's surprise, they all looked at each other, momentarily forgetting there was still a world and people outside their quiet, still four walls. As usual, Charlie was first to the door, his little legs scooting as fast as they could.

Becca caught up and opened it to Mrs. Cecillia, the neighbor from across the street. Mom loved Mrs. Cecillia, saying more than once that "she's good people." With a half smile, Mrs. Cecillia asked how everyone was and spoke with Becca for a bit. Losing interest, the younger boys drifted back into the house.

Still concerned, Cecillia asked if they'd heard any updates about what was going on. Logan shook his head.

"No, we haven't heard anything," Becca said. "How about you guys?"

"Well, not really," Cecillia said. "But it's more about what Erik saw. It's terrifying. Erik was in Nashville when everything happened yesterday." She paused to gather her thoughts. "He had to walk all the way back. The whole twenty-three miles. None of the cars were working, no lights, no engines. People just abandoned their cars and started walking."

Her voice broke slightly. "Erik said there were cars and people everywhere on the roads. Everyone seemed lost."

Becca and Logan exchanged wide-eyed looks.

"He said it took hours to get back," Cecillia continued. "He had to stop and sleep in the back of an abandoned truck." Her voice dropped. "The scary part was when he got back to town.

The grocery stores, convenience stores, even the pharmacy were overrun. He stayed clear and came home. People were panicking, acting erratically."

Becca crossed her arms and leaned back against the door. "Everyone's just scared, I bet. I'm so glad he made it home safely. Do you all need anything?"

"Not for now," Mrs. Cecillia said. "But who knows how long this will go or how bad it'll get. I was hoping to hear something." She paused. "I'll let you get back to your morning."

"Maybe check with Mr. Ira," Logan added. "He's been working on ways to communicate with people. He might've learned something."

Walking back inside, Logan looked up at Becca. "Yeah. I don't think we're having school today."

After a pause, wide-eyed, she said, "No...I guess not."

By mid-morning, the family decided to go back to the park. It didn't require electricity or a car. On the way, they saw familiar neighbors everywhere, all apparently arriving at the same conclusion and needing to escape their quiet, stuffy houses.

At the park, Logan and Becca stayed close, watching the boys as a team. There were so many kids, it was hard to keep up while also listening to the chatter of nervous parents. From what he overheard, Logan couldn't tell if anyone really knew what was happening. Every explanation sounded confident until someone else contradicted it. One dad whispered about a nuke. Another swore it was grid failure. Someone laughed nervously and mentioned self-aware AI, Terminator style. Concerned and amused, Logan thought that Dad would probably get along just fine with these people.

With nothing else to do, the Hopkins bunch stayed at the park for hours. It was a beautiful spring day and the perfect temperature. The grass was just starting to come in thick, and the smell of it mixed with whatever someone was grilling a few streets over.

Distracting the littles seemed like the best medicine, anyway. It helped quiet the constant questions about when Mom and Dad would be back. A raised voice cut through the noise. Logan turned just in time to see two dads arguing, hands up, faces red. Someone pulled them apart quickly, laughter following like it was a joke, but the laughter felt wrong.

Goldfish and Cheez-Its had held hunger at bay, but now the boys needed real food. They headed home again. The now-familiar smell of grills filled the air, which Logan suspected was the last fresh meat available. It had been over thirty-six hours since the lights went out. Without a generator or some kind of power source, everything was likely bad now.

Tripp, just noticing the empty streets, asked, "Why aren't there any cars going, Bee? And why are some just parked in the middle of the road?"

Becca kept walking, eyes forward. “I think...because they're all broken.”

"All of them?" Charlie asked.

"Yeah, I think so, boys..." She trailed off.

Near the house, they passed Mr. Ira tinkering in his garage again, the generator humming loudly beside him. They waved and kept walking. Back home, Becca sent the boys to wash up and get ready for dinner. Outside, Logan, now the de facto generator expert, brought the unit back to life, quicker this time. He listened to it run a second longer than necessary, suddenly aware of how loud it sounded in the quiet neighborhood. Still, some power felt better than none. Logan wanted the win. Something he could fix, even if nothing else made sense.

As he stepped through the side door, he heard Becca cry out, "Oh nooo!"

The dread in her voice hit him before he even reached the kitchen. Everyone stood around the sink. The faucet hung open, useless. Silence had replaced the steady pressure that had been there just hours earlier. Becca looked back over her shoulder at Logan, a tear already tracking down her cheek. She whispered, "The water's out. The sinks and toilets aren't working."

No one spoke.

CHAPTER 6

NOW WHAT

Becca turned the faucet on and off a couple more times in disbelief. Logan checked the bathroom sink, finding the same thing. The toilets didn't refill either.

Nobody moved for a moment. The only sound was the last drip from the faucet Becca had just turned off.

"How much backup water do we actually have?" Logan asked.

Becca leaned against the counter, arms crossed, running through it out loud. "We have some bottles in the fridge, several cases in the storage room, and a few big jugs in the garage."

"Is that a lot?" one of the little boys questioned.

Becca glanced at Logan before answering. "No, it's not."

Logan pulled open the storage room door and stood in the doorway, looking at the shelves. Dad had stacked water in every available space, but looking at it now with fresh eyes, it didn't seem like nearly enough. Four people. No timeline. No guarantee of anything coming back.

They talked through the rules quietly, away from the little boys. Drinking water first, obviously. No showers or baths for now. No flushing unless it really mattered. Dishes could wait.

"How about the pool?" Logan said.

Becca nodded. "It's green. But it's water."

"We could use it for flushing and washing, at least," Logan said. "Dad has a filter in the garage. And purification tablets in the go-bag. If we had to, we could try to make some of it drinkable. But that's a last resort."

She started writing it all down.

Everything suddenly had a cost. Becca reached for the sink again out of habit, then stopped. She dropped her hand back to her side and didn't say anything.

After snacking, they drifted back to the table. It had become the center of everything now. The place where they landed when they didn't know what else to do. The fireplace hummed behind them, keeping the chill off.

Becca had her notepad out. She went through the numbers out loud. Logan followed along, doing the same math in his head.

"About three weeks of food if we stretch it," she said. "Water is going to be tighter. Maybe a week and a half."

Logan nodded. "That should be enough time for something to change."

Becca didn't respond right away. She just looked at her notepad.

Charlie was nearby, scribbling on a piece of paper, completely unbothered. Tripp sat quietly at the end of the table, watching them both.

As the last bits of sunlight faded, the radio crackled to life on the kitchen counter. Everyone went still. Even Charlie looked up from whatever he was doing.

"...repeat—this is an emergency announcement issued by state and federal authorities."

The broadcast was different this time. A real voice, not the robotic one. Measured and deliberate, like someone choosing every word carefully.

"Widespread infrastructure failure has been confirmed across multiple regions. Power restoration efforts are ongoing, but officials now report critical failures at water treatment and pumping facilities."

Becca glanced back toward the sink.

"Residents should prepare for limited or complete loss of municipal water service. If water is still available, conserve immediately. Do not assume service will return."

A pause of static, then the message repeated from the beginning. When it was over, nobody said anything for a moment. Logan stared at the table.

Tripp broke the silence first. "What does that mean, Lo?"

Logan looked at him. "It means we were right to save the water."

It wasn't the whole truth, but it was all he could offer for now.

Out of habit, he pulled out his phone, then set it back down. It was still dead. Dallas and six hundred miles was a long way. And now the water systems were failing. Everything was failing. He pushed the thought down and got up from the table.

After the shock wore off, the house settled into its new nighttime version of quiet and dark. Just the fireplace, the generator outside at Ira's place, and the occasional creak of the house. They rationed candles, one in the kitchen and one in the living room, none upstairs unless someone needed to go up. Flashlights stayed off unless absolutely necessary. Batteries mattered now.

Becca wrote things down, sharing her thoughts with Logan. Water counts. Food rations. What could wait. What couldn't.

The boys slept in the living room, closer together than usual. Logan stayed awake longer than he meant to, staring at the ceiling and listening for sounds or signals, good or bad. Somewhere in the distance, a dog barked, then several more. Even an owl joined in behind the house. The hum of a couple of generators. The quiet was truly unnerving.

The radio stayed on low, just in case. There was only static and fragments of voices. Nothing new or helpful. Eventually, the house went still. Sleep came in pieces for Logan and the others. The night felt obnoxiously long.

Logan was already up when the knock came. Frozen, he didn't know what to do. He waited, hoping it would just go away. At this hour, in this situation, it couldn't be good.

Again, the knock came. Even and persistent.

Shaking Becca awake, Logan pointed toward the door. She seemed confused as the third knock came, followed by a soft voice. Sleepy-eyed, they both eased toward the door. Looking out, they saw a young couple, likely in their late twenties. The guy wore a hat pulled down low, and the woman's arms were tightly wrapped around her stomach and waist.

Logan's eyes dropped to the man's hands before he realized he was even doing it. Both wore backpacks that looked overly full and heavy.

Becca barely cracked the door open. "Can we help you?"

The young woman responded first. "Yes, thank God. We've been walking for hours. We got lost off the interstate."

The man added, "Could you spare some water or food? We left Nashville with basically nothing to eat or drink. We didn't have much in our apartment, and the stores were all empty. It was falling apart there." He dropped his head, sounding defeated.

Logan looked at Becca. She gave a small nod.

Becca stayed on watch and asked Logan to grab some food and water for them. Logan ran to the storage room, grabbing some granola bars, a few cans of soup, and several bottles of water. He hesitated for a moment, then put one can back.

"Here you go," he said as he handed over the items. The young couple thanked them, grateful, as they backed off the porch and stood there, just looking around.

"The interstate is that way," Logan called out, pointing down the end of the road. "Make a right at the park, then another right at the main road."

The guy nodded, and they moved off down the road, packs shifting with each step. Logan watched them go until they cleared the neighbor's driveway.

Becca closed the door and turned both locks. They stood there without moving, listening to the quiet on the other side.

After a moment, Logan said it out loud. "That's not the first visitors we'll have."

Becca didn't respond right away. She was still looking at the door. When she found her voice, she said, "It's only been forty-eight hours since the event. There are already refugees." She looked at Logan, eyes wide. "How does it get this bad so quickly?"

Logan didn't answer. He didn't have one.

Becca straightened up, ran a hand through her hair, and walked back toward the kitchen.

The younger boys were up now. The commotion must have woken them. Tripp asked, excitement in his voice, "Is that Mom and Dad?"

Logan looked at him and shook his head slowly.

CHAPTER 7
NEWS

By late morning, Logan decided to explore a bit and make a stop at Mr. Ira's, hoping he might have learned something new by now. On the short walk over, he took note of fewer neighbors and an increase of people he didn't recognize. Like the young couple from that morning, he suspected they were transplants from somewhere less-safe.

Arriving at Ira's, he knocked on the door. Mrs. Rose cautiously opened it, then relaxed when she saw his familiar shape.

"Hi, Logan," she said. "So glad to see you. We've had a couple of strangers this morning, and I thought you were another."

He smiled. "Nope. Just me."

"Well, come on in and visit," she said warmly. "Do you want some tea or soda?"

"Sure! Do you have Sprite?"

Mrs. Rose disappeared for a moment, returning with the green can. Grabbing it, he thanked her. "Oh, it's cold too!"

Mrs. Rose showed him the way to see Ira in his office. He was sitting at a large wooden desk that looked about as old as he was.

"I'll let you boys chat," she said as she scooted off.

Ira was wearing a headset and working the controls of a black box about the size of a shoebox with a bunch of buttons and knobs on it. Several wires ran out of it, including a long one strung across the ceiling.

"Hey, Mr. Ira," Logan said with no response. Not wanting to startle him, he cleared his throat and said it louder, finally catching the old man's attention.

Ira turned and smiled at Logan. "Hey there, young man. Good to see you. How are you guys holding up?"

Logan paused. "We're okay. Mostly thanks to Dad, though. Luckily, he planned ahead and had so much stuff put away. We're fine for now, I think."

"Good to hear," Ira said. "I knew you all should be okay. Your dad was sharp. We had discussed the possibility of something like this happening often. We always seem to be on the same page."

"Ira...do you think my parents are okay?" Logan's voice broke up a little.

Ira put his hands flat on the desk and sat up straight. "Son, if I know your mom and dad, they are just fine. They're smart and resourceful. I bet they're spending all their energy trying to find a way home to you guys."

"Hope so," Logan said, thinking the journey from Dallas would be all but impossible without a mode of transportation.

Changing the subject, he pointed at all the gear strewn about. "Is that your ham setup?"

"Sure is," Ira said, perking up. "Most everything got fried during the event. Luckily, a couple things survived. This HF rig made it somehow." Pointing at the black shoebox thing, he continued, "This radio was in a metal cabinet in the garage. I had it lined with cardboard and completely disconnected. Usually, you put them in Faraday bags, but I didn't have one big enough."

Laughing, Ira added that the cabinet wasn't magic, just steel and luck.

"So, is it actually working now?" Logan asked, taking a sip of his Sprite. The carbonation burned just a bit.

"It is now," Ira said. "I thought it was fried for a while, too. Then I realized the storm, or event, whatever it was, scrambled the sky for a bit. None of the bands were open."

Confused, Logan asked, "The sky was scrambled?"

"Yes, sorry. Basically, the atmosphere wouldn't support or transmit the radio waves," Ira said, making a wave motion with his hand. "It took about forty-eight hours for things to settle down and open some of the bands. I've started having luck in the twenty- and forty-meter bands now."

"That's great!" Logan said. "Finally, some good news. What are you hearing?"

"Unfortunately, nothing good," Ira said plainly. "I've heard from some hams on the East Coast. One in Charlotte and one near Savannah, Georgia. They're in the exact same position we are." He paused. "Whatever happened was big and must have hit most of the US."

Logan asked, "Any word on Dallas?"

"No, not Dallas. But I did hear someone from Abilene, which is near Dallas, relaying info." Ira measured his response. "Sorry, Logan, but they were impacted, too. Same as here." Logan nodded.

With watery eyes, Logan thanked Ira and said he needed to get back to check on the boys. As Logan took his final sip of Sprite and walked toward the front door, Ira stopped him for a moment. "Keep your head up, son. Your folks will make it back to you. I know your dad, he'll find a way." Logan nodded.

"One more thing," Ira added. "The game's changed. People are getting desperate, especially those who had little and were unprepared. Keep an eye out. Be safe."

Logan looked back at the street, then nodded once and headed for the door.

As he stepped out of Ira's house, he heard the oddest sound, motorized and moving toward him. Looking down the street, he saw the culprit. An ATV, with two neighbors from another section of the neighborhood aboard. He sort of just waved as they cruised by, the back storage rack completely loaded like they were heading somewhere and not coming back. That was the first motorized vehicle he had seen in days. He hurried home, turning the question over in his head. Why was it running when the cars weren't?

Inside, he found the boys and Becca playing cards on the floor. Before being dealt in, he told them, mostly Becca, about all the news and updates he had gotten from Ira, and then about seeing the ATV.

Becca glanced at the boys, then back at Logan. "This is good news. At least now we know that some things survived."

The news was both scary and encouraging in a way. Maybe everything didn't get fried.

"That really sucks about Mom and Dad," Tripp said.

"I wonder if our golf cart would work since the ATV was running," Tripp said, curious.

The family had a gas-powered golf cart that was pretty old, a hand-me-down from Nicole's parents. They used it to tool around the neighborhood, to and from the park, and just for fun.

Logan and Becca looked at each other.

"That's a great question, dude!" Logan yelled, running out the side door toward the separate storage garage, the group in tow.

Logan pulled up the door and rounded the back of the golf cart. Sliding into the seat, he turned the old Yamaha key to on and gradually pressed the gas pedal, almost like he didn't want an answer. The parking brake released. He pushed just a bit further and the engine came to life.

"We have wheels!" Logan yelled, and the family cheered.

Charlie immediately tried to climb up into the seat beside him. Tripp was already asking where they were going first. Becca stood in the garage doorway, arms crossed, shaking her head with a grin she couldn't hide. Logan laughed, actually laughed, for the first time in days. He let the engine run a little longer than necessary, just to hear it.

CHAPTER 8
STRANGERS

By Wednesday morning, day three since the lights went out, Logan could see the neighborhood had already changed.

Looking out, Logan noticed a particularly troubling problem developing. Trash cans had been lining the street for days now. Nobody had come to pick them up. Bags were piling up, and between the animals and the heat, there was quite the smelly mess. It was another reminder of the new world they lived in, and the lack of help or support from any external sources.

Additionally, Logan continued to notice the ever-increasing presence of strange people in his neighborhood. The numbers were growing, and they were moving through the streets more slowly than they should've been. Their eyes worked over the neighborhood as they passed. He saw people of all sorts, bags slung over shoulders, strollers filled with random goods, shopping carts and wagons carrying everything they owned at this point.

As Wednesday morning wore on, the knocks kept coming.

A woman knocked just before noon. She was young, maybe mid-twenties, with a backpack that looked like it was packed in a hurry. She asked for water first, and then food if they had it, then she asked which direction the interstate was.

Logan answered all three for her. Becca filled a water bottle from their supply and added a few packs of crackers.

The woman thanked them and started walking.

Becca closed the door. Neither of them said anything for a moment.

"That's the third one today," Becca said.

Logan looked out the door and then back at the storage room. He didn't respond.

The family collectively decided the best place to be at this point was out of sight. Anytime they ventured outside, it brought conversations with outsiders. People asking for help or resources in some form or another. Becca and Logan wanted to help all they could, but the ever-pressing issue of resources had to be managed closely now. The reality continued to push in on them: what they had might be all they were ever going to get.

A late-afternoon lunch of canned chicken, white rice, and saltine crackers was rudely interrupted. This time, it was another announcement from the enemy emergency radio, still sitting on the kitchen counter. The now-too-familiar deep beeps, followed by a pause, gave way to the message. This time it was a formal, official voice, not the robot, that came over the waves.

"This is an official federal emergency announcement. Nationwide infrastructure disruptions remain ongoing. Restoration timelines are indefinite. Citizens must immediately transition to long-term self-sustainment. Conserve water, food, and fuel. Limit movement. Secure homes and personal property. Emergency services may be unavailable or significantly delayed. Do not rely on law enforcement or medical response for routine assistance."

As usual, the message repeated twice and then vanished back into the radio world.

Logan looked at Becca. "Bee, you've been doing the math. How much food and water do you think we have left?"

Becca hesitated for a moment and picked up her running list from the table. "Based on my math, we have about three weeks of food and a week and a half of water."

She added, "Surely things will come back by then. There has to be help, or a plan of some sort." It sounded like she was trying to convince herself.

Logan answered back firmly. "What if they don't have a plan? What if everything is truly ruined?" He raised his voice just a bit to emphasize it. "If everything is truly fried, it will take months or even years to bring back. How can we make it that long?"

Charlie didn't understand the full weight of that statement. Tripp did, and asked quietly, "What happens if we run out of water or food, Bee?"

Logan looked at Becca.

"Don't worry, little man. We don't have to worry about that," she said, forcing a half-smile. "We'll come up with a plan. Besides, we have all the green pool water we could ever drink."

She continued, "We'll just need to limit what we use, and we'll have to stop giving things out to the commuters. I want to help, but we also have to look out for ourselves now."

Logan nodded in agreement.

Charlie had been quiet through most of it, pushing a saltine around his plate. He looked up at Becca. "When are Mom and Dad coming home?"

Nobody answered right away.

"Soon, bud," Becca said. "Soon."

Logan looked down at his plate, took a heavy breath, and didn't say anything.

Later in the day, another knock came at the door. Logan looked out and incorrectly assumed it was another transplant needing something. To his surprise, it was Mrs. Cecillia.

Opening the door and greeting her warmly alongside Becca, they caught up on the changes and happenings throughout the neighborhood. She, too, expressed concern about all the strangers passing through.

She asked, "Has either of you noticed anything weird over here or around? We've had a couple things come up missing."

Vance's bike had disappeared, along with a large wheeled cooler.

Looking back toward the garage, Logan said, "Not that we know of. We've kept everything locked up for the most part. We didn't see anyone around your house either."

"I'm worried that some of the people passing through may have taken it," Cecillia said, frustrated.

Becca chimed in, "I'm so sorry to hear that. I know Vance loved his bike. He was always on it."

"Yeah," Logan added, "Mr. Ira said we need to keep our eyes and ears open for this kind of stuff. People are getting desperate, and that makes them scary."

The three of them fell quiet.

Speaking of Ira, Logan noticed there were far fewer small-engine noises now. The generators were going quiet, likely out of fuel, he thought. They had been trying to conserve fuel as well, only running their generator when necessary to power necessities or charge batteries.

Another piece of information Mrs. Cecillia shared was that she and Erik had seen an old Chevrolet pickup truck driving down the main road by the park while they were outside with Vance. The best explanation they could come up with was that it was old enough not to be impacted by the event, mostly analog technology, Erik guessed.

The sun was beginning to set, and Logan wanted to check in on Ira before it got too late.

He decided to take the golf cart this time, just to mix it up. The engine whined to life, and he pulled out of the garage, the familiar hum of it settling under him. The streets were quieter than they should have been for a Wednesday afternoon. No kids outside. No one walking dogs. Just the occasional face appearing at a window as he rolled past.

On the short ride over, he noticed new handwritten messages taped to several nearby doors and windows. Neighbors were writing in large block letters and posting them.

NO TRESPASSING

DO NOT KNOCK

NO FOOD

The most concerning one read: **WE HAVE KIDS.**

Just before finding Ira in his driveway, filling his generator, Logan noticed one final sign:

LEAVE US ALONE.

The friendly neighborhood no longer looked or felt friendly. It was tense and closed off. Cautious seemed to be the new normal.

Before setting the parking brake, Logan realized he had become the center of attention. Curtains shifted. Doors cracked open.

Eyes followed him from all directions. Motorized vehicles were no longer normal.

Maybe taking the cart had been a mistake.

"Hi, Mr. Ira," Logan said once he was on foot. "Everything feels so nuts. Like one of those movies or a bad dream."

Ira shook Logan's hand. "Unfortunately, you're right, my boy. Everyone's locked up now. Curtains closed. Quiet." He chuckled softly. "Well...until you showed up on that golf cart. I never thought I'd see this neighborhood so quiet. Folks used to be talking to, or about, someone all the time."

Logan gave a short laugh in return.

"I see you're filling your generator," Logan said. "How much gas do you have left? It can't be much."

Looking around and lowering his voice, Ira said, "About two days." He glanced down the street. "We have to be careful what we say now. Resources like food, water, and gas, they're the new currency."

Logan didn't respond. His face must have shown it, because Ira continued.

"Money doesn't mean much anymore," Ira said. "What people need is food, water, and shelter." He paused, scanning the street. "The scary part is...people haven't gotten desperate yet."

He let the words hang.

"What do you think will happen?" Logan asked.

"Just think about what your parents would do to get to you, or to protect you," Ira said, meeting Logan's eyes. "That's what these people will do soon."

"Alright, bud," Ira said. "Why don't you head back before it gets any darker? I'll keep an eye on you while you drive back."

"Okay," Logan said. "Thanks."

Logan climbed back onto the old Yamaha and headed home, passing a few more strangers along the way. Eyes shifted toward him as he drove by. He found himself going faster than normal, not entirely sure why.

Whatever rules he thought still existed no longer did.

When he reached home, Logan quickly parked the cart inside the extra storage garage, pulled the door down, and locked it tight.

CHAPTER 9

THE GAME HAS CHANGED

The dark set in fast. Without light or power, the neighborhood vanished almost instantly.

Inside, the house settled into the new, now-familiar routine. Snacks. A small dinner from the food storage room. Working together to fill toilets with pool water and counting food. Checking the flashlights, inspecting batteries, and double-checking the door locks.

They blew out the few candles illuminating the lonely house. They drifted toward the living room, finding a pallet or couch to snuggle into for the night.

The little boys said their prayers in innocent voices. Tripp looked up. "Bee, when will Mom and Dad be home?"

Becca looked at Tripp and then at the other boys. "Hopefully soon, buddy. Right now, the cars and planes don't work. That's why it's taking them so long."

Charlie asked, "How long will it be? I REALLY miss them."

Logan looked away.

"I don't know, guys, but I do know they are trying their best to get to you," Becca said. "Now let's get some rest."

Without screens or other distractions, the group fell asleep quickly. Logan lay there for a while before sleep came.

Logan woke before he knew why. There was an odd clang of metal on metal coming from the back of the house, or maybe the backyard. The gate, maybe?

He jumped up, startling Becca in the process. "I heard something out back," he said as he walked toward the back door, grabbing a flashlight. Unlocking the bolt lock and then the doorknob, he eased the back door open. Nothing but pitch black greeted him.

He clicked the button on top of the flashlight, scanning the porch and making his way toward the pool. Near the edge, something moved. The figure was big.

Focusing the beam on the figure, he instantly recognized it as a person. A large man dressed in dark clothing. The man was squatting down, reaching into the pool with something.

Becca, just catching up and now noticing the large man, let out a scream or a gasp—both.

Everyone just paused, looking at each other for what felt like minutes. Logan blurted out, "What are you doing?!" followed by Becca, "Can we help you...?"

The stranger stood up slowly, staring back with sharp eyes. Tall as Dad, but thicker. There was a sense of authority about him.

In a low, measured tone, the man said, "I'm getting some water. I'm thirsty and haven't had anything to drink in a day or so." He just stared longer, adding, "Do you have any fresh water or food?"

Becca looked hard at Logan, then back to the burly guy. "We don't have much either. Everything's mostly run out. We'll get you a bottle of water and a snack." She added, "That's all we can spare. Then we'll need you to leave the property."

"Logan, go grab it, please. I'll stay here," she said.

Logan ran through the house, grabbing a bottle and a bag of potato chips out of the storage room. His hands moved faster than his brain. He was back on the porch in under a minute, but it felt much longer than that.

Back on the porch, he held them up for Becca to see and tossed the man the items.

"Thanks," the man said flatly.

He stared at Becca and Logan for a moment longer, his eyes moving from one to the other. Then to the house. He didn't seem to be in any hurry. Logan kept very still. Finally, the man turned and headed back toward the gate. He slowly disappeared out of the flashlight's beam.

Logan and Becca quickly went back inside, locking the top and bottom locks of the back door while making sure the blinds were shut.

They were both breathing harder than they should. Becca's eyes were wide as she said, "That was nerve-wracking! He just came into our backyard and took what he wanted!" Her voice grew higher now. "Since when is that okay?"

Logan responded, "That was scary. What if he comes back?! What do we do?"

Becca just shook her head, still looking stunned. "We'll have to be more alert moving forward."

The two sat mostly quiet until the first glimpse of sun started making its way through the windows.

The sun eventually came up. They had made it through the night. Logan looked at the back door, then at the storage room, then at his brothers still asleep on the couch. He didn't go back to sleep.

CHAPTER 10

TRADE

Thursday morning, and the family was already getting restless. The young boys had not been out for a while and needed something to do.

Becca recommended taking the golf cart to the park so everyone could get some fresh air and stretch their legs. The house just didn't feel inviting this morning. Still air and no circulation gave it a lived-in smell that Logan wanted to escape, even if only for a little while.

Logan talked to Becca, advising against taking the golf cart this time. He mentioned the looks and attention it had drawn on their last short trip. "Maybe we should walk," he said.

"No," Becca said flatly. "We need to have some fun, and we need fresh air. Charlie and Tripp need this mini-adventure, Logan."

Still hesitant, Logan tried another angle. "Shouldn't we conserve gas?"

"No, we should be fine. We have six jugs thanks to your dad, so we don't have to worry about that, at least," Becca rebutted.

Logan conceded, but with reservations. The neighborhood had already changed so much, he didn't know what to expect at this point.

Becca was right, though. The little boys were elated to be going on the journey. They were bouncing off the walls and couldn't contain themselves. Grabbing hoodies, hats, and balls, they darted out the side door to the storage garage.

Logan and Becca caught up. Opening the lock, the cart sat safely inside. Everyone piled on. Logan and Becca up front, Charlie in Becca's lap, Tripp on the back seat facing away from them, bouncing his legs. Like they were going for a ride around the neighborhood, like any other day. They had done this hundreds of times. They backed out of the side garage and onto the street. It was a beautiful spring day, just like many before it.

The smell hit first—old trash, thick and sour. Mixed with it was the heavy odor of things that shouldn't be burning. Paper. Plastics. Rubber. Smoke drifted from makeshift burn barrels and shallow pits. The neighbors were getting creative, trying to solve one of the most basic problems—trash.

As they drove, everything looked vaguely familiar but not quite right. The grass was too high, cars scattered about, nobody in their yards.

Logan searched his memory and made an odd connection to the old movies Grandpa Jake used to watch nonstop. Old westerns. It felt like that moment in the show right before a duel, or when the bad guys came into town. Everyone sort of just disappeared.

Before making the left turn to the park, the family spotted Mrs. Rowe walking Molly along the sidewalk. She was a fixture in this part of the neighborhood, late thirties, always in workout clothes, the kind of person who knew everyone's name and wasn't shy about using it. Today, though, she looked different. Her eyes were scanning. They slowed to say hello.

"Hi, Mrs. Rowe." Logan waved.

"Hi, everyone," Mrs. Rowe replied, holding her golden tightly.

The young boys jumped off to pet the wiggly dog. Smiling and giggling, they fought over Molly's attention.

Becca asked Mrs. Rowe, "How have you and the family been? We've been holding it together down our way. It's been exhausting with all the transplants coming through from Nashville or wherever they came from."

Mrs. Rowe's eyes widened a bit. "Yeah, we've had things go missing," she said quietly. "More than once." She tightened her grip on Molly's leash. "Honestly, we're running out of food and water. We just never thought it would be this long."

"Yeah, we've heard of a good bit of theft down our way too," Becca said. "It seems everyone just takes what they want all of a sudden."

Logan jumped in, telling her about the strange man from the night before at the pool.

Shaking her head and looking down, Mrs. Rowe said, "I just don't know what we're going to do, any of us, if this doesn't get better."

"Boys, where are your parents? I haven't seen them around," Mrs. Rowe added.

Logan looked back at his brothers. "They're in Dallas. They were there when everything went out."

"Oh dear, I'm so sorry, boys. I'm sure you're worried sick. I bet they're just fine, though," she said, forcing extra enthusiasm.

Pulling Molly back toward her house, she said, "I guess I should get back. I don't want my husband to worry about me. Y'all stay safe, okay?" They said their goodbyes. Charlie yelled after her, "Take care of Molly!" She smiled and kept walking.

The family moved on. Near the intersection of the neighborhood and the park, a man stood on the sidewalk. Someone Logan didn't recognize. He was well dressed, wearing business-casual clothing, but with sneakers. He also wore a very nice watch that Logan noticed immediately because it looked similar to his dad's.

The man waved them down with an easy smile. "Hi there, boys—and Miss," he said, nodding toward Becca.

Logan and Becca gave polite smiles while Tripp said, "Hey, Mister!"

The businessman looked over the cart. "That's a nice ride you have there. Only one of a few vehicles I've seen moving in the last several days."

Logan laughed. "Yeah, I guess we got lucky because it's so old."

The man turned his attention to Becca, getting straight to the point. "Would you consider a trade, or maybe selling it?" Pulling his hand from his pocket and revealing the watch Logan had noticed earlier, he said, "This is a Rolex Submariner. They're pretty hard to come by and worth a lot." Making sure everyone could see it, he continued, "Probably worth twelve or thirteen thousand dollars. I'll trade you right now."

Becca's eyebrows rose. She glanced at Logan, then back at the man. "Sir, that's nice, but we need this for the family. Plus, it's not mine to trade." She added, "Nice watch, though."

Yesterday, this wouldn't have happened.

The man's voice rose. "Look, I have family in Huntsville, Alabama. I have to get to them. I can't walk that far!" He pointed to the shoulder bag at his side. "I'll give you ten thousand dollars in cash. I have it right here. That's a deal. Take it."

Logan straightened, pulling his shoulders back and lifting his chin slightly. "Thank you, but that money, or the watch, doesn't help us. Not now."

The man's face flushed, and he stepped closer than he needed to, now almost within arm's length. His hand disappeared back into his pocket.

Becca didn't say anything. She slammed her foot down on top of Logan's, driving it into the gas pedal. The cart wasn't fast, but thanks to Dad's carburetor modifications, it could reach about twenty miles per hour.

They left the man behind, furious and helpless in his expensive clothes.

CHAPTER 11

NO LONGER OURS

Logan didn't slow down until the neighboring houses disappeared behind them. Even then, he kept going faster than necessary, the cart engine loud beneath them and impossible to hide. The rest of the short trip was quiet. He kept coming back to the man's eyes more than his words.

The park should have been a relief. A sort of reward for the boys after a traumatic morning. Instead, they found themselves in disbelief. Two days ago, it had been empty. There were a few kids playing and parents half paying attention.

Now it was occupied.

Trash and people were everywhere. People lay in boxes, tents dotted the green space, makeshift lean-tos had sprung up along the edges. Their slides were being used as shelters. Monkey bars framed with tarps. Swings drifted slowly, with no kids on them.

Logan noticed an assortment of bikes, chairs, and other household items that oddly matched things recently reported missing in the neighborhood. There were dozens of people, more than they could count. Unclaimed dogs roamed between the camps. Kids, dirty and unkempt, played amongst the shelters.

As the cart rolled in, conversations stopped and heads turned toward them. They were fed, clean, and mobile. Everything these people weren't.

Charlie broke the silence. "Who are all these people, Bee?"

Becca hesitated. "I don't know, bud. They must be from out of town or...somewhere else."

"But they are taking up the park and our slides!" Tripp said, his voice deflated. "Those are our slides!"

"They are, aren't they?" Becca replied calmly. "I'm not sure it's safe to play here right now. How about we just go back home and find something sweet to eat?"

Charlie frowned. "Why isn't it safe, Bee? We just want to play."

"We don't know them, bud, and they don't look very friendly," Becca said, looking over the impromptu camp.

The boys looked back at their park. The swings. The slides. The things that used to belong to them.

They nodded reluctantly.

Logan had already made the decision before anyone said it out loud. He'd been watching the crowd since they pulled in. This wasn't their park anymore. He turned the cart around without a word.

CHAPTER 12

FIRST WATCH

Logan took a different route home, steering wide of the corner where the businessman had been. He hoped the rest of the trip back would be uneventful. Luckily, it was—at least until the last few houses. They had almost made it home when a uniformed man walked out of the treeline at the end of the cul-de-sac by their house.

He was walking straight toward them, clearly intending to intercept them before the driveway. Dark uniform. Black tactical boots. A duty belt with equipment, including a holstered gun, and a large pack on his back.

As they got closer, Logan and Becca realized this person was law enforcement. They met the man almost at the end of the driveway. He waved politely with a smile. The man was much more broad up close. He had short, dark hair and a stubby beard.

"Hi, guys, my name is Officer Owen, but you can call me Blake." He grinned.

The boys respectfully said, "Hello, sir." They had always been taught to appreciate military and law enforcement.

Becca sat up straight, smiling a little extra. "Hi, Officer!" Logan shot her a quick look and smirked. Becca saw it but ignored him.

Blake said, "Good to see everyone. I've been walking for the last couple of days. I had to get out of Nashville. It's gotten bad up there," as he looked back toward the north.

Tripp volunteered, "We just got back from a ride to the park. We couldn't play. It was full of people."

"I'm sorry to hear that, little man," the officer said sympathetically.

Turning back to the family, he added, "I know it's a lot to ask, but do you have any extra water or food to share, by chance? I had to leave in a hurry. There was nothing left anyway." His voice got quiet.

Logan and Becca exchanged a look. Logan noticed Blake hadn't moved. He stood where he was, hands visible, waiting.

"You're welcome to come in," Becca said carefully. "Just the kitchen for now. Honestly, we'd love an update on what's going on out there, if possible."

"I can handle that," Blake said. "Thank you all so much."

Logan turned into the driveway, then pulled into the storage garage. Everyone hopped off to meet the officer at the side door. Logan took an extra second to pull the door down and secure the lock.

Inside, Becca instinctively said, "Excuse the mess. With everything going on, we haven't kept the house up like we should. It's hard without power and running water."

"No worries, ma'am," he said politely. "I can understand. I'm not sure it matters anyway..." He trailed off.

The house was dim, lit by a single candle on the counter. It probably looked as strange to him as he did to them.

Becca and Logan turned toward the storage room to find dinner options. Logan glanced back once more. Blake was still standing near the table, pack on, posture rigid. He hadn't settled in yet. His eyes moved around the room, doors, windows, and then back to the boys.

Logan and Becca settled on a couple of cans of SPAM, canned chicken, rice, and mixed vegetables. When they came back, they saw Blake sitting at the table talking to the younger boys. He was telling them a story about the time he was in a car chase through downtown Nashville. He was being very animated, and the boys were hanging on every word. The story ended with the bad guy crashing into a pole and leading them on a foot chase. Blake ultimately made the arrest and locked the bad guy up, to cheers from the boys.

After some small talk and more pleasantries, the group decided it was time to piece together dinner. Logan now had to manually light the stove, but it still worked. He started frying the SPAM with some seasoning while also boiling the rice and warming the vegetables.

The smell of fried pork, or whatever SPAM was, along with the seasonings, took him back for a moment to watching Mom and Dad work the stove during family dinners.

The boys, including Logan, looked at Blake's cool equipment and even his gun while Becca finished up. Logan couldn't help noticing how the officer always seemed aware of where everyone was in the room, even while smiling at the boys.

Announcing that dinner was ready, they set the table and sat down to eat on their paper plates. Only after everyone had taken a seat did Blake finally slide his pack off and lean it against the wall close by. Logan hadn't realized he'd been holding onto it.

The boys had Sprite, their favorite soda, and the adults opted for something a little stronger tonight, courtesy of Dad's special cabinet. The makeshift family sat around the table enjoying a comfort that few had now. The fireplace threw uneven light across the room, and for a moment it almost felt normal.

Becca asked the officer, "So where are you going? What's your plan?"

He took another bite and paused for a second. "I have some family in Chapel Hill. I guess I'll head that way. I'm not sure what else to do. My aunt and uncle live down there. They have some land and livestock. I'm hoping they can use some help or even security. I'll earn my way somehow," he said.

Becca quizzed a bit further. "How about you? Do you have any other family? Were you in Nashville alone?"

"Yeah, it was just me and my border collie, Mocha. When everything went sideways in town, I had to get out. Everything was breaking down, so I decided to leave, even though the higher-ups told us to stay."

He took another bite and washed it down with his dark brown drink. "When I went back to my apartment, it had been looted. Door busted in. Everything trashed." His voice dropped. "Mocha was nowhere to be found. He must have been terrified and ran off. I looked for him, all over the apartment building, outside, everywhere."

Logan set his fork down. "How long did you look?"

"Long enough that I knew I was running out of time," Blake said. "It was getting so bad. I couldn't wait around anymore. I had to leave." He paused. "I left Mocha. I didn't have a choice."

The table went quiet.

Becca put a hand on his shoulder. "I'm so sorry. That sounds horrible. Poor Mocha..."

Logan had to question a bit further. "Sir, what was so bad out there? Like...what's it like?"

Blake took another sip and looked toward Becca, then back at Logan. "Well, the problem is, in the city, nobody was ready for something like this. Normally the power goes off for an hour or two. No harm, no foul. It's been out for days. Plus, the city has never lost water like this."

"How fast did it fall apart?" Logan asked.

"Faster than I ever thought possible," Blake said. "With no food for days and water gone soon after, thousands of people flooded the streets at once. The stores were overrun within hours. Then it turned to looting. And in some cases, violence." He shook his head. "So much faster than I would have ever imagined."

Logan thought about the young couple at their door. The man in the backyard. The businessman on the corner. And that was just here, a small suburb twenty miles south of the city.

The officer took a minute to gather his thoughts and finish his plate. He stood up, walked to the trash to deposit his plate, and wiped his fork in the sink. "The city leadership told us to stay put. They posted us on corners and told us to keep the peace. Strict orders of no violence toward civilians, period. The problem is, as soon as everyone figures that out, there's no respect and no safety. We were sitting ducks."

Logan watched his jaw tighten.

"For some reason, when things like this happen, the police become the enemy. We had no way of protecting anyone, or ourselves. Our people just started disappearing. Leaving their posts. Pretty soon, it was just me and a lot of angry people." He looked down at the sink. "That's when I decided to get out and head south. I had to, you know."

Nobody said anything for a moment.

"You made it here," Logan said. "That counts for something."

Blake nodded once and didn't respond.

Brightening now, he smiled. "And here I am with you fine folks. Although I do worry that all of those people will head this way looking for resources like you guys have." More serious now, he added, "It could get dangerous. You all will have to be careful. I guess we all will."

Becca jumped in with the story from the night before, the guy in the backyard. Blake nodded and added, "Exactly. That's what I'm afraid of for good people like you all."

Everyone cleaned up their plates, still trying to digest the stories and news the officer had shared.

The officer finished his drink and stood. "Thank you all for the hospitality. I better get back on the road toward my aunt and uncle's. I still have about twenty miles to go."

Becca asked, "Why don't you stay here tonight? It's a long way, and you have to be tired. We have plenty of room. Plus, we all sleep in the living room, anyway. You can have Charlie's room down the hall."

"No, ma'am, I can't do that. I don't want to impose. I'm just a stranger here eating your food," he said plainly.

Logan came back quickly. "No, for real—stay with us tonight. We'd like to have you, and honestly, it would be nice to have some reassurance in the house."

Blake looked at the boys, then at Becca. "Are you sure? Only if everyone is comfortable."

Unanimously, everyone agreed. "It's settled," Logan said.

Blake hesitated, then nodded. "Alright. Just for tonight. Only if you let me take the first watch, though."

Becca and Logan shared a puzzled look. "What do you mean, watch?" they asked.

"Well, since you've had visitors now, and we know it's only going to get worse, I suggest you set up a night watch. We take turns keeping an eye and an ear out while the others sleep. That way, there will be no surprises."

"That's such a great idea," Logan shot back.

With the new routine now almost a habit, the gang slipped into their normal spots, cozy and comfortable. Tonight felt different with Blake in the house.

The officer took watch on a chair near the back door, the fireplace casting shadows on him as he looked out. He would be up for three hours, then Becca, then Logan. That was the plan.

Logan lay there listening, replaying the night in his head. The business guy on the corner had seemed genuine too.

Logan didn't realize he had drifted asleep until he was woken by footsteps. He raised his head. Blake was standing completely still at the front window, not moving, just watching the street. He stood there long enough that Logan wasn't sure what to make of it. Then Blake turned, caught his eyes, and smiled. "It's all good, chief. Just keeping an eye on things. Get your rest." Logan held his gaze for a second, then lay back down. Sleep came slower the second time.

Next, he woke up to someone shaking his shoulder. It was Becca. "Time for your watch, Lo."

He wiped the sleep from his eyes and stretched. Glancing over at the battery-powered wall clock, it was almost 3:00 AM. Reluctantly, he crawled out of his cocoon and took a seat near the back door. As Becca lay down near Tripp on the couch and pulled the covers up, she whispered, "If you see or hear anything, let us know, okay?"

Logan nodded and took his seat near the back door where Blake, then Becca, had taken their turns before him.

The night unfolded easily. The pitch-dark and painful quiet played tricks on his mind. He thought he saw movement several times, luckily just the wind or shadows moving in the moonlight. He never noticed just how much noise a still house can make. Settling, popping, and creaking all danced around in his ears and mind.

He thought about Blake's words, the way he'd scanned the house, the way he never fully relaxed. Maybe that was what survival looked like now.

As 6:00 AM rolled around, he got up quietly and stood at the front window, the same spot where Blake had been standing in the middle of the night. He looked out at the empty street and understood, maybe for the first time, what it actually meant to be on watch.

CHAPTER 13
THE MEETING

Making another pass to the front door and then over to the side window overlooking the storage garage where the fuel and golf cart were stored, he had a rhythm now.

He was exceptionally tired. Running on a handful of hours of sleep and being up for the last three had taken its toll on him. He decided to head to the storage room and do something he'd never thought he would—break into Dad's coffee supply. It was stored in mason jars, sealed and fresh. He loved the smell of it, but hated the taste.

He thought back on the many mornings. Every morning...Dad made coffee without fail. There must be something to it, he thought. Like he had seen Dad do a thousand times, he grabbed a small stainless pot and filled it with fresh water from one of the large blue jugs they'd brought in from the garage.

Water didn't feel like the problem yet. They still had plenty, and the pool, if it came to that. It could be purified with the filter and boiled when needed.

Back at the stove, he lit a burner with the long-reach lighter. To his delight, it worked, and a blue flame sprang to life beneath the pot. He prepared the shiny steel French press with a few scoops of coffee.

Behind him, he heard the house begin to wake in pieces. People moving about, doors closing, someone using the bathroom, the quiet sounds of stretching and waking. Logan felt relief as his watch finally came to an end.

Blake came up the hall from Charlie's room. He was wearing gym shorts and a gray shirt that read MNPD.

"Looks like you made it through the night," Blake said with a smile.

"Barely," Logan replied. "It was tough. Everything in me wanted to fall asleep."

Blake nodded. "Well, good job staying up and keeping us safe." He disappeared back into the room.

Logan poured the hot water over the coffee and let it steep.

"Good job, dude," Becca told him. "That was a long night."

Logan shook his head in agreement.

Blake reappeared from the hall, now fully dressed in his uniform, boots included. "Any way I can get some of that coffee, my man?" He nodded toward the press.

"Sure thing," Logan replied, pressing down the handle.

Becca looked at Blake. "Are you leaving already?"

"Yes, ma'am. I need to get on the road to Chapel Hill. If I start early, I should be able to make it just after nightfall," Blake said. "I need to get there before it gets any worse. I don't have any resources or external help, and I'm sure my family could use me. I know I could use them."

The little boys chimed in, having overheard. "No, Mr. Blake! Stay with us. We like having you here."

He walked over and patted both of them on the head. "I think you guys will be just fine with Becca and Logan here."

With sad looks on their faces, they replied, "Okay..."

Logan slid a warm cup of coffee over to Blake. Feeling the warmth hit his hands, Blake smiled. "Ahh. Nice and warm. This should fuel me for the trip."

He took a few sips, then looked at Becca and Logan. "You guys are doing great. Keep your eyes open. Lock everything down. Don't be predictable. Pay attention to who's watching, okay?"

The room felt heavier as they sipped their coffee.

Blake continued, "It's day five now. I think it's going to keep getting worse. You can't trust strangers anymore. Just know, you have resources people will want to take." He took another gulp, bigger this time. "Stick together. Protect what you have."

He finished his mug, shouldered his pack, and thanked them once more. Logan handed him a granola bar for the road as Blake headed toward the door. With the family waving, he slipped outside and down the street, his boots steady. They watched from the windows until he disappeared from sight.

The house was quieter without him.

After Blake's departure, the group settled back into the new normal. Straightening up, filling toilets, checking food and water counts, and trying to entertain the younger boys. Staving off questions about Blake and their parents, they moved through the agenda.

It must have been late morning or early afternoon when a knock came at the front door. The family froze, now associating knocks with concern—or danger. Becca and Logan exchanged a glance and moved toward the door.

The face standing there was odd, but familiar. Logan wondered why Richard Lawson was on their porch. He lived on the other side of the neighborhood, in a separate section. Early fifties, mostly gray hair, wrinkles set in from decades of running construction crews. They recognized him vaguely from Fourth of July and Memorial Day gatherings. They opened the door cautiously, noticing Richard had a holstered pistol on his hip. A couple of other men stood with him. They, too, looked familiar in that vague, neighborly way.

Becca spoke first. "Hi. Can we help you guys?"

"Hey there, folks. Sorry to startle you," Richard said. "Me and some of the guys are doing door-to-door check-ins." His eyes drifted past them into the house, scanning. "We want to bring everyone together and talk about how we might work together for the safety of the neighborhood."

Becca and Logan nodded, noticing that De'andre Nolan and Mitch Collins were armed with rifles slung across their chests. They were scanning the street and nearby houses closely. Their rifles sat at low ready, grips tight, fingers resting just above the trigger. Logan recognized the grip and stance. His dad had taught him the same one at the range. Seeing it in his front yard felt different. His pulse rose in his ears.

Both men were in their late twenties or early thirties. Logan thought they looked strong and capable. He remembered seeing them working out at the park and running together on the trails.

Richard continued, "We're setting up a meeting in the green space between our two sections this afternoon. We'd love to have you come listen in." Then he paused. "Where are your parents, Logan? I haven't seen them."

Logan answered carefully. "They're stuck in Dallas, we think. They were there when everything shut off."

"Oh no," Richard said. "I'm really sorry to hear that. You'll definitely want to come to the meeting, then. We're going to talk about neighborhood security and resources. You're going to need some help with them gone, I bet." He held Logan's eyes for a moment. "The meeting's at two o'clock. We'd love to have you. We all need to stick together now."

Becca nodded. "Okay. Thank you. We'll be there." She shut the door.

Logan and Becca stayed by the window, watching the armed men move door-to-door, delivering their message.

As they walked back into the house, Becca said quietly, "That was odd. Do you think guns are necessary? I mean, it's not that bad...is it?"

Logan replied confidently, "Blake told us how bad it already was in the city. It might be smart to have a plan before that gets here."

"Maybe so," Becca said after a moment.

Logan thought about what Blake had said that morning. Pay attention to who's watching. He turned back to the window. The men were still moving door to door, still scanning. They were watching everything.

CHAPTER 14
LINE IN THE SAND

The early afternoon passed quickly. The family decided it was time to head out on their short walk to the green space separating the two sections of the neighborhood. Logan recommended—and Becca agreed—that they would leave the cart at home this time. Unwanted attention was not the goal of this trip.

When the family arrived at the meeting place, there were already a couple dozen people gathered, talking quietly among themselves. Nobody was laughing or carrying on. People observed others in the crowd while glancing down the road, as if waiting for someone else to arrive.

Richard was standing in the back of a very old-looking Jeep. It was faded orange, with several rusty spots around the edges. He was holding onto a big metal bar that ran across the top rear of the vehicle. He was flanked closely by De'andre and Mitch.

Logan noticed the addition of Carol Jensen, also from the other side of the neighborhood. A clipboard was tucked under one arm. She was a short woman, probably in her early forties, though it was hard to be sure due to all the "upgrades" she'd had over the years. She was never particularly friendly and definitely didn't care for kids. Watching her eyes, Logan saw her counting and sorting as neighbors moved about the space.

Ira caught eyes with Logan from the back of the crowd, keeping his distance. He gave Logan that familiar smile and a nod. Logan started to work his way toward him, edging along the back of the group. But the crowd tightened as Richard climbed up higher on the Jeep, and by the time Logan looked back, Ira had shifted further away. Logan decided to go back to where Becca was standing.

Richard waited until the murmurs died down enough to get started. It didn't take long.

"Alright," he said, voice steady. "Thanks for coming out."

He looked the crowd over. Families. Couples. A few people standing alone. Some with arms crossed. Parents holding kids close.

"I won't waste your time," Richard continued. "You all know why we're here. Whatever happened out there"—he pointed beyond the houses—"it isn't getting fixed today or tomorrow. And nobody's coming to sort it out for us."

A few heads nodded.

"We've all seen the changes already. Unknown people passing through. No information from outside. No real leadership." He paused. "That doesn't mean panic. It means we have to adapt." Richard shifted his weight, settling in. "This neighborhood is a good one. Strong and connected. But only if we stay that way. And that means looking out for each other. Not just inside your homes, but outside too."

He pointed toward the entrances of the neighborhood. "We've got access points. Streets that funnel traffic. Blind spots. Right now, anyone can walk through here without being noticed and take what they want. That's a problem."

"So we're setting up a patrol. Nothing crazy. Just a few groups working together. We'll operate day and night." He glanced at the men nearby with slung rifles, then back to the crowd. "Presence alone goes a long way."

A man near the front spoke up loudly enough for others to hear. "What if we don't want armed people walking around the neighborhood?"

Richard looked over at him, expression unchanged. "Then don't join the patrol," he said. "But the patrol will still walk the streets protecting all of us."

This brought on a quick burst of chatter, but no more objections for the time being.

He then held up a clipboard for everyone to see. Conversations dropped. The crowd focused in. Logan watched Carol's eyes move to it immediately, like she'd been waiting for that moment.

"We'll have sign-ups after this. Nobody's being forced. But if you're able, we need you. Every extra set of eyes matters."

"Now, another thing we need to be honest about." Richard's tone shifted slightly. More serious. "Resources. Water. Food. Fuel. Medical supplies. Some of us are doing okay right now. Some of us aren't." He shrugged. "That gap is only going to get wider. I know several folks are out of fresh water."

Logan turned to Becca. She was already looking at him. Neither of them said anything. He turned back to Richard and crossed his arms. They had plenty of food, water, and fuel. For now. He kept his face still and listened.

"I'm not saying hand over anything. I'm saying we need to know what we're all working with. If we don't manage this together, we'll all be in trouble sooner rather than later." He leaned slightly in toward the crowd. "We'll be putting together a basic inventory. Your responses will be voluntary and private. Just so we can plan. Share when it makes sense. Fill gaps before they turn into emergencies."

"Carol will be helping with inventory and resource management," Richard said, already moving past the comment.

Carol nodded at him, as if the role had been decided well before the meeting.

Richard straightened. "The people who stick together will get through this. The ones who isolate...won't." He nodded once. "Stick around. Sign up if you can. Ask questions. Talk to your neighbors. Let's do this the right way."

Logan glanced toward the back of the crowd, instinctively searching for Ira. He was gone. Logan scanned the edges of the green space, the road, and around the nearest houses. Nothing. He hadn't seen him leave. One second he was there, and then he wasn't.

Looking back toward the Jeep and the line of people beginning to form, Logan paused. He watched for a moment, then looked back at Becca and the boys. He didn't move toward the line. He took Becca's arm lightly and steered them toward the edge of the crowd. They needed to talk before anyone put their name on anything.

This wasn't just planning. It felt decided.

Was this a line being drawn?

CHAPTER 15

THE SAFE

The walk home felt longer than it should have. The neighborhood looked the same, but Logan noticed things he hadn't paid attention to before. Who watched from behind windows, who lingered on their porch, and who had skipped the meeting entirely.

Nobody spoke at first. The boys just sensed it, staying close without being told.

By the time they reached the house, Logan understood one thing clearly. The meeting hadn't really been about safety. Not entirely. Something else had been underneath it.

The house was quiet when they returned. Just the same stale air locked inside. Logan and Becca moved through the rooms out of habit, checking doors and windows even though nothing had changed. Everything was locked. Everything was where it should be. Still, the sense of ease they'd felt earlier in the day was gone. Logan missed the comfort Officer Blake had brought during his short visit.

The neighborhood meeting replayed itself in Logan's mind. The way some people nodded while others stayed silent. It bothered him how quickly everyone had agreed and how little pushback there'd been. Nobody asked who was in charge. Nobody objected as decisions were made. It had all happened quickly, wrapped in the language of help and safety.

Logan found himself back near the front door, lingering longer than necessary. He understood now that what came next wouldn't be announced. It would arrive politely. With expectations. With a clipboard just like the one Carol had held.

Outside the glass of the door, the first patrol walked past. Two men and a woman Logan recognized from the meeting. All three carried AR-style rifles and moved together down the street. It didn't look especially organized, and the way they handled the rifles showed a lack of experience, or at least confidence. Logan noticed muzzles drifting where they shouldn't and poor spacing between them.

He had an eye for those things now, after years of shooting and training with his dad. His father had been a stickler for firearm safety, muzzle awareness, trigger-finger discipline, all of it drilled in relentlessly. Logan could hear his dad's voice as clearly as if he were standing there: Treat every gun like it's loaded. Never point it at something you don't want to destroy. Never put your finger on the trigger until it's time to shoot. He never thought those lessons would have a practical application like this.

Logan didn't tell anyone. He just went to the closet and paused in the doorway, taking in how much his parents had stashed away over the years.

A large gray safe sat in the back left corner. Next to it were several gear bags he'd have to explore later. On the shelf above the safe rested a heavy-looking go-bag, clearly packed with equipment his dad believed would be necessary for moments exactly like this. To the right of the safe were green metal army-style ammo cans, each labeled by caliber.

He approached the safe. It felt wrong. For years it had been strictly off-limits. Only Mom and Dad could open it, or even see what was inside. He knew the code, or at least he thought he did. It had to be the same one they used everywhere else: the door locks, the garage keypad, even the TV passcode. Mom and Dad's anniversary. The numbers ran through his mind. 0218.

His hands shook as he tapped the numbers into the keypad. For half a second nothing happened, and he thought he'd gotten it wrong, or that maybe it hadn't been the anniversary after all. Then came a beep, followed by a heavy clunk from inside the safe. Logan turned the handle, and the thick door swung open. The interior came alive with light.

The amount of gear crammed inside was overwhelming. There were more firearms than Logan had expected, various scopes and optics, magazines stacked on nearly every flat surface, and countless boxes of ammunition. It was clear his parents had prepared. Logan had always known his dad owned a lot of guns and equipment, but he'd never seen it all together in one place. Seeing it like this made it real. He made a mental note of a large black lockbox on the top shelf, something he might explore later.

Safety was no longer guaranteed, and by the look of things, protection might be needed sooner rather than later.

He called out for Becca. A moment later, she stepped into the closet, her eyes widening. "Wow, Logan. I don't think you're supposed to be in here. You know the rules. Your parents are adamant; none of us go near the closet or the safe."

Kneeling, Logan glanced back over his shoulder. "I know. I know. But the circumstances are different now. Everything's different." He turned to face her fully. "You heard what everyone's been saying. What Blake said. What Richard and the neighbors are pushing. It's not safe. We're going to have to look out for ourselves."

Becca's eyes moved around the closet before settling back on the safe. "I don't know, Lo. I'm not sure we need to do this yet. We have patrols out there. It seems like the neighbors are looking out for us."

"That's what worries me," Logan said. "It sounded like they're more concerned about resources than actually helping. This stuff is ours. We have to keep it safe and quiet. We have enough right now, but not if we're pressured to give most of it away for the 'greater good.'"

"I still don't think it's necessary," Becca said firmly. "Not yet."

Logan didn't answer right away. He looked at the ammo cans, the gear bags, the go-bag on the shelf. His dad had put all of this here for a reason. He thought about the man in the backyard. The businessman. The patrol walking past with rifles they may or may not know how to handle. "Okay," he said. "Then at least a pistol."

Becca exhaled. "Okay. One pistol. Somewhere close, but safe. And definitely away from the little guys."

Logan nodded. Reaching into the safe, his nerves spiking again, he picked up a pistol he recognized from past range days, the Glock 48. The weight of it felt familiar, the rough grip in his hand. Slim. Balanced. It fit perfectly. He checked it the way his dad had taught him. Slowly and deliberately. He grabbed an extra magazine, then shut and locked the safe.

"We can put it on top of the refrigerator," Becca said quietly. "The boys won't be able to reach it."

"Yeah," Logan said. "That makes sense. It's safe and central to the house."

In the kitchen, keeping it out of sight, Logan placed the pistol on top of the refrigerator.

Once the weapon was in the house, there was no pretending this was still normal.

CHAPTER 16
REMEMBER THE PLAN

The night had passed without incident. No voices in the distance. No movement near the house. No reason for alarm. Logan felt tired in his bones as the sky began to lighten, the kind of tired that didn't go away with sunrise.

By midmorning Saturday, the boys were outside, barefoot in the grass, tossing a football back and forth and arguing about rules that seemed to change freely. Their laughter carried in the quiet of the neighborhood now. It sounded almost out of place, like something from before all the lights went out. Logan watched them from the porch, coffee mug warm in his hands. He was suddenly a coffee fan and realized why his dad had required it to function all those mornings.

Becca stepped out beside him, her hair pulled back hastily, her eyes giving away the night they'd split between them. She leaned against the porch post without saying anything. They didn't need to. The watch had gone smoothly, but it had been exhausting, nonetheless.

The sound of footsteps came first, then hushed voices.

Logan straightened as two people appeared in sight around one of the neighboring houses, moving at an unhurried pace. A patrol, one he recognized now. That alone reminded him that something had changed. This wasn't a one-off anymore. This was the new normal, stacked on top of all the other new normals.

Carol Jensen walked with them. The street behind her was empty except for the two patrol members, who hung back near the sidewalk.

She held her clipboard tight against her chest, papers clipped neatly in place. She smiled when she saw Logan, lifting a hand in a small wave as if this were a casual visit.

"Morning," she called out. "Everyone doing okay?"

Logan nodded. "We're good, Mrs. Jensen."

Her eyes drifted briefly to the boys, then back to him. "Good. That's good." She glanced down at her clipboard, flipped a page, and sighed lightly. "I just wanted to check in. We're going around today making sure everyone's accounted for."

She hesitated, the pause measured. "We haven't seen your names on any of the duty rotations yet," she said. "Or the resource list."

Logan felt Becca shift beside him.

"And," Carol added, her gaze sliding past him toward the driveway, "there's the golf cart. Mobility like that could really help the neighborhood right now."

Carol smiled again, nodded to herself, and made a small note on her clipboard.

Becca spoke up, firm. "Logan and I were actually talking about that. Logan is only thirteen, and I'm the only other adult in the house." She paused, letting it sit. "I can't leave the boys alone, not during all of this. There's too much unknown around here."

Finding some strength in Becca's words, Logan added, "Yeah, Mrs. Jensen, I'm not sure how much help I'd be. I'm certainly nowhere near as useful as those two guys." He nodded toward the men on patrol. Adults wielding rifles like the rest.

"You both have good points," Carol conceded. "We'll find a way to plug you in. We all need to work together now." She paused. "It's only fair to your neighbors, you know?"

She nodded toward the storage garage. "We understand you have a working golf cart. That would be hugely helpful to the neighborhood. We only have a few vehicles running."

Logan's shoulders tensed. "Yeah, we're basically out of fuel for it. Too bad, really. You're probably right."

Becca glanced at him, then back to the three visitors.

"That's no problem, Logan. Luckily, many of your neighbors have volunteered their gas, along with other items, to help out," Carol said without hesitation.

"Oh, cool, that's nice of everyone," Logan said, watching Carol scribble on her clipboard. "We're not planning on going anywhere anytime soon, so we should be good for now."

Looking from Logan to Becca, Carol said, "If the need arises, we'll make sure it's put to good use."

Becca spoke instinctively. "It's not mine to loan out. It's the Hopkinses, and they aren't here to give permission."

"Oh, hun, I understand," Carol said smoothly. "I don't think they'd be worried about it. I think they'd recognize the importance of working together."

Logan almost smiled. Knowing his father, giving up important resources would never have been part of the plan. The thought brought a twinge of humor and despair.

He and Becca simply nodded.

Turning toward the next house, Carol said, "We'd better get going. We have a lot of people to catch up with today. If you would, please put together a list of your key resources. It would be most helpful for our planning."

"Will do, Mrs. Jensen," Becca said.

The group moved farther up the street, knocking on doors and holding muffled conversations with other neighbors. Logan and Becca tried to listen, but they were too far away, and the boys had grown louder in their football game.

Becca turned to Logan. "Hey, let's step inside for a moment."

She closed the front door behind them, the thud echoing through the foyer. The kitchen was visible from where they stood. The pistol was still sitting on top of the refrigerator where they'd left it.

They stood there without speaking. The house was quiet. The boys' laughter drifted in from outside, muted by walls and glass.

"That wasn't a check-in," Becca said.

Logan nodded. "It felt like an inventory checkbox."

She smiled at him, approving. "Exactly. She wasn't asking how we were doing. She was figuring out where we fit and what we have."

Logan leaned against the wall, coffee now cool in his hand. "The clipboard," he said. "Once your name's on it..."

"You don't come off," Becca finished. "And I bet you don't get a say."

They let that settle.

"She smiled the whole time," Logan said.

"That's how people don't notice what's happening," Becca replied.

Logan exhaled. "Yeah. She didn't care about patrols."

"No," Becca said. "She cared about the golf cart."

"Mobility is like gold now. And fuel." Logan set his coffee mug down on the counter. "And who controls both."

"She already assumed she could borrow it," Becca said. "That wasn't a question. That was her testing how much we'd push back."

Logan stared at the floor. "I lied to her."

Becca didn't hesitate. "You protected your family. You did what you had to do."

He nodded slowly. "If we give them anything, it's not ours anymore."

"No," Becca said. "It becomes shared. And shared never comes back, especially now."

"And if we give them a list, they decide what's fair." Logan looked up. "That's not safety."

"That's control," Becca said.

Outside, the boys shouted again, the thump of the football hitting hands.

"They'll be back," Logan said. "And next time it won't sound optional."

He swallowed. "So what do we do?"

"We stay quiet," she said. "We don't volunteer. We don't stand out. The cart stays hidden unless we have to use it. Fuel too." She crossed her arms. "No lists. No sharing."

Logan hesitated. "What if they push harder?"

Becca looked toward the front window. The patrol was gone, but the feeling hadn't left. "We need a backup plan. We need to be ready if it comes to that."

"Like leaving," Logan said

"Possibly. I don't see this getting better, and I don't see them ignoring us now," Becca said.

The boys laughed again, loud and careless.

Logan shook his head. "I don't like this."

"I know," Becca said. "But you saw it. That matters."

He nodded.

Becca looked out the window toward the boys. "Hey, Lo. When your dad left, he mentioned knowing the plan. What did he mean by that?"

Logan didn't answer right away. After a slow breath, he said, "Well...Dad liked to think about this kind of stuff. Backup plans. Just in case." He paused. "I used to think he was kind of crazy." He wasn't sure he thought that anymore.

"Dad always said there would be a line," Logan said quietly.

Becca waited.

"If we crossed it, we were supposed to leave. All of us were supposed to head to Grandpa Jake's house in Mississippi, if things got really bad."

Becca frowned. "Kind of like now? What else was there?"

"Yeah," Logan said. "This would probably qualify." He swallowed. "We were supposed to load up, whatever supplies we could carry. Guns. Food. Water. And go."

"Why their house?"

"Grandpa Jake believed in backups too," Logan said. "Even more than my dad. He has land. A big garden. Animals. Everything we'd need." He looked down. "That was the plan. That was our backup." His voice broke. "Now they're six hundred miles away, and we're stuck here, and nothing works."

Becca pulled him into a hug. "I'm here. We have each other. Your brothers need us to be strong."

Logan wiped his eyes on his sleeve and straightened. "Then we should think about that plan. Because if we don't..." He trailed off. "Carol and Richard will make use of our stuff, and then we really will be stuck."

Becca nodded once, hard. "Then we'd better start planning."

CHAPTER 17
NO ONE IS COMING

The house settled into night without issue. Dinner had come and gone early, a mixture of cooked pasta noodles, canned tomato sauce, and saltine crackers. The rooms felt dark even before the sun had fully set, shadows filling the corners.

The family sat around reading books, telling jokes, and waiting for sleep to come. It felt strange to Logan how time had shifted now. They woke up early and went to sleep early. There was no reason to stay up late when there was nothing to do except stare at the fireplace or candles.

At night, the fear crept in. He could manage it during the day when there was something to do, or a problem to solve. But when everything went quiet, his mind went straight to Dallas. Six hundred miles away. No phone. No way to know if they were okay, where they were, or if they were trying to get back. He didn't let himself go too far down that road. But it was always there chewing at him.

As usual, the radio had been on all day, running on rechargeable batteries and the crank when needed. It sat on the counter, low but constant, cycling through static and random tones. Logan had gotten used to its presence, stuck somewhere between background noise and a lifeline. It hadn't said anything useful in days.

Suddenly, the beeps. Those stupid beeps, followed by the voice that came through without warning.

"...this is an emergency broadcast update."

Logan looked up immediately. Everyone else did too. The tone was calm, projecting confidence and control, even when control was in short supply. There was no good news. Power restoration efforts continued. Critical systems remained offline. No estimated timeline was available.

Then the confirmation came. Logan had known. He just hadn't wanted to say it out loud.

"...we can now confirm the disruption was caused by a large coronal mass ejection impacting infrastructure across multiple regions..."

The announcement continued, explaining that assessments were ongoing and that damage to electrical and communication systems was extensive. The language stayed careful. There were no promises. No suggestion that anything had improved, only that they understood more now than they had before. Now it had a label.

The message ended the same way it always did. Stay calm. Conserve resources. Look out for one another. The radio faded back into static.

No one spoke for a moment. The word confirmed hung in the air. There was no more speculation.

Logan thought about the news broadcasts from weeks ago. The calm language. The reassurances. How small it had all sounded back then. Whatever had happened wasn't temporary. It wasn't getting better anytime soon. If it ever did, it would take a lot of rebuilding.

Eventually, they settled back in. The boys were tucked into their pallets layered around the living room. Everything was as it should be.

By the time Logan took second watch, the neighborhood was completely still. He sat near the front window, watching the street without being seen, trying to stay invisible in his own house. The moonlight washed the pavement a dull gray. Houses stood dark and silent. No movement. No sound beyond crickets, locusts, and the low hum of bullfrogs nearby.

Occasionally, he made a trip through the house to look out the side door and window, then the back door.

Time moved differently at night. Mostly just slow. Painfully slow. He checked his watch. 4:15. He sighed and leaned his head back against the wall, counting breaths instead of minutes. Playing a computer game in his head. Building fun houses and battling PvP enemies.

He adjusted his position, carefully scanning the street again, when the sound cut through the quiet.

Three hurried, sharp pops echoed in the distance, followed by two more cracks of a different pitch. Logan froze.

A moment passed, then two more shots followed. Slower. Intentional. Then silence, perfect and still, set back in.

The sound hadn't come from nearby houses, but it wasn't far either. Somewhere beyond the direction of the park, he thought. Close enough to matter. Logan stayed still, listening.

He waited for sirens. For shouting. For anything that showed something happening. Nothing came. The silence returned, heavier than before.

Had he imagined it? Logan exhaled, realizing he'd been holding his breath. Someone had fired a gun, or guns. There were shots, then others that sounded different. Answering.

And no one was coming.

He glanced down the hallway toward his sleeping family. The night no longer felt empty. It felt active and dangerous.

After staying statue-still for too long, he decided it was time for his sweep through the house. He checked on his brothers and Becca. Everyone was still asleep, oblivious to what had just happened outside, just hundreds of yards away. He decided not to wake Becca. There was nothing that could be done, and they were in no immediate danger that he could tell.

For the next couple of hours, he thought through different scenarios, weighing options. Violence was creeping toward them. Richard and Carol wanted their resources. What they had would eventually run out.

Around 6:00 AM, he decided they had to develop a plan to get to Grandpa Jake's. The signs were there, whether they chose to acknowledge them or not. Dad had been right. He wished his mom and dad were here. To give him advice. To have his back. To coach him through it.

Finally, everyone began to stir. The little boys jumped up, telling Logan good morning before racing off to get breakfast. Today, that consisted of Rice Krispies Treats and granola bars.

Becca and Logan decided on apple cinnamon oatmeal. They filled a small metal pot with water from their jug and placed it on the stove. Becca turned the burner on high and held the lighter against it. She tried again. Then again.

Logan noticed the confusion and stepped over to investigate. He leaned in close to the burner. Nothing. No smell. He pulled back, shoulders slack, gut heavy.

"The gas is out," he said flatly.

"No, no, no, no." Becca moved around, turning on more burners. They were empty. No smell. No gas. The last sense of normal was gone.

Before this, they could cook. They had the fireplace to keep them warm at night, even though the temperature was tolerable. There had been safety in that. Comfort. Now it was gone. All of it.

Becca took a step back, disbelief on her face. "Now what? We can't catch a break, Logan."

"No, no, we can't." Logan's head slumped.

Charlie chirped up. "Hey, what's wrong, guys? Do you want my Rice Krispy treat?" he asked, smiling innocently.

"No, bud. We're good," Logan said. "Just trying to figure out how to warm our water now."

Tripp popped his head over the couch. "Well, just use the grill. It's hot, right? Geez." Then he returned to his book of wild animal trivia.

Becca smiled at him. "That's a great idea, Tripp. We do have propane left in the grill. You know what, let's use that. I need coffee too."

The two of them went outside and fired up Dad's Weber. It heated both pots of water nicely. It accomplished the goal and put a quick bandage on a terrible morning.

Sitting inside, Logan took the time to update Becca on the night and the shots he'd heard. Becca looked genuinely disturbed, the same way Logan had felt when it first happened, holding his breath, waiting.

"It feels like things are coming apart," Logan said. "I don't think we have what we need long-term, especially after the radio announcement. It doesn't feel safe, and Richard and Carol are going to come for our stuff sooner rather than later. I think we need a plan. We need to do what Dad said. We need to get to Grandpa Jake's."

"Lo, I wish you were wrong. I really do," Becca said. "But I think you're right. I don't feel like we're safe or stable here anymore."

Logan nodded hard. "Then we know what we have to do. We have to get out of here. It's decided."

CHAPTER 18
A DECISION IS MADE

With the decision behind them, Logan and Becca started planning. One question sat at the center of it all. How do you make a 160-mile trek to Mississippi with two little boys?

They circled around the kitchen table. Becca grabbed some paper and a pencil and started sketching ideas. They both landed on the same conclusion almost immediately. The only way to make it with Charlie and Tripp was in the golf cart. There was no chance everyone could walk that distance. The boys wouldn't keep up, and even if they tried, they wouldn't cover enough ground. It would take weeks on the road, exposed and unknown.

Becca talked through it out loud. "Gas. I think the cart holds about four or five gallons. It doesn't use much to run, but we'll need a good bit to go that far. I think we'll need two or three tanks to make it." She did the math, writing as she went. Ten to fifteen gallons.

Luckily, they still had that much. They'd been careful. The generator had stayed silent for days now. The noise and attention it drew just wasn't worth it.

Logan added, "If we can average ten to fifteen miles an hour, we could get there in about fifteen hours total. I think we could ride five or six hours a day." He rubbed his temple. "I just don't think the little boys could make it much further than that in a single stretch." He stared down at the numbers. "That puts the trip at three days."

His eyes drifted to Charlie and Tripp, sitting on the floor nearby, playing cards and laughing quietly. "And we have to watch out for them," he said, lowering his voice.

"We do," Becca said. "But I don't think it's safe here anymore. Not now. I think this is the right call. Grandpa Jake will know what to do. He'll have resources. He'll take care of us." She straightened in her chair. "Okay. Golf cart it is. Three days. A couple of gas jugs. What else?"

"We'll need food for three or four days and plenty of water," Logan said. "Water comes first. Space is going to be an issue. The storage rack isn't very big."

Logan leaned closer, lowering his voice again. "What about guns? I think we need to be armed. If we run into trouble, or more people like that business guy in the neighborhood."

"You're right," Becca said calmly. "People are going to want what we have. And they'll be more desperate once we're out there." She ran a hand through her hair. "Lo, it could get dangerous. We haven't been outside the neighborhood in seven days. We have no idea what we're heading into."

Logan thought of something Richard had said during his speech, how presence alone might discourage trouble.

"I think we should both carry pistols," he said. "And bring a rifle or two. Just in case."

"Yeah," Becca said after a moment. "Let's start there. We'll need somewhere to sleep. We can grab the camping gear from the garage."

"That's easy," Logan said. He scratched his chin. "We should grab Dad's big bug-out bag too. I bet it's already packed with half of what we need."

Becca nodded. "And a bag of extra clothes. At least it's not cold yet."

By then, the boys had lost interest in cards. Charlie climbed into Becca's lap while Tripp stood nearby.

"What are you guys whispering about, Bee?" Tripp asked.

"Well," Becca said gently, "it looks like we're going to take a trip to see Grandma and Grandpa in Mississippi."

Both boys erupted. "Yes! Yes! Yes!" Tripp yelled. "We love their house!"

"They have ATVs, tractors, and chickens!" Charlie added, grinning.

Tripp hesitated. "But...how are we going to get there? All the cars are broken."

Becca smiled. "That's what Lo and I were just talking about. We're taking an adventure on the golf cart."

"The golf cart?" Tripp said. "That'll take forever."

Laughing, Becca said, "We think about three days. We'll camp together along the way."

"That sounds fun!" Charlie yelled.

"All right," Becca said. "Go play while Logan and I get ready." They didn't argue. They scattered back to the living room, Connect Four pieces clacking while monster trucks crashed into each other.

"Okay," Becca said, her tone shifting. "Let's get to work."

"But when do we leave?" Logan asked. "We can't just load up and roll through the neighborhood."

"Middle of the night," she said. "Between patrols. That's our safest window."

Logan nodded. "Yeah. That makes sense."

"I'll gather food and water," Becca said. "You grab the go-bag, guns, and ammo." They split up, moving from room to room with purpose. Food. Water. Clothes. Bags filling quickly.

Then a knock hit the front door. Hard.

Becca froze. Their eyes met. Logan leaned around the corner, heart sinking. Carol stood on the porch. Richard was beside her.

They came together in the hallway, nerves rising. Gear was spread out just behind them. Becca opened the door, Logan at her side. "Hello, Mrs. Carol. Mr. Richard." The street behind them was quiet. One of the patrol members hung back near the sidewalk, watching.

"Hello, Hopkins bunch," Carol said smoothly. "After our talk yesterday, we were hoping to add you to the list."

"Of course," Becca said. "We just got tied up."

Logan quickly suggested, "We can sign up now."

Richard smiled. "Perfect. Logan, we'll put you down for resource pickup and delivery. Becca, we'll need you on patrol duty. Logan, here, can watch the boys while you're out." He clapped Logan on the shoulder and squeezed.

Logan forced a smile.

"Yes, sir," Becca said. "Happy to help."

"We're also putting our supply list together," Becca said. "Can we bring it by in the morning?"

"That would be wonderful," Carol said. "Thank you for your compliance. It takes a village."

"It sure does. So glad you're taking the lead on this." Logan said evenly.

They left. As Carol turned away, Logan saw her eyes linger just a moment, past them, into the house.

Becca shut the door and jabbed Logan in the ribs. "Really? So glad you're taking the lead?"

He grinned. "It bought us time, didn't it?"

They got back to work. Both now in the closet, Logan punched in the code. Beep. Thunk. He grabbed another handgun and chose a shorter 5.56 rifle, one he knew well. He cleared it, grabbed a handful of magazines and extra ammo. For Becca, he took his dad's favorite rifle, a camo-painted DD4 AR. If it was good enough for Dad, it was good enough for them. He finished up the kit with holsters, belts, and slings.

Glancing up at the black box on the top shelf, he knew it was now or never. He slid it down and set it between them. To his surprise, the key was already in the lock.

Inside were family photos. Passports. A hard drive. Documents. Cash.

"I think we should take all of this. It looks important," Logan said.

"Yeah," Becca agreed. "Cash could especially come in handy. Cards don't matter anymore." They packed everything together.

Then Becca spotted the atlas. She grabbed it. Logan frowned. "What's that?"

"A book of maps," she said, smiling. "Your parents thought of everything."

Logan nodded. "They're saving us again."

They stacked everything in the living room, bags and cases lined up against the wall like they were ready to move out. Trimming where they could, they wouldn't know what had to be left behind until the early morning hours.

Logan wondered if they'd make it out before anyone noticed, before the neighborhood closed in.

CHAPTER 19

IT BEGINS

Later in the evening, Becca and Logan were finalizing their route with the atlas. It was the last piece of the puzzle besides actually executing the plan.

They decided to work their way around Spring Hill and Columbia. Too many people. Too many unknowns. Avoidance was the plan. Instead, they'd start near the park, then pick up a southbound road and stay on it for miles, skirting towns wherever possible. Somewhere past Lewisburg, they'd have to cross the interstate and find a way west. None of it felt certain to Logan, but it felt better than the alternatives.

The hurried planning and packing fell into silence. The adrenaline wore off, leaving Logan and Becca sunk into the couch, quiet but not settled.

Did Carol and Richard notice? Could they know they were planning to leave? Too many questions. No answers. Logan pushed it all aside. They would move forward.

After a moment of quiet, they prepared their final meal in the house. Their home. Soon the familiarity would be gone. Whatever safety it still offered would go with it.

After executing the nighttime routine with the boys, everyone got comfortable. But for Logan and Becca, there would be no sleep tonight. There would be watches, timing, math, and Tetris with gear on a small golf cart storage rack.

Logan kept running through the logistics. Clearing the patrols and the neighborhood boundary. Then what came after that. His imagination filled in the blanks. He'd watched too many movies growing up. Would it be chaos right away? Or something quieter and emptier?

They took turns watching the front door, careful to stay out of sight, jotting down times. They weren't sure how many patrols existed or how far they reached. But the same two shadowed figures kept returning to their stretch of the street, and that was what they could control. Logan tracked the gaps, twenty minutes, then twenty-three, twenty-one, twenty-six.

Not perfect. But close.

"There's a pattern," Logan whispered. "About a twenty-minute window."

Becca nodded, still scratching notes while pacing between the windows and the back door.

The old analogue clock on the wall read 10:58 PM.

Becca came back over to him. "I think it's time we start loading. After the next patrol goes by, give me a signal and I'll start moving things to the cart."

Logan nodded. "Okay." They would have to load quietly and in the dark. Light and sound carried through the still night. Something they couldn't risk.

As the next set of lights faded past the neighbor's house, Logan turned to see Becca already holding bags on each shoulder. He nodded hard and flashed a thumbs-up. She slipped out the side door toward the storage garage. Logan watched from the window as she unlocked it, eased the door up, and disappeared inside.

He retreated back to his post. Nerves climbing. The plan had started, and he felt the weight of it settle in his gut. He kept one eye on the clock. Fifteen minutes had already passed. No Becca.

He tapped lightly on the glass. Then harder. Her face appeared at the corner of the garage door, caught just enough by moonlight. Logan pointed to his arm, where a watch would be, mouthing Time.

She nodded and slipped back inside the house.

"How's it going?" he whispered.

"Good so far," she said quietly. "I got the bags, camping gear, and two gas jugs loaded. I folded out the storage area on the cart. It gives us more room, but it takes the back seat. Tripp can sit back there, and Charlie can sit between us up front."

"That's a great idea," Logan said. "That gives us more space. What do we have left?"

Before she could answer, a beam of light cut through the front window, bouncing across the walls and framed pictures. They both froze, ducking into opposite sides of the foyer. Logan pressed his back flat against the wall. He could hear his own breathing.

Becca crept closer to the door. "We're good," she whispered. "Just the patrol."

Logan exhaled, realizing he hadn't breathed in what felt like forever.

"We've still got the water jugs, go-bag, guns, and atlas," Becca said. "I'll grab those next. Then the boys, radio, and flashlights. That should be it. Then we're on the road."

She gathered the next load. Logan waited until the street settled before giving her the signal. She stepped outside again. Logan stayed where he was, listening. The house felt smaller now. Already starting to feel like something they didn't belong to anymore.

Then metal clanged. Loud. Too loud.

Logan's stomach dropped before he even moved. He rushed to the window. Becca eased the garage door shut and darted back inside.

"I'm sorry, sorry," she whispered, panicked. "I knocked over the bikes. It's so dark out there. I can't see anything."

They stood frozen, listening. No voices. No shouting. Just the night.

Becca pressed her back against the wall, breathing hard. "Logan...if that brought someone, if I just ruined this—"

"You didn't," he whispered. His jaw clenched as he checked the clock.

Twenty-four minutes.

Right on cue, the shadows returned. Rifles slung low. Slow steps. No urgency. Their lights swept across siding and pavement, then moved on.

"I think we're okay," Logan said quietly. "They kept moving."

Becca let out a breath and rested her hands on her knees. "I thought that was it," she said. "I really did."

"It wasn't," Logan said. "We're still good."

She straightened. "I'll go back out and strap everything down."

"Yeah," Logan said. "What if we cover it with something, to hide it? A tarp or something. Grab straps from Dad's truck."

She nodded, moving toward the main garage. She returned with a blue tarp and green cinch straps. "I'll be back."

"You've got twelve, maybe fifteen minutes," Logan said.

This time there were no crashes. No patrols. Becca came back, rubbing her hands together. "Okay. We're good. We just need the boys, the radio, and the guns."

Logan nodded. Neither of them moved for a second.

"I'm going to grab more food," Becca said. "Whatever I can carry."

As the patrol passed on schedule, Logan slipped the holster belt on. It felt stiff. Awkward. Necessary. The Glock clicked into place. He turned off the radio and slid it into his hoodie pocket.

It was just after 12:30 AM. He didn't feel tired. There was electricity in his veins now. Something sharper than adrenaline. Determination.

Becca returned with more food. They stuffed it into a backpack. Logan handed her a belt. She clipped it on and looked down at it for a second. "I can't believe this," she said quietly. "Armed. Leaving on a golf cart. After the world just...stopped."

Then she added, softer, "I can't believe we're leaving all that food."

"I wish we had a way to carry it," Logan said.

"Me too."

The boys were curled together, closer than they'd ever been before. Logan noticed how they'd changed. Less fighting. More sharing. Growing up without being asked.

Becca gently woke them. Candlelight flickered across the walls. Logan took it in one last time.

Home.

Charlie rubbed his eyes. "It's dark, Bee. I'm scared."

"I know," she said, pulling him close. "But we're together. We'll keep you safe."

Logan watched her hand out snacks and juice boxes, hoping it would cut down on questions.

At 1:16, the final patrol passed. Logan didn't write it down. He wouldn't forget this one.

"They just passed," he whispered. "It's time."

Becca blew out the candles.

Logan took a moment to scribble a quick note to Ira.

Ira, we've decided it was time. We are going to my grandparents' house. It doesn't feel safe here anymore, and as you've probably already figured out, I don't think this can last long term. Grandpa has food, water, and safety. We can't do this alone. Good luck to you and Mrs. Rose. Thanks for all you've done to help. P.S. Here is a key to the back door. We had to leave behind some fuel, water, and a lot of food. Please make use of it. Logan H.

Logan folded the note and grabbed the key as he ran out the door to join Becca and the boys. "What's that, Lo?" Becca asked. He told her what it was. She smiled in response. "That's a great idea. I would hate for that to go to waste."

In the garage, Logan slid the gear selector to neutral and released the parking brake. With some extra effort, he pushed the cart back out of the garage, gear and family included. When it cleared, he stepped up and pulled the door down out of instinct.

Sliding the gear selector forward, Logan stepped on the gas while pulling the choke button out. The cart came to life, and they were off.

The sound felt enormous. The engine coughed, rattled, vibrated through the frame and into his bones. Too loud. No hiding it now. Logan imagined the whole neighborhood hearing it.

He looked back once. The house sat quietly in the moonlight. His room. The yard. The driveway.

For the first time, doubt flickered, not about leaving, but about whether he'd ever see it again.

They left home. The memories. What safety they had left.

CHAPTER 20

INTO THE OPEN

They took the long way out, hugging side streets and taking cut-throughs. They used back paths they'd learned over the years, avoiding the patrol routes they'd noticed over the last couple of days. The cart stayed dark, lights off, just a shadow moving through familiar streets that no longer felt like theirs.

Logan's shoulders and chest stayed tight. Every moment, he kept expecting a flashlight beam to hit them. A voice to yell out. A hand to grab him from behind, pulling them back. Nothing happened. Still, he didn't relax.

They cleared the last row of houses and rolled past the treeline that marked the edge of the neighborhood. Once they were sure they were clear, Logan flipped the switch. The headlights snapped on, highlighting the pavement ahead.

The park came into view as they slowed near the turn. It wasn't quiet anymore. Not like it used to be. Fires burned in scattered pockets, uneven and low, smoke hanging in the air instead of rising. Shapes moved in and out of the glow. Some stood close to the flames. Others wandered aimlessly, heads down, dragging their feet like they didn't know where they were going, or where to go next. Becca leaned forward slightly, eyes scanning. This was the last turn before the main road. The last bit of familiar ground before everything opened up.

He didn't like how busy the park felt. Didn't like that there were more people here than on their last visit. Didn't like knowing that once they turned, there would be no more slipping through unnoticed. No more pretending they were just neighbors out for a drive. Staying still wasn't safe anymore, though. He eased the cart toward the road, anyway.

They made a right onto the main road out of the neighborhood. Their lights swept across multiple cars, just sitting there, parked and still. Open doors, along with trunks and some hoods. Their engines long cold. All of them seemed to have been abandoned in haste. Luxury cars stranded right beside rusted beaters.

The CME hadn't discriminated. It had taken everything the same.

Logan slowly weaved through the maze of cars, eyes darting ahead and to the sides. The family followed the headlights and the glow of the moon illuminating the landscape around them. They hummed along at a much slower pace than expected, but crashing into something unseen would be worse.

The boys gave in to exhaustion. Charlie lay sprawled across Becca's lap, breathing deep and steady. Behind him, Tripp had folded himself into the gear, buried under soft bags and blankets.

They turned onto the southbound road they'd marked earlier. It was a smaller, two-lane road. It looked far less traveled as the parking lot of stranded vehicles became less and less dense with each mile. As they continued, the roads they had recognized became less and less familiar.

Outside the cart, the engine's whine sounded too loud. The rattling was too sharp. Every vibration felt like an invitation for discovery. Logan reached down instinctively to kill the lights. Darkness swallowed everything around them. There wasn't enough visibility to make any meaningful progress. He let out a heavy breath and flipped them back on.

Neither of them spoke. Silence felt safer. Becca stayed alert, her eyes constantly moving, watching the road, the trees, and the ditches. Logan focused on keeping them moving without drawing more attention than they already were.

The family rumbled along further. They did their best to avoid any form of light, movement, or towns along the way, sliding past a couple more populated areas and neighborhoods.

The road curved just ahead. Logan let off the gas, coming to a stop. Becca turned to look at him. "What's up?"

He nodded up ahead. "That's the 840 overpass."

Her eyes strained forward. "Oh yeah. You're right."

"There could be people. That's a big intersection," he said.

Becca thought for a second. "There will be people," she said. "But we have to go south. 840 wraps around everything. We don't have a choice." Logan took a deep breath, dropped his shoulders, and agreed. He knew it, but didn't like it.

"Keep your eyes out," he said. He eased off the brake and back onto the accelerator, the engine jumping back to life. Loud and ominous.

As they got closer, Logan caught the smell first. That familiar smell of things burning and trash that had soured. A small fire flickered ahead. Then another. Then more.

As they approached the overpass, tents came into view, clustered beneath the concrete. Makeshift shelters pressed together. Figures moved among them.

They were almost under the bridge when a beam of light locked onto them. Movement erupted around the overpass. People stood up. Shadows moved. Voices shouted indistinctly.

"Punch it!" Becca yelled, gripping Logan's shoulder.

The cart surged forward as Logan mashed the gas, weaving between stalled cars and debris piles. Tents and people blurred past on either side. Another shadowy figure yelled from the abutment above as another light flared on them from behind. Logan didn't look back, the cart still racing ahead.

They cleared the bridge and kept going, the engine revving high as the concrete and street signs faded into the dark behind them as fast as the cart would allow.

"I think we surprised them," Logan said, breath tight in his chest.

"Yeah," Becca said. "I think so."

After another ten or fifteen minutes, enough time Logan hoped, he noticed a gravel road cutting off to the left. It looked like a good spot to pull over. Turning in, he drove another couple hundred feet and finally took his foot off the gas. He locked the parking brake with a click and sat for a moment, arms resting over the wheel. The adrenaline drained out of him all at once.

"I think we need to stop," he said quietly. "We're all tired. We haven't slept in almost twenty-four hours."

Becca nodded, squeezing Charlie. No argument from her.

He climbed off the cart quietly and walked a short distance up the road. Gravel crunching under his feet. No flashlight. Just moonlight to guide him. He scanned ahead and to the sides, checking the treeline and ditches, then glanced back toward the road behind them. For now, it felt empty.

He climbed back aboard the cart. "It looks clear from what I can tell," he told Becca, while taking his hoodie off and pulling the radio out of the pocket. He set the radio in the front storage area and rolled his hoodie up into a makeshift pillow, trying to get comfortable.

"A couple hours," he said. "That's all."

The night was calm. Cool enough to be comfortable. No wind, no distant voices, and no danger that he could determine. As exhaustion pulled him under, Logan knew there would be no watch tonight. Everyone was spent. It was a gamble. They didn't have another choice.

CHAPTER 21

EXPOSED

They woke up late. The kind of sleep that only came from exhaustion. Sunday was gone. It was Monday morning.

The sky was already bright by the time Logan opened his eyes. A brilliant blue, clear and wide, with only a few clouds drifting by. Birds chirped and sang in the trees nearby like nothing had changed. For a few seconds, it almost felt normal. Like a Saturday morning before everything. Logan let himself stay there longer than he should have, soaking in the sounds. Then his thoughts drifted to his parents, just for a second, then he pushed it away.

Everyone was quiet. The boys were curled up and still. Becca hadn't moved yet. No sounds nearby. No voices. No engines. No reason to panic.

It still didn't feel real that it was Monday. Eight days since their world had started over.

Logan sat up and immediately winced. His neck protested, stiff and angry from the hours before. His body was pushing back now, unprepared for this kind of fatigue. For this kind of journey.

Instantly, he realized the dark didn't disguise them anymore. They were exposed. The gravel road stretched open in both directions, empty and unforgiving. Anyone looking could see them coming from a good way off.

Becca caught his look before he said anything. She followed his eyes down the road, then back behind them. She didn't comment, just nodded slightly. They were thinking the same thing. She slid out from under Charlie carefully and stood, stretching her back and legs. She moved like someone who hadn't slept well either.

It was a beautiful day, the kind Logan would've trusted before, the kind that once meant things were going to be okay.

They dug through the bags for breakfast. Nothing fancy. No cooking. Nutri-Grain bars, juice boxes, and water. The boys sat on the edge of the cart, legs dangling, still groggy. Nobody complained. Nobody talked. They ate because it was time to eat. Charlie held his juice box with both hands like it was something precious. Tripp stared down the road and didn't ask where they were going.

Logan rationed the water silently in his head.

Burning daylight now, Becca and Logan reviewed their route. They would keep heading straight south, working their way around the town of Lewisburg. The goal for the day was Pulaski, then west from there. Best case, they hoped to cover about fifty miles. Added to the twenty or so from the night before, it would feel like real progress.

They packed back up and rolled south.

The road felt different in the daylight. Too open. Houses passed slowly on either side. People stood on porches with arms crossed, eyes tracking them as they went by. No waves. No hellos. Just blank stares on dirty, tired faces.

A family sat off the road beneath a tree, their belongings piled around them. They didn't ask for help. They didn't flag anyone down. They just watched, defeated. As the cart passed, their small child chased after them for a few seconds before stopping, her head held low. Tripp smiled and waved from the back as they left her behind.

Farther down the road, smoke curled into the sky from a house that was already gone, nothing left but a blackened shell.

Tripp broke the silence. "When can we go back home?" The words landed heavier than Logan expected. He kept his eyes on the road. There wasn't an answer that wouldn't feel like a lie, so he let it hang there. Becca reached back and rested a hand on Tripp's shoulder. "Not yet," she said. "We still have a long way to go to Mississippi." Her voice was gentle but final. They kept moving.

The farther they went, the more rural it became. For once, Logan welcomed the nothing. Trees and open fields felt safer than people now. People meant danger. They made good time over the next hour, just fence posts blurring past and the occasional farmhouse.

Up ahead, a large brown sign came into view: LEWISBURG, Population 13,000.

Becca leaned forward, eyes narrowing. "Not a huge town," she said, "but that's still a lot of people. We should go around."

Logan nodded and pulled to the shoulder, spreading the map across the seat. On paper, the county roads looked quiet enough, thin gray lines looping around the town instead of cutting straight through. That was preferable.

In reality, those roads weren't empty at all. As they approached the outskirts, houses began clustering closer together. Logan scanned constantly now, hands tight on the wheel. There was nowhere to disappear. Pulling off the road would only draw attention.

People weren't staying downtown anymore. They were spreading outward, settling wherever there was land, shade, or something worth taking. This wasn't going to work the way they'd planned it. Anyone traveling like this was trying to avoid attention, and that made them worth watching. People were adapting quickly.

Daylight had taken away what little advantage they had. At night, they could disappear. Now there was nowhere to hide. It had taken eight days for daylight to become more dangerous than night.

They skirted the outskirts of town, dipping in and out of narrow two-lane roads, the cart still pointing south. Once they were clear, they rolled on for a short stint before coming over a steep hill. Logan caught something ahead. Far down the road, something blocked it completely.

At first, it looked like debris. Too even. Too deliberate. He eased off the gas. The engine dropped to a low hum. Becca stiffened beside him. Charlie sat up straighter and Tripp grabbed the back of Logan's seat.

As they eased closer, shapes took form. A truck angled sideways. Something large stretched across the road. It wasn't wreckage. Then a silhouette shifted near the blockage, someone ducking back out of sight.

Logan didn't hesitate. He veered hard off the road toward the first open structure he saw, an empty-looking house with a garage door hanging halfway up. They rolled inside and killed the engine.

The sudden silence pressed in on them. Becca moved fast, grabbing the door and bringing it down with a hard pull. Logan leaned forward, eyes locked on the thin strip of daylight beneath it, heart pounding in his ears as he listened.

The boys shifted, whispering questions he couldn't answer. In the hint of light, he turned to them without speaking and pressed a finger to his lips.

Logan silently prayed the house was empty, that whoever had lived here had already moved on, and that whoever was manning the roadblock didn't notice them. One thing was clear now. Whatever waited on that road, they weren't ready for it yet.

CHAPTER 22
CLOSE CALL

Logan and the family climbed off the golf cart, fumbling in the dark. The only light came from the thin strip glowing beneath the garage door.

They gathered behind the cart without speaking, crouching out of instinct. The smell of gas and hot plastic hung in the air, sharp and heavy, mixing with pine needles from outside. No one moved. No one breathed louder than they had to.

They didn't know if they'd been seen. They didn't know how long it would take for someone to reach them if they had.

They waited.

What felt like an eternity, though it was probably only minutes, was broken by a low rumble.

It grew gradually at first. Uneven. Wrong. A mix of sputtering and rattling that Logan couldn't quite place. His mind latched onto it anyway. An old truck, maybe. A busted muffler. A tractor. The sound grew louder.

Logan's body went rigid. He squeezed the back of the cart and pulled Tripp tighter against his shoulder. He couldn't see Becca in the dark, but he could feel her beside him, stiff and unmoving, as Charlie pressed tight against her chest.

Then voices. At first muffled, lost beneath the engine noise. Then closer.

"I think they turned in here."

He went still.

The engine coughed once more and then cut, the sudden silence almost worse than the noise. Footsteps followed. Gravel crunching, slow and deliberate.

"There's only a few houses," another man said. "Cover's not great."

Logan swallowed. There was nowhere else to go.

A shadow passed across the thin strip of light under the garage door.

"Ben, check around that house," someone said with authority.

Footsteps moved off to the right, toward the main house.

"I don't see their cart," a voice called out.

"Me either," another answered. "Let's keep looking. Maybe they went deeper into the neighborhood."

"Maybe," the first man said. "But let's clear here first."

Multiple footsteps moving around them.

The front door of the house, not the garage, opened.

Logan's grip tightened until his hand hurt. His throat closed. He leaned down, whispering to Tripp, then to Charlie, he wasn't even sure they could hear. "Shhh."

Inside the house, footsteps moved across the floor. Cabinets shifted. A drawer opened and closed. The sounds were close now. Too close. Logan thought he could hear the man breathing, only a side door separating them.

A voice from outside broke the moment. "Ben. Come on. We're giving them time to get away."

"I don't see anything in here," Ben shouted back.

A pause.

"Alright. Coming."

Footsteps moved away from the side garage entrance door. The front door slammed shut.

Two shadows crossed the strip of light once more, moving in the opposite direction. Their voices faded as they walked away, swallowed by distance.

The loud vehicle, whatever it was, fired back up without warning, breaking the eerie silence. The sound made everyone jump, and the boys whimpered, squeezing even tighter.

It faded off behind them, presumably deeper into the neighborhood.

Stillness fell again. Only then did Logan realize how hard he was shaking.

Ben had been right outside the door.

Logan had no way of knowing what that really meant, or how close they'd come to things going very wrong. He didn't know what those men would have done if they'd found them. Hurt them? Taken their supplies? Taken the cart?

He settled on one answer. Wheels. Resources. Mobility. That had to be it.

It was another reminder of how much things had changed. Their fear wasn't the CME anymore. It was people.

They stayed where they were, quiet and unmoving, hoping the men wouldn't return. There was no real way to measure what a "safe" amount of time looked like, so they waited longer than felt reasonable. Minutes stretched. Maybe an hour. No one dared move.

The stuttering engine never came back.

They kept expecting it, the rattling noise, the voices, but it never returned. Either the men were still searching elsewhere, or they'd found another way out of the neighborhood.

Finally, Logan clicked on his flashlight.

Both boys let out shaky breaths they'd clearly been holding. The dark had been brutal for all of them. The beam swept across the garage, and Logan let out a slow breath. It felt risky, but the exposure was minimal and worth it.

"Everybody okay?" Logan whispered.

The boys nodded, eyes wet but silent.

Becca loosened her grip on Charlie. "Wow," she whispered. "That was close. Absolutely terrifying."

"It really was," Logan said quietly. "We got incredibly lucky. I guess they didn't think about us pulling in here. I'm glad they moved on."

He glanced toward the house. "It seems empty, the way that guy just walked in and searched around, but I want to make sure we're alone before we get too comfortable."

As he stood, he remembered the gun. He touched it without thinking, just enough to remind himself it was there.

A question flashed in his mind. Would he use it? What would he do?

Becca was already reaching for one of the bags on the cart. "I'll get some food going," she said. Logan nodded and turned toward the door into the house.

The boys perked up immediately. A snack always helped. Even now.

Logan stood, legs shaky at first, then steadier as he crossed the garage. He eased it open and slipped inside, staying low, careful not to silhouette himself against any windows. Even with the sun beginning to lower, he wasn't taking chances.

He moved from room to room, quiet and deliberate. The house was empty and stale. Whoever lived there had either left days ago, or never made it home at all.

For now, they'd be squatters. And he was grateful for it.

When Logan returned to the garage, a couple of candles cast a soft light across the space. The family's voices were low, echoing faintly off the bare walls. He took a quick look around: yard tools, bikes hanging from hooks, a large red toolbox shoved into a corner. Nothing useful. Nothing untouched. The open door told him that the place had already been picked over.

Becca had set up Dad's little propane camp stove and was warming chicken noodle soup. A warm meal, something almost normal, was exactly what they needed after the tension.

At first, Logan didn't sit down. He moved around, keeping an eye on the door.

They were all starving. They'd just forgotten. The meal was a success.

Their confidence came back a notch. Just enough to feel human again. Bellies full. Spirits steadier. Then the exhaustion hit hard and all at once.

Logan looked at Becca. Her eyes were glassy, shoulders slumped. The boys had gone quiet in that boneless way that meant they were almost out already.

He turned to them. "Why don't we roll out the sleeping bags in here," he said quietly. "We're safe for now. It's good shelter. Let's get some rest before we try to figure out how to get out of here."

"I'll take first watch."

Becca didn't argue. The exhaustion was written all over her face. She just nodded and got to work.

She unrolled the sleeping bags and tucked the boys in, curling up beside them. They fell asleep almost immediately.

Logan climbed back into the golf cart and sat on the seat, listening to nothing in particular. He flipped through the map again, more out of habit than usefulness. He checked his pistol, cleared it, loaded it, then cleared it again, his hands moving on autopilot. He was getting more and more comfortable manipulating the weapon.

Every so often, a sound pulled his attention sharp. A tree cracking somewhere outside. The garage settling. Dogs barking in the distance, on and off. It was unsettling and unfamiliar, but nothing that felt immediate. Nothing that demanded action.

The thin strip of light beneath the door had disappeared. Night had fallen, he thought.

Locked inside the garage, there was no way to know what time it was anymore. Logan found himself longing for his now dead Apple Watch.

After what felt like a few hours, Logan gently shook Becca awake and traded places with her. His body was done. His mind wasn't far behind.

He closed his eyes and was gone. It felt like seconds later when Becca nudged his shoulder.

"I think you've been out a few hours," she whispered. "We should probably put our heads together and figure out a way out of here before the sun comes up."

Logan groaned softly and sat up, rubbing his shoulder, trying to wake the arm that had gone numb beneath him.

Becca already had the camp stove going. Instant coffee, warmed and waiting.

The smell hit him harder than he had expected. It reminded him of his parents. Morning routines. A different life, before a dumb three-letter thing crashed everything around them.

Logan figured it was now Tuesday morning, somewhere just past midnight. Maybe an hour on either side.

As good a time as any to leave. Quietly.

The two of them sat close together, heads bent over the map.

It didn't take long to see the problem. Pushing farther south wasn't an option, not with the roadblock and the population of Lewisburg sitting directly in their path. Too many people. Too many unknowns. Too much exposure.

Planning quietly, they paused at every sound outside.

Becca traced a finger back along the route they'd taken in. "What if we backtrack a couple of miles?" she said, hushed.

She pointed to a thin line on the map, a narrow, two-lane road that wound west through nothing in particular.

It wasn't part of their original plan. It wasn't even close. But it was an option.

"That should take us under I-65," Logan said, following it with his eyes. "Then we can pick up Highway 31 and head south from there."

"Back toward Pulaski," Becca said.

Logan nodded. It wasn't ideal, but it avoided Lewisburg entirely. That alone made it worth considering.

They figured it would add distance, maybe twenty-five or thirty miles from where they were now. More than they wanted, but in the right direction.

Logan did the math in his head and didn't like the answer. The detour would eat into their fuel more than he was comfortable with, but there wasn't a better option.

"We'll do it tonight," Becca said. "Daylight hasn't exactly worked in our favor."

"No," Logan agreed. "Night's better for sure."

They estimated three, maybe four hours of travel time if nothing slowed them down. That would put them moving through the last stretch right around sunrise.

"When we get close," Logan said, "we can stop. We'll set up camp, rest, and eat. Then we figure out the next leg."

Becca nodded. "One problem at a time."

It wasn't the route they'd planned, but it should work.

They had a plan, and now they needed to move. Time was ticking.

CHAPTER 23
THE LONG WAY

With the planning complete and Tuesday morning bearing down on them, it was time to move.

Logan stepped over to the golf cart and lifted the seat. He leaned in, squinting at the semi-clear plastic of the gas tank, trying to judge the fuel level in the dim light. It looked like they'd burned a little more than half a tank.

He paused for a moment, running the numbers in his head. Half a tank had gotten them roughly forty miles. Maybe a little more...or less, he couldn't be sure. That meant they were still tracking with their original estimates. Still within the margins they'd talked through on paper.

He grabbed one of the full gas jugs from the back rack and tipped it carefully into the tank. When he finished, he expected the jug to be completely empty, but when he straightened it back up, it still had some fuel in it. Only about half gone, he thought.

He tightened the gas cap back on, then slid the jug back into place on the rack. The smell of gasoline filled the air in the garage now. Normally he liked the smell, but in this confined space, it was a lot, stinging the eyes and settling in his nose and mouth.

They didn't dare open the garage door to air it out. Not yet. Not until they were ready to roll.

They woke the boys.

Tripp came to first, eyes wandering, blinking hard like he wasn't sure if he was dreaming or awake. He scanned the garage, the cart, the gear piled around him, confusion settling in fast.

"Where are we—"

Becca cut him off, pulling him close and whispering reassurance. Charlie stirred a moment later. He looked up at the dark ceiling, then found Becca without a word and pressed himself against her side. She wrapped an arm around him. With both boys now awake, she worked on packing the sleeping gear while they shook off the last bit of sleepiness.

Logan froze.

A sound. Outside.

It was faint. A cracking noise. Maybe a footstep. Maybe a branch snapping.

He lifted a hand instinctively.

Everyone followed his cue without a word. Becca stopped mid-motion. The boys went still. The garage felt impossibly quiet, every breath loud.

Seconds passed. Then a few more. Logan strained to hear anything: voices, movement, another step. Luckily, nothing came. They could just hear the low hum of night insects.

He dropped his hand. "I think we're good. Sorry..."

They went back to work, moving quickly and quietly.

Once everything was packed and loaded, Logan took an extra minute to inspect the load. He tugged on straps, shifted gear, double-checked that nothing could slide or rattle loose. Every sound mattered. Every mistake cost something.

Everyone climbed into their spots, the boys still groggy and quiet. No one was excited to be back on the cart. It was time, though.

"I'm going to check out front," Logan whispered to Becca. "I want to make sure the coast is clear before we open the door and drive out. Just real quick."

She nodded in agreement.

He slipped through the inside door from the garage into the house, the same way he had earlier. Again, he was careful not to expose himself to the outside. He moved slowly, every step deliberate.

He paused at the front door, then eased it open and stepped out into the night, crouching low as he moved into the yard. He only took a few steps at a time, sticking close to cover until he reached a large tree. He pressed his body against it, studying his surroundings.

The area was still. No engines. No voices. No movement he could pick out. He took extra time to make sure there were no immediate threats.

After a few minutes, he slipped back inside and closed the door behind him. He moved quietly back to the garage.

The crew was waiting. Logan climbed into the driver's seat. Becca's face was tight, focused. The boys sat hunched, wrapped in layers, eyes heavy.

"You guys ready?" he whispered.

There was no response, just a stare back. As ready as they'll ever be, he thought.

Becca slid off the seat and walked over to the garage door. Logan met her eyes and gave a nod. She gripped the handle and started lifting it, inch by inch.

The sound was piercing in the cold air outside.

Metal ground against metal, the spring winding, louder than it had any right to be in this situation. Logan flinched, certain the noise carried far beyond the house. He imagined faces turning, people listening, the search party coming for them.

Becca raised it just enough.

She jumped back onto the cart, and Logan released the brake. The cart rolled forward gradually, methodically. No lights for now. He kept the RPMs low, willing it along as they eased out of the garage and into the driveway.

At the edge of the neighborhood, Logan slowed and looked downhill toward where the roadblock had been.

He didn't see people moving, but the truck was there, or at least he thought it was. It was parked near a couple of barrels with fire burning inside them, orange light flickering against the darkness.

His jaw tightened, knowing the people down there had been hunting them just hours before.

He kept moving, pointing the cart back up the hill they'd climbed the day before. The same hill that had hidden the road-block from them. The same hill that had boxed them in. No one spoke.

At the top, Logan slipped the cart into neutral and killed the engine. Gravity pulled them down the backside, the silence broken only by rubber tires thumping on pavement. For once, the terrain worked in their favor, shielding them from the other side and the roadblock.

At the bottom, he pushed the gear to forward and flicked the lights on. With a hard push of the gas pedal, the engine jumped back to life. He pressed the gas harder now, wanting distance. Wanting space between them and whoever might come chasing.

A couple of miles later, they reached the cutoff road they'd marked on the map. Logan took the left turn clean and steady. Just like they'd planned. The tension eased slightly. They only passed a few signs of life as they moved, candles glowing in windows, small fires burning in front yards. A couple of people stepped out to listen as they went by, trying to place the sound. No one waved. No one followed.

After forty-five minutes or so, a large bridge structure appeared ahead in the moonlight.

"I-65," Logan muttered.

Everyone stiffened, remembering the last underpass had been chaos: people, noise, desperation. Logan sat up straighter, scanning ahead, slowing the cart. This intersection was smaller. Quieter. Not much around it.

As they drew closer, they noticed one tent set off to the side. No debris. No crowd. Just the tent.

It shifted as a woman unzipped the front flap and poked her head out, watching them pass. No waves. No calls. Just observation. A simple look of what Logan pegged as amazement, maybe.

They rolled under the interstate without incident. Logan kept his eyes moving until the concrete was well behind them, then let out a slow breath.

"That was...uneventful. Maybe this backup route isn't so bad."

"Good luck for once," Becca said softly.

They pushed on into the early morning hours. Tuesday. Day ten.

It was chilly, colder than it should've been for April. The boys huddled against Becca, their hoodies pulled tight, knees tucked into their chests. Logan felt the chill through his jacket and was even more thankful for the warm house they'd borrowed.

"I feel like we should've hit 31 by now," Logan said quietly as they pushed on.

"I was just thinking that," Becca replied. "We didn't miss anything, did we? The plan was solid."

"I know," he said. He kept his eyes on the road.

The darkness felt endless, no signs or landmarks to tell them how far they'd gone. Just fields and power poles sliding past in the moonlight.

A large yellow sign finally appeared, black arrows pointing left and right. Highway 31. He exhaled and pulled to a stop. He scanned both directions and saw nothing, then turned left. South again.

He pressed the accelerator harder. For now, the plan was working. The wind cut through his jacket as they picked up speed. He pulled his collar up with a hand and kept the other on the wheel.

"Night's definitely the time to travel," Logan said. "Fewer people and less visibility."

"Yeah," Becca replied. "I just want to be there. We're freezing."

They pushed on. Logan glanced back over his shoulder. Tripp was out again, his head leaned against the bags. Charlie wasn't. He was curled into Becca, shoulders shaking, his breathing uneven. Logan tightened his grip on the wheel. Stopping out here wasn't smart. He scanned the road ahead, then the dark behind them. He thought a moment longer, then eased off the accelerator and pulled over.

"Hey, bud," he said, keeping his voice low. "Talk to me."

"I just want to go home," Charlie cried.

Logan swallowed hard and said patiently, "I know, buddy. It wasn't safe for us anymore. I wish it was."

"It was warm," Charlie shot back. "And we had all of our stuff—my toys."

Becca brushed his hair. "People were trying to take what we had."

Logan leaned in. "We're almost to a stopping point. When we get there, we're going to set up our tent, sleeping bags, and maybe even have a fire. It'll be like camping with Dad."

Charlie sniffed. "Yeah, that sounds kinda fun."

"Do we have any marshmallows?"

Logan laughed. "No—but I bet Grandma and Grandpa will when we get there!"

"Oookay," Charlie conceded.

They moved on, Charlie pacified for the moment.

Before Pulaski, they had planned on turning off earlier than they would have, learning from the Lewisburg mistakes. As they approached, they turned off onto Guthrie Road. It was a small cut-through that would lead them toward 64, where they planned to make their big move westward.

Just as dawn began to break, they found a narrow opening in the woods, an old logging road barely visible.

They followed it a couple of hundred yards in and shut the cart down. This time, they were surrounded by trees and cover. A much better position than their haphazard first night.

Everyone slumped in defeat.

Four hours in the cold. Sore legs. Cramped backs. Faces streaked with dried tears from the cold wind beating on them.

But they were hidden, and they were done.

For now.

CHAPTER 24

TRESPASS

The crew climbed off the cart, trying to settle in. There was work to be done before they could get some much-needed rest.

The woods were quiet around them. Just the sound of the cart ticking as it cooled and birds up in the tree line.

The sun was already climbing through the trees as the morning moved in. The cold still hung in the air, nagging at them. They couldn't seem to escape it, but they certainly wanted to.

Logan thought of warmth first. He took Dad's go-bag off the cart, pulling it free of the straps and other gear it was tangled in. Searching through the small front pocket, he found a lighter. Using his foot, he cleared an open area, trying to get down to soil. The last thing he wanted was a big fire in some random field while they were trying to hide from prying eyes.

After opening up a large circle, he found some dead limbs at the bases of the trees around them. He stacked them in a neat, teepee-style triangle, then filled the opening underneath with dried grass he'd balled up. He used the lighter to ignite several sections of the grass while lightly blowing on the flames. It caught and began to spread through the grass and into the limbs. They had fire.

The smoke rose steadily now. Logan glanced up, noticing it was higher than he would have liked. Maybe a little too much.

His little brothers were elated. He laughed, knowing every kid loves fire, and was happy to bring them at least a pinch of joy. Charlie seemed to be in better spirits, the glow and warmth soaking into him.

Becca grabbed the other black bag from the back, the one with all the food. She pulled out some instant oatmeal, Spam, and trail mix for a small treat. She threw the Spam and oatmeal into small metal pots and placed them right next to the fire. Logan found the small coffee percolator mixed in with the camping gear. Taking some precious water from their jugs, he filled both the coffee and oatmeal pots, still keeping ration counts in mind.

The Spam started sizzling almost immediately, the salty smell spreading fast through their makeshift camp. This pulled the boys' attention.

Logan thought, now it's the small things that bring joy. Just like camping, there was something about a decent meal that brought you back to center.

Once everything was done, the food was divided up, and everyone dug in. The young boys were ravenous and seemed appreciative. Their diet was far from structured now that everyone was only eating once or twice a day.

The food seemed to lift everyone, especially the now-common staple of coffee. Holding his cup out and pointing, Logan laughed. "Now I get it. I see why everyone is nuts about coffee. It all makes sense finally."

Becca laughed with him as she took a sip.

Thawing out and finding some life again, Logan set to work putting up the tent. Tripp was right beside him, trying to help and asking question after question. Why this, why that, on repeat.

Logan normally would have gotten frustrated and told him to get lost, but now he found more patience. He worked closely with his middle brother, showing him how to attach the poles. How to pull up from the middle. How to push the stakes down at an angle. The same kinds of things Dad had shown him. In no time, the two boys had the tent up. The woods had started to come alive around them. Birds called back and forth above, and the fire had burned down to a steady, quiet crackle.

They piled the sleeping bags and extra clothes inside for warmth and pillows. For the next several hours, this was going to be their new home.

After the meal and tent setup, the sun was now solidly in the sky. Logan noted it was somewhere between morning and midday. It took him a second to realize it was still only Tuesday.

With everyone relatively full, and after several broken nights of sleep weighing on them, it was time to crash.

Becca looked over at Logan. "I'll take first watch this time. You need the rest, and you took the first watch last time." Logan tried to rebut, but Becca wouldn't have it.

He watched her take her post on the cart. She stretched out, propping her feet up on the plastic dash, finding a comfortable position.

Logan conceded and crawled in with the other two boys. He zipped himself into the tent and then into the sleeping bags. He unsnapped his belt, unholstering the sidearm at his hip. He'd almost gotten used to the weight, but it certainly wasn't comfortable to lie on. He set it aside and laid his head down next to Tripp and Charlie.

They were warm and safe, for the time being.

He lay there, almost comfortable, briefly listening to the fire crackle and pop before he faded.

It couldn't have been long.

He woke to a loud, even voice.

"Mornin'."

It took him a second for the word to register as he tried to connect fuzzy dots. The voice wasn't one of theirs. His eyes snapped open, and he glanced at his belt lying beside him while grasping the tent zipper.

At the same time, he heard Becca's startled reaction. She only sleepily managed, "—Huh?"

Logan opened the tent flap, seeing the voice's owner now. The fire had burned down to coals. Smoke still curled up through the trees, thin but visible. The morning air was sharp and cold.

A man stood with his hands in his pockets, weight shifting slowly from side to side. He was older, with broad shoulders. He wore an old fleece shirt and work boots. A beard that was mostly gray, with some black mixed in. His face was calm and unreadable.

Just watching.

Logan and Becca paused.

"Didn't mean to scare you," the man said. His voice was deep and steady, the kind that carried without effort. "I saw the smoke."

Behind Logan, the tent shifted. The boys murmured, half-awake, confused by the voices.

Logan swallowed. "We're just passing through. We don't mean any trouble."

The man nodded, eyes drifting to the cart, the gear, the tent. He didn't linger long on any one thing, but he didn't miss anything either.

"Yeah, I figured," he said. "This road doesn't see much traffic anymore since...whatever happened."

Logan looked to Becca. Her eyes were wide, now fully awake and speechless. She must have dozed off.

"You're on my land," the man said, not unkindly. More matter-of-fact than anything. "You're a bit off the road in here."

Logan nodded. "Sorry. We were just trying to find a safe place to rest. We drove all night."

"Is that so?" the man said. He shifted his weight again. He glanced at the fire. "It was a cold night for April, huh?"

Logan followed his gaze. "Yes, sir, it was. That's why we had to stop and warm up."

The man pointed toward the smoke as it curled upward, thin but visible in the daylight. A knot tightened in his chest.

"You might want to be careful with fires," the man said flatly, "if you're trying to stay hidden."

Logan didn't respond. He climbed out of the tent, making his way toward Becca.

"It's hard on kids out here," the man said.

He nodded toward the trees behind him. "I've got a place back there. Not far. I have a wood stove that still works and coffee, if you drink it." He paused. "I even have eggs."

He said it casually, like it was no trouble at all.

Becca stepped closer to Logan, not touching him, but close enough that he felt it.

Tripp blurted out, "Oh, I love eggs..."

"We're okay," Logan jumped back in. "We've got food."

The man nodded, looking back at the fire. "Yeah. I figured I'd offer." His eyes moved to the cart. "Is that thing still running?"

"For now," Logan said.

"Huh." The man scratched at his beard. "That one gas or electric?"

"Gas," Logan replied.

"Fuel's getting hard to come by now," the man said matter-of-factly.

He waited.

"Kids eat better inside," he added. "It's warmer, too. Plus, you won't be advertising yourselves." He gestured toward the smoke.

Becca cleared her throat. "We're going to get moving soon."

"Sure," the man said. "I didn't mean to rush you." He glanced back at the boys peeking through the tent. "Those yours?"

Logan stiffened. "Yeah. My brothers."

"How old?"

"Eight and four."

The man nodded slowly. "That's a lot to keep up with."

"Who are you?" He tipped his nose toward Becca.

"I'm the nanny," she said. "We're all in this together now."

He was quiet for a moment, then said, "You guys headed somewhere specific?"

Logan hesitated, just a second too long. "Southwest, into Mississippi," he said. "For now."

The man nodded again. "You know, the road you're on doesn't go through."

That landed. "What do you mean?"

"It's a dead end," the man said simply. "Runs out a couple of miles past here."

Logan looked at Becca. She didn't say anything, but her face tightened.

"Most folks miss it on the map," the man went on. "It looks like it connects."

"Is there another way?" Logan asked.

"It depends on what you're driving," the man said, glancing at the cart again. "That might make it. There are trails and old ATV paths. They'll get you where you're going if you don't mind it being slow and rough."

He continued, "When you get to the end of the trail, that'll put you out by an old church on 166. If you head south, you'll hit 64."

When they heard 64, Logan and Becca both straightened up. That was where they wanted to go anyway. They were thinking the same thing without saying it.

"Would you show us?" Becca asked.

"I don't have wheels like you, but I can tell you where they start." He paused. "Or you can follow me back and eat first. Warm up."

The offer hung there.

Logan looked past the man, toward where the trees thinned—toward the idea of walls. Warmth. A table. Actual cooked food.

Then he looked back at the cart. The gear. The kids.

"We really appreciate it," Logan said. "But if we sit down, we won't get moving again. We've still got a long way to go."

The man studied him for a second. Then he nodded. "Fair enough, boy."

He pointed down the road. "The trailhead's just to the left of the dead end. It looks like nothing. You'll miss it if you're not looking closely. Follow it for about half a mile, and you'll T into 166. Turn left onto that."

"Thank you," Becca said.

"Stay on dry ground," he added. "And I wouldn't be out there after dark."

Logan nodded. "Yes, sir. We won't."

The man took a step back, giving them space. "Good luck," he said.

As he retreated toward his place, Logan caught the man glancing back at the cart one last time before the trees swallowed him. He wished, suddenly, that it didn't stand out so much.

They packed quickly after that.

CHAPTER 25

STUCK IN A HARD PLACE

After breaking down the tent and packing the rest of the gear, the fire was the last thing Logan killed. As the smoke vanished, he couldn't shake the feeling that it had already done its damage.

His stomach had stayed tight and uneasy since the encounter. The man had been odd, not threatening, just wrong in a way Logan couldn't explain. The kind of feeling that gnawed at him, compelling him to move.

Everyone hopped aboard the cart, ready to go. Logan and Becca spent an extra second consulting the map to be sure. Now, looking closer, Logan could tell the man had actually been right. The road didn't extend all the way through. There was a green blob of landscape between them and the 166 they were seeking.

Talking out loud, there were three options as Logan saw it. One, they risk passing through Pulaski. Two, they could head north, away from Pulaski, and try to find another way over to 166. Tracing the route with his finger, Logan saw how long it would take. There were no other roads moving westward for miles and miles. Lastly, they could take the old man's advice and try navigating the trails.

Logan dropped his head to the wheel in thought.

Becca spoke up. "I think we back out of this mess and head north to find a safer way around."

"That will take miles—maybe an hour or more," he said. "That's fuel we don't have."

"I say we push through. I don't see where we have a choice." Logan said.

More serious now, Becca pushed back. "Lo, we don't know what's out there in those trails—and we certainly aren't on an ATV."

He switched to reverse. "I think that's what we need to do." He wasn't taking no for an answer this time.

Coming out of the logging road and field, he made the right toward the dead end. They passed a couple of houses, but otherwise nothing else. One of them must have belonged to the creepy guy. He pressed the gas a little harder, even though it was already maxed.

The family made it to the trailhead without issue. Surprisingly, it was exactly where the old man had said it would be. The trail had grown up with tall grass, but the rough outline was still visible if you paid attention. Logan glanced around one more time, scanning for anything out of place. He noticed the sun falling toward the three o'clock position. Quick math suggested they should be well on the other side of the trail by nightfall. It was, after all, only a half-mile stretch.

They bounced off the road and worked their way into the dense brush and tree cover. Luckily, the trail opened up a bit once they got into the trees. It was extraordinarily rough going, though. The ground was hard and deeply rutted. Old ATV tracks littered the main path, converging and diverging in and out.

As Becca had pointed out, the cart wasn't designed for this kind of abuse. Logan stayed firm on the wheel and gentle on the throttle, trying not to bounce his passengers, or their cargo, out. They dodged downed limbs, deep mudholes, and the occasional household appliance that had been conveniently abandoned.

They were moving much slower than he'd anticipated, every bump fighting their progress.

The sun continued to drop right in front of their eyes, and with visibility shrinking by the minute, their pace slowed to a painful crawl.

Logan glanced at Becca out of the corner of his eye. Her body was rigid, teeth clenched tight as she held Charlie close to keep him from bouncing out. He wasn't sure if it was the terrain, the closing darkness, or the way she'd gone quiet after he overrode her.

Distracted by the thought, Logan didn't notice the large ruts just ahead. Becca pointed and went to yell, but it was too late. The cart sank hard, perfectly centering itself on the raised middle section. The engine screamed as the cart dropped, the revs spiking before Logan could even process what had happened. He looked back at the rear tires, off the ground by a few inches, spinning uselessly.

The boys started crying from the jolt and the sudden roar of the engine. Logan turned to Tripp, telling him it would be okay, while Becca rubbed Charlie's back, trying to calm him.

The light continued to fade. They weren't going anywhere.

Becca covered her face with her hands and took a deep breath. Speaking through her palms, she said, "Logan, this was a dumb idea." Her voice climbed. "I told you not to take this way. We had no idea what was out here, and now we're stuck. Like—big stuck."

She pressed on. "The guy specifically told us not to be out here in the dark."

Her shoulders shook. She kept her head down, breathing shallow, quiet enough that the boys wouldn't hear.

"You're right. Maybe this wasn't the play," Logan said. "But now we're here, and we have to get out of this."

He jumped off without further argument and started doing. He tried rocking the cart side to side, hoping it might shift. No luck. It was solidly mounted on the center ridge and too heavy to budge.

"Help me push it," he snapped.

He walked around back while Becca gathered herself. "Look, I'm sorry. Right now, we don't need to argue about who was right. I just want to get out of here and put some distance between us and this place."

Becca sat Charlie down and joined him. They dug in and shoved with everything they had.

Nothing. Not an inch.

The cart weighed hundreds of pounds, and the gear didn't help. "Let's unload it," Becca said. "Drop some weight. Maybe."

They pulled the boys off and stacked the gear to one side. Full dark was almost upon them. It all stacked together: the lack of sleep, the stuck cart, the man, the darkness pressing closer by the second.

They tried pushing the now-empty cart again. The boys stood off to the side, holding each other and crying.

Nothing. No movement.

Logan dropped to his knees. "It's not moving. It didn't freaking budge."

Becca stood staring at the problem, arms crossed. Slow tears slid down her cold, nipped cheeks. "The tires aren't even touching. We can't push it. What do we do?"

Bile rose in Logan's throat, and he thought he might be sick. This was their only transportation. They were still at least 110, maybe 120, miles from their destination.

They wouldn't make it. Not like this. Too far from home. Too far from their grandparents.

Becca walked over and wrapped the boys in her arms. They sobbed quietly together. Now fully dark, the unknown pressed in from all sides.

Through tears, Tripp asked, "Why can't we go?"

Logan barked back, "Because the stupid wheels aren't even touching, and we can't push it. It's too heavy. That's why!"

He heard it the second it came out. Still crying, Tripp asked again, softer now. "But how do we get the wheels to touch? I want to go. It's scary here."

Becca brushed his long blond hair from his face but didn't answer.

It hit Logan.

He spun around and crouched beneath the cart, staring at the gap under the tires. Just enough light to see. "Tripp," he said, eyes wide. "You're a genius."

He hurried over and kissed him on the forehead. "Everyone grab a flashlight. Help me find branches."

The others stared at him, confused. "We're going to make the wheels touch," he said, already moving.

"What?" Becca asked.

"If we put branches and limbs under the tires, it'll fill the gap. The tires can get traction on them."

Something clicked. No one argued. They just moved, grabbing branches and dragging limbs into place.

After shoving several thick chunks beneath each tire, Logan slid back into the seat and eased on the throttle. The tires caught, lurching the cart forward a few feet before settling again. They repeated the process, inch by inch, until the cart finally climbed free of the ruts.

They cheered, but quietly. Celebration could wait. They wanted to get out of there.

The rest of the trail was rough, but the worst was behind them.

Logan exhaled as they broke out onto the road, right beside the church, just like the man had said. To his credit, everything the man had told them so far had been true.

"Should we stay here?" Becca asked. "Maybe behind the church or something?"

"No," Logan said. "Let's put some miles between us." She nodded.

They turned left onto Road 166, pointing south once again.

A few miles later, they reached it: Highway 64. The main road west. The small two-lane feeding into a slightly larger four-lane stretch.

Logan turned right and accelerated. They successfully navigated around the larger town. According to the map, there wasn't much out here, and that seemed accurate. After a few more miles, he finally felt comfortable pulling over. Like before, he found a small gravel road and guided the cart onto it.

They crept along, searching for anything settled. Nothing. Just the backside of a golf course, trees to the left and open greens to the right. In the headlights, a few flags waved weakly over overgrown fairways.

Logan steered into the trees and parked.

"There will be no fire tonight," he said to no one in particular.

Nobody argued. Becca got the boys settled without a word, tucking them into the tent with the sleeping bags pulled tight. Logan stood outside for a moment, listening. The golf course sat quiet in the dark, left behind like everything else. Out on the fairways, the flags barely moved.

He thought about Tripp's question. *How do we make the wheels touch?* Eight years old and the sharpest one out there in that moment.

Becca came and stood beside him after a few minutes. She didn't say anything, and neither did he. There wasn't much left to say tonight.

Logan took first watch.

CHAPTER 26
NOT ALONE

They climbed off in silence. No talking. No bickering. Just the sounds of packs shifting and feet moving in the tall grass. Logan scanned the treeline out of habit now. He kept replaying the last stretch of road and the trail in his head. He didn't think anything had followed them. Nothing that he could see, at least. That didn't mean much anymore, though. Surprise was one of the new rules now.

It was fully dark. Tuesday was almost over. They had only been on their journey for two days, but to Logan it felt like a week already.

Every sound seemed louder now that the cart was quiet. It settled into him then, not relief, not safety, but exhaustion. The kind that made decisions slower. The kind that made mistakes easier. They couldn't keep pushing like this. Not without paying for it.

They needed rest. Even if it meant risking safety.

There would be no watch tonight.

Becca had fallen asleep on hers earlier, just as Logan probably would have done the same, he bet. They would gamble it. All of them tucked in. All of them asleep. Together.

At the mention of this, Becca dropped her head and simply nodded. By the look of it, she didn't have anything left to give.

The four made short work of setting up camp, as uneventful and efficient as they could manage in their current state. The little boys looked like walking zombies. Mentally and physically spent. Logan was proud of how they were holding on. Still moving. Still listening.

Still kids.

He was watching them grow up on the road. Too fast.

They piled into their home for the night. Logan laid the firearm near his head, close enough to touch. He still wasn't sure how he would respond if his brothers, or Becca, were seriously threatened. But he knew he needed the option to make that choice. Becca brought the rifles in and placed them in a corner with the bug-out bag. Everything inside. Everything together. They exchanged a quick glance of agreement.

The little boys were asleep before their heads hit the padded portion of their sleeping bags.

"We need to get some rest, or we're both going to be worthless," Logan said quietly as he leaned over and zipped them in.

Becca nodded. "I'm sorry I fell asleep, Lo. That could have been really bad." She hesitated. "I don't know what he—" She stopped. Swallowed. "I'm just sorry."

He didn't answer right away. His eyes moved to the boys, then back to her.

"Let's keep our ears out and work together," Logan replied.

He didn't acknowledge the apology. He wasn't sure how to feel about it. How exposed they'd been. About how thin the margin had become. But he also understood. He could have done the same thing.

He lay there, listening to the noises of the night in yet another unfamiliar place.

Becca closed her eyes and put her arm around Tripp. Her breathing slowed almost immediately, now even and steady.

Logan lay still, listening to the dark settle around them. At some point, without meaning to, he let go.

A fluttering noise—then a branch snapping—pulled Logan out of deep sleep.

He froze.

Then the whooo...whooo of an owl swept over the tent.

It made him jump anyway. His heart kicked hard before he could stop it. Realizing it wasn't a threat, he forced himself to breathe.

Nobody else stirred.

That was good. And it wasn't.

Was he the only one still listening? The only one trying to sort threats from noise?

He lay back down and pulled the sleeping bag tighter. The night had gone quiet again. He told himself to rest. That the threat was gone. His body agreed before his mind did, and eventually sleep found him again, uneven and shallow.

He woke suddenly, certain he'd heard something. Voices.

His eyes opened, staring into the dark. He turned his head slightly toward the gun.

But he didn't reach for it.

His arms felt stuck. Heavy. Like they were buried in quicksand. His body refused the command.

He listened. Hard.

Nothing.

No footsteps. No whispering. No follow-up sound. Just the night.

Was his mind playing tricks on him?

Time stretched. Eventually, he told himself it was nothing. That there was no threat. Not this time.

But the question stayed with him, cold and sharp.

Why couldn't he grab his gun? Would he hesitate if it mattered?

The thought followed him until daylight crept in.

Sunlight filtered through the netting at the top of the tent, breaking into tiny octagon shapes. Logan stared at them, studying the pattern, trying to decide how much of last night had been real.

Exhaustion blurred the edges of everything. It had to be that.

He felt half-human when he finally moved. Not rested. Just functional enough.

He slid out from beside Charlie and unzipped the tent. The lack of weight at his waist caught him instantly. He turned back for his gun and belt. It was now part of his uniform. A necessity. He clipped it back into place before stepping fully outside.

The sun was already up. Judging the angle against an imaginary clock face, he guessed it was around nine.

The morning was quiet. No threats he could identify. His family slept on.

The sky was clear, the air already warming. It would be warmer today than the last few. A small mercy.

He climbed onto the golf cart as it squeaked beneath him and stretched out for a beat, soaking in the sun as the rest of the family began to stir. He actually longed for coffee this morning. Funny how quickly that happens, he thought with a quiet laugh.

Finally, everyone was up and milling about. The little guys complained of hunger. Logan had forgotten how hungry he was until opening the bags and searching for breakfast options, his mouth watering now and a pang of hunger stabbing his lower belly. He would have killed for bacon, eggs, and pancakes.

His mind drifted to Waffle House on Saturday mornings. Dad always ordered the same thing. Mom always said she wasn't that hungry and then ate half of everyone else's food. The table would be covered in plates and the boys would eat until they couldn't move. Nobody was in a hurry to go anywhere. Just noise and syrup and country music playing on the jukebox.

He hadn't thought about that in days. It felt both close and impossibly far away.

They still weren't willing to risk a fire. They would have to eat quick and easy meals, no cooking. Chocolate Clif Bars and trail mix. They were careful to continue rationing food and water. The trip had already used more resources than they had planned, and at this pace it would take them closer to five days instead of the planned three.

After breakfast, Logan and Becca discussed travel plans for the next leg of the journey. They easily agreed that night travel was the only option moving forward. It had its challenges and dangers, but it far outweighed the exposure of daytime travel.

They would leave tonight, giving them the day to plan, organize, and get much-needed rest.

Pulling out Dad's atlas once more, they focused on their position. They were on 64, a couple miles west of Pulaski. This road would take them straight west, which was perfect. It wound around another large town, Lawrenceburg, and continued on.

That led to basically nothing until Waynesboro, the next town with any sort of measurable population.

They thought if they could get around Lawrenceburg without incident, it would be smooth sailing. Managing forty or fifty miles would be a huge win.

Inventory came next. Food was manageable. If they had to, they could ration further or go without for the last stretch. Logan remembered Dad saying you could survive weeks without food if you had to. Water was the real danger. With the extra days added, it was thin to start with, and they'd have to stop cooking with it entirely. They had a filter and purification tablets in the go bag if it came to that. Fuel was also a concern. Depending on mileage, they should get there, or close enough. Zero room for error.

Logan topped off the cart's tank, leaving a couple of gallons plus the extra jug.

Charlie wandered over mid-count, trail mix spilling from his hand.

"What are we doing out here by this golf course?" he asked. "Are we hiding?"

Logan and Becca exchanged a look.

"We're just resting, bud," Logan said. "Everyone was tired."

Charlie frowned. "Then why do you guys have guns? And why do we have to be so quiet all the time?"

Becca answered before Logan could. "Just to keep you safe. There might be some bad people out here, but we'll protect you."

She smiled, trying to make it light. "Why don't you go play with Tripp for a bit while we finish up?"

"Okay..." Charlie said. He didn't sound convinced.

Once he was gone, Logan said it. "We don't have any room left for mistakes." Saying it out loud landed hard, even on his own shoulders. "As of right now, we barely have enough to get there. If we even do."

Becca looked at him. She didn't have a response, just took a couple of deep breaths, trying to shoulder the message.

They cleaned everything back up and reloaded the cart. They would leave in four or five hours, based on the sun's current position.

They sat under the trees, finally able to breathe. Nobody rushed to move or plan or check anything. They just sat. Talked quietly. Laughed a little.

The stories came easy once they started. Logan brought up the soccer game, final penalty kick, season on the line, and somehow he'd put it in for the win. Tripp reminded him he'd cried afterward, which Logan denied, which made everyone laugh harder. Tripp had his own stories remembering his two baseball championships, both of which he described in exhausting detail. Charlie listened with wide eyes like he was hearing them for the first time, even though he wasn't. Charlie talked about his little buddies from the neighborhood, whom he missed now, thinking about them.

A low growl popped up in the distance, and grew.

The bunch froze.

The sound was moving east to west, in the direction of 64. It grew louder, then passed near their position without slowing. Logan placed it. An ATV. It was moving quickly, fading out just as fast.

Logan leaned toward Becca, his voice low. "We're not alone out here."

She shook her head. "Nope."

They went back to talking about the time Tripp got stuck on the zipline while camping, yelling, "This is the worst day ever!" over and over while Dad had to rescue him and Mom filmed the whole thing.

Everyone smiled at the memory. A great one. An unfortunate contrast to recent events.

The trees cracked softly in the breeze between stories.

They were interrupted.

Pop.

Pop-pop.

Then another burst—sharp, clean cracks. Distant, but not far.

The sound came from the same direction the ATV had gone. The direction they needed to travel.

Logan's grip tightened, knuckles whitening as he angled his head, listening for more. Nothing followed. No shouting. Just silence.

Whatever was happening out there—it wasn't good. It was violent and within earshot.

Suddenly, their laughter felt reckless. He kept his eyes on the tree line in the direction of 64. Whatever was out there was between them and where they needed to go. How would they navigate the miles and the human danger safely?

The little boys waited a moment, then Tripp asked the question burning in them both. "What was that? Were those fireworks?"

"No," Logan said quietly. "I don't think those were fireworks, bud. I'm not really sure what that was."

He looked at Becca, wide-eyed.

Nobody spoke for a while after that. The boys stayed close, quieter than usual, no longer asking questions. Becca had pulled Charlie into her lap and was running her hand through his hair. Tripp sat with his knees pulled up, staring at the ground.

Logan kept his eyes on the tree line in the direction the sound had come from. He turned it over in his head. How many shots. How far. What it might mean for the road tonight.

He didn't share any of that out loud. He sat with his back against a tree, eyes and ears open.

The hours passed. The light shifted. Nobody made it back to the stories.

Logan saw it first. He sat up deliberately.

He nudged Becca with his elbow and pointed east. A dark column of smoke was rising now, thick and steady against the sky. It hadn't been there earlier.

CHAPTER 27

CONTACT

The rest of Wednesday afternoon was ominous. The dark smoke they had noticed earlier continued into the sky all afternoon. A reminder that they weren't safe. Violence was just right around the corner.

Night crept in. It was the family's eleventh day since the lights went out.

The next leg of the trip loomed over them, just like the smoke.

Logan stared into the night sky longer than he needed to, not wanting to move.

Everyone did their part, packing the few remaining items. They took their usual seats and prepared to move.

Logan had to turn on the golf cart lights tonight. It was dark in the wooded area, and there was next to zero visibility due to the cloud cover.

They navigated the couple hundred yards back to 64 and proceeded west, still hoping to put in a solid forty or fifty miles. They desperately needed to make up time and distance.

They made it a few miles down the road and saw a faint glow just off the right side. As they approached, Logan could tell it was a house, or what was left of a house. It was still smoldering. It had recently finished burning itself out, by the look of it.

He didn't want to talk about it or bring more attention than necessary. It might frighten the little boys even more. This must've been the source of the black smoke from earlier, and likely the area of all the gunfire too.

They were just before the house now. The headlights of the cart splashed into the front yard, illuminating more of the scene. There was basically only one side of the house still standing, including the garage. His eyes drifted toward the driveway and across the front yard. Something caught his attention, drawing his gaze back between the porch and the driveway. Something his mind registered before he understood it.

He slowed just barely as he made out a shape on the ground. The dim light caught it only at the edge of his vision. Long and rounded. Wrong. The shape lay still.

His mind tried to dismiss it. Then it caught up.

The conscious and subconscious connected all at once as they rolled past.

Throat heavy and stomach turning, he looked to Becca to see if she had caught a glimpse of the same thing he had seen. In the faint backlight, he could see her face. It was straight, jaw muscles flexed, eyes as wide as he'd ever seen. She had noticed it too.

No words were needed. The terror flowed between them without saying a thing. Logan focused forward on the road. His hands tightened on the wheel. The rules had changed again.

"If you had to," Logan said, nodding toward the gun at her hip, "can you use that?"

Becca didn't answer right away. "Yeah," she said. "If I had to."

Logan responded flatly. "Good."

He wanted to get out of this area as fast as possible. There were dangerous people hunting on this particular stretch of road. The road they had to take.

He pushed the gas down as far as it would go. Becca sat rigid, holding Charlie in her lap as usual. Tripp was sitting up in the back, holding onto Logan's shoulder. Everyone kept an eye out for anything and everything.

The question he had asked Becca lingered. Logan turned it inward. What would he do? Did he have what it would take to defend his family, or himself? He still didn't have an answer, and didn't want to find out.

Their pace was solid, Logan thought. No issues so far.

They were coming up on a decent-sized intersection a few miles south of Lawrenceburg. Logan hoped it would be enough of a buffer, given the minimal sprawl of the town. His guard stayed up now: people, threats, roadblocks. He wanted to be proactive instead of reactive, spotting issues before they were dire. Their safety depended on it.

He spoke up to the family. "We're getting close to Lawrenceburg. Keep a close watch. Let me know if you see anything—anything at all."

They passed a few houses with various lights in and around them. Some looked to be small fires, some candles, but nothing of concern. They hadn't even seen a person on this stretch yet.

They successfully made it around the south end of Lawrenceburg, still cruising. Logan estimated they were about halfway to their goal of forty to fifty miles.

It was still very dark out with the cloud cover. Visibility was a constant concern. He wished they could run dark.

They were coming up on a stretch marked as the Laurel Hill Wildlife Management Area.

Logan knew that part of the journey should be quiet. There were no houses. No driveways. No reason for anyone to be out here.

Somewhere like that might be a great place to camp, he thought. Not now, though. They still planned to push on and put in another twenty or thirty miles.

By now they were well into the wildlife area. They had only passed a couple of access roads here and there. A few hunting areas tucked off the road were marked by signs. Much of the land was fenced in. The road ran straight and dark between the tree lines, quiet except for the hum of the cart.

"Lo..." Tripp said nervously from the back. "There are lights behind us."

Logan and Becca both snapped around.

A faint light swept across them from behind, appearing to the left before sliding back to the right. It moved side to side, catching the trees and the edge of the cart as it followed them.

Two small lights trailed them on the road. They were dim, almost yellow-tinted. Evenly spaced. Moving together. Growing.

Not flashlights. Too uniform.

"It's an ATV," Becca croaked. It was moving fast now, much faster than the cart could achieve.

"We can't outrun them, Becca," Logan yelled over the engine. "I can't turn off—there are ditches and fences on both sides." Desperation rose in his voice. "Tripp, lie down in the back. Stay low."

He thought about turning the lights off, but that wouldn't help. They couldn't hide, and there was nowhere to go. The lack of visibility wouldn't allow them to get far. The ATV was bearing down on them quickly.

A single, bright flash burst above the headlights, followed by a loud, echoing pop.

Logan flinched. He didn't know if it missed on purpose.

Becca ducked instinctively. "Did they shoot at us?"

"I'm not sure. Maybe a warning?" Logan said as he leaned low over the wheel. Becca pulled Charlie down between them and yelled back to Tripp, "Stay down!"

"They'll be on us in just a second, Becca," Logan said, squeezing the wheel tight. His mind raced, trying to come up with a plan. "Any ideas?"

"No. We can't hide now. I don't think they're friendly either," she managed.

"We can't stop," Logan said. "If we have to fight or dodge them, that's what we'll do. But if we stop, bad things will happen."

Becca squeezed Charlie and agreed.

Logan kept turning around, keeping an eye on the threat. It would be there in seconds. The lights obscured his view of the rider, or riders. He didn't know who or what was after them, but like Becca, he knew they didn't have good intentions.

No other shots came. It must have been a warning.

He could hear their engine now. Someone was yelling at them, but Logan couldn't make out the words over the engines and wind. The voice was loud. Angry.

Becca unholstered her pistol and held it in her right hand while shielding Charlie with her left.

The ATV was now just off the left rear corner, still surging forward. The glow of the lights illuminated two large frames sitting atop the machine. The person in the back was clearly holding a handgun pointed in their direction.

"Pull over now!"

Logan glanced over, taking in the full picture. Two large people, likely men. Camouflage coats. Black head coverings that only showed their eyes. Menacing.

The sound of the ATV, the gunshots, the burned-out house, and the victim in the yard. The math added up. He did not want to be the next one.

The front wheels were even with Logan now. Side by side, racing down the road as fast as the golf cart could manage. Another shot rang out to his left. The rider in back fired into the air again.

"Next one's for you, boy," one of them yelled.

Logan turned hard left. With only inches separating them, they collided, smashing into the ATV's front tire. The driver didn't react fast enough. The ATV skidded, then barrel-rolled, sending the riders flying.

At the same time, Becca had just turned to say something.

There was a scream as she was thrown from the cart, unprepared for the sudden jerk. Logan caught a glimpse of her hitting the pavement, tumbling with a heavy grunt.

Charlie lay flat in the seat, screaming, reaching for where Becca had been.

Realizing he'd lost Becca, Logan slammed on the brakes, holding Charlie up with his right arm so he wouldn't slide onto the floor. He glanced back at Tripp. He was still lying flat in the storage area, gripping the gear bags and the rack, sobbing.

Logan grabbed his flashlight from the storage compartment. Looking out the rear of the cart, he clicked it on, searching for Becca. He found her. She was lying flat on her back, holding the back of her head and moving slowly.

He scanned to his right, looking for the ATV and its occupants. He saw it about fifteen yards away, adjacent to Becca, in the opposite ditch. The lights faced toward the woods. One of the riders was on his feet, hobbling toward the cart, cussing at the three boys. In the beam, a pistol glinted ready in the man's hand.

Logan reached for his own pistol.

Several shots rang out from behind the man, from Becca's position. Two quick flashes, followed by a third. The man crumpled, hitting the pavement unnaturally.

Follow-up shots sounded from behind the ATV. This time, the flashes came from the other man's position.

Logan could tell they were aimed toward Becca. There were several.

Becca screamed loudly, the sound echoing off the trees. She returned fire, focusing on the ATV now. One- and two-shot bursts for what felt like an eternity.

Logan had to help Becca. She was out in the open, lying on the road. No cover.

He took aim at the crouched figure kneeling behind the ATV, trained on Becca's position, exchanging fire with her. He pulled the sights down onto his target. He squeezed the trigger.

Pop.

He got his sight picture back. Patiently now—Pop. Pop. Pop.

It sounded like a war zone. The figure stopped firing and went flat.

Logan shook his head, his ears ringing badly from the exchange. "Stay here! Don't move!" he yelled at the boys as he exited the driver's side of the cart.

His gun tracked the first shape on the road.

He approached slowly. It was a large man. He wasn't moving, and it was obvious he was gone by the way he lay and the large puddle of blood surrounding him. Logan grabbed the man's pistol and threw it toward the cart.

He knew he should clear the second guy, but Becca mattered more. He ran toward her, glancing back at the ATV a couple of times, not seeing any movement or follow-up shots.

He could hear his brothers wailing behind him. They were yelling for Logan and Becca to come back.

When Logan reached Becca, she was still moving.

Relief hit him, sharp and brief.

Then he saw the blood.

His protector and caretaker of four years held a massive wound on the back of her head with one hand and pressed the other against her upper chest. She was moving, moaning loudly.

"Oh, Becca..." was all he could manage.

Looking over the situation, it appeared the head wound was from the fall, not a gunshot. But lower on her chest, the blood was spreading from beneath her hand. She pressed down harder, but it didn't seem to help.

"I'm hit, Lo," she said, lowering her head toward her chest.

He pushed his hand over hers as hard as he could. She let out a high-pitched shriek.

"Oh no. No. No." He shook his head, like he wanted to wake up, or disappear.

In the reflection of his flashlight, he saw her eyes. Wide. Terrified. Tears streamed from the corners.

"Check on the other guy," she pushed out between heavy breaths. "I'm not sure if we got him."

"Okay. Okay. I'll be right back. I'm getting the med kit too," he yelled as he stood and moved toward the ATV, pistol at the ready.

The machine lay on its side, angled diagonally in the ditch. He couldn't see behind it, which worried him. His sights moved from the back corner to the front to the middle as he inched forward. He had no idea where the man might be.

He eased around the front. Shoes. Then legs. He crouched, sights up and ready.

The guy lay there clutching his abdomen, maybe his stomach. His gun lay beside him. He didn't look like he had any interest in reaching for it. Logan stepped closer and kicked it farther into the ditch.

The man looked up at him and reached out with an open hand.

"Help me, boy," the man gasped. "Don't let me die in this ditch."

Logan stopped.

Just long enough to hear Becca screaming behind him.

"You shot Becca," Logan said. "You're on your own."

He turned and ran back to the cart, ripping open the go-bag. As he searched for the med kit, he tried to calm his brothers. They were hysterical.

"I'll be right back, guys. I have to help Becca," he yelled, already turning toward her.

As he reached her, he slowed. She wasn't moaning or holding her head anymore. Her hand had slipped from her chest. He grabbed it, pressing it back onto the wound. No yell this time.

Her eyes shifted toward him.

"I love you guys, Lo," she whispered. "Get home."

"We will," he yelled. "And you're coming with us!"

Her grip on his hand loosened slightly. Her eyes drifted, still open.

Logan grew heavy, shrinking into the road.

"No. No. No."

He felt her neck. Nothing. Her wrist. Nothing. He pressed his ear to her mouth...nothing.

His Becca was gone.

He fell back onto the road, hurting, aching, crying.

He could still hear the other man yelling from behind the ATV.

Logan didn't care. There was nothing he could do to help him anyway. He was the reason Becca was gone now. He was on his own. Let him stay in that ditch, Logan told himself.

CHAPTER 28
THREE

Logan sat in silence, holding Becca's hand, willing her to come back. Tears streamed down his face unchecked. He was struggling to understand how everything had changed so fast. Just minutes ago they'd been rolling along, making good time. They'd been laughing and talking about foods they missed, things that felt so far away. Now she lay still.

He heard soft footsteps behind him and twisted around, heart jumping, to see a flashlight bobbing through the darkness toward him. Tripp's voice cut through the night.

"Logan? Are you okay?"

"Go back to the cart, Tripp," Logan managed between sniffles. "Please stay with Charlie. I'm okay."

The lie hurt.

Tripp hesitated, then the light turned away.

Logan sat there a moment longer, staring at Becca's face. Her eyes were still open, her expression strangely calm, as if she might wake up any second and scold him for worrying.

Then something shifted inside him, demanding movement.

He gently let go of her hand.

Logan picked up Becca's gun and tucked it into the back of his jeans. He turned toward the ATV and forced himself forward. He was afraid of what he'd find. Afraid of seeing the man dead—but even more afraid of finding him alive. Alive and suffering. Alive and begging for help he couldn't give.

The man lay on his side, one arm wrapped around his stomach. Logan nudged him with his shoe.

Nothing.

He nudged him again, harder this time.

There was still no response.

Logan looked down at him briefly, anger and grief boiling together in his chest. Then he turned away and didn't look back.

He searched around the ATV, scanning quickly, mechanically. There was a camouflage bag strapped to the back and a gray backpack half-submerged in the ditch nearby. He grabbed both and set them aside. They might have something useful. They had to now.

Using his light, he swept the ditch until it caught a dull reflection. The man's gun lay a few yards away. Logan scooped it up and took a moment to clear it, hands steady despite everything. He unloaded it and placed it in one of the bags, making a mental note to go through everything later.

He backtracked toward the cart and found the other man, the one who had rushed them first. The one Becca had stopped. The masked man had almost nothing on him. Just an extra magazine for the pistol Logan had already taken. He added it to the gray bag as well.

As Logan turned back toward the cart, his thoughts caught up to him all at once. How was he supposed to explain this? How could he possibly say the right words to his little brothers? Words they could understand. Words that wouldn't destroy them.

Or maybe worse—words they would understand.

He reached the cart.

The boys weren't there.

"Tripp?" he shouted. "Charlie?"

A moment later, Tripp's voice came back, sharp and broken. "Over here, Lo! Hurry—Becca's hurt!"

Logan was already running.

He sprinted back, the flashlight beam bouncing wildly ahead of him. When he reached them, both boys were huddled around Becca's body. Tripp was shaking her, tugging at her arm and shoulder. Charlie kneeled at her waist, his small hand pressed flat against her belly, eyes fixed on her face.

"Logan," Tripp cried, tears streaking down his cheeks. "We have to help her. She's bleeding."

Logan dropped to his knees and wrapped an arm around Tripp, pulling him close. He rested his forehead against his brother's.

"We can't help her, bud," he said softly. "She's already gone."

"I tried," Logan sobbed, clutching them both now. "I tried to help her. She was just hurt too bad..."

They stayed like that for a long moment, the three of them clinging together in the dark, mourning someone who was still there—but already gone.

Eventually, Logan pulled back. He wiped his face with the heel of his hand and looked down at Becca again. He didn't know what to do with her. Every option felt wrong. They couldn't bring her with them. They didn't have a way to bury her. None of it was enough.

She deserved better than this.

Logan had to make the decision, anyway.

He carefully moved her to the other side of the ditch. It wasn't deep or wide, but she was heavy, almost a foot taller than him. He strained and stumbled, muscles screaming as he fought to keep her from slipping or rolling awkwardly. When he finally got her settled, he stood there for a second, bent over and shaking. The road was completely silent. The air still smelled faintly of gunpowder, mixing with the damp of the ditch.

He ran back to the cart and grabbed her extra coat. When he returned, he draped it gently over her face and upper body. He placed his hand just above the wound, then looked back at his brothers and bowed his head. He whispered a short, silent prayer. It didn't feel like enough.

The question crept in. What if he hadn't jerked the wheel? What if he'd reacted faster? Was this his fault?

He shoved the thought aside, for now.

Logan told the boys it was time to go. There was nothing else they could do. They hugged her one last time before walking back toward the cart. Logan spared a brief glance toward the other bodies in the ditch, then looked away.

Whatever happened to them wasn't his problem. Not anymore.

They loaded the extra bags and strapped everything down. Logan pulled Becca's gun from his waistband and placed it in the storage compartment.

In the glow of his flashlight, he saw the blood on his hands and forearms. Becca's.

He tried wiping it away on the damp grass, then with an old shirt, but it didn't help. He needed water, but they didn't have enough to spare. He'd have to make the remainder of the trip with his hands reminding him of their loss each time he looked down.

They climbed back aboard the cart. Tripp automatically moved to his usual spot in the back.

Logan glanced over and saw Charlie sitting in the middle. The empty seat beside him caught his breath.

"Hey, Tripp," Logan said after a moment. "You can sit up here now."

No one answered.

Tripp simply climbed down and slid into the empty seat.

Becca's seat.

Logan swallowed hard, pressed the pedal, and the cart lurched forward.

They were back underway.

Three instead of four.

CHAPTER 29
CARRY ON

The cart hummed steadily beneath them as the road stretched out ahead. No one spoke. The night wrapped around them, cool and still, broken only by the tires on pavement and the faint rattle of gear and bags strapped behind them. Logan kept his eyes forward, hands fixed on the wheel, aware of the empty space beside him.

He was the one in charge now, the weight of everything settling heavily on his mind and shoulders. He thought about Dad. About what he would do right now, standing in Logan's place.

He couldn't escape the overwhelming feeling that they had forgotten something, or left something behind.

They had about twenty miles left to cover. Logan knew, without needing to check the map again, that it would feel longer than anything they'd traveled so far. Every mile pressed on him differently now.

They rode mostly in silence. Tears still dotted their faces. Tripp stared straight ahead, his jaw tight, his hands folded together in his lap. He didn't fidget. He didn't ask how much farther. Charlie leaned against him, small and still, already half-asleep but waking every time the cart hit a bump.

They passed a couple of lit houses, most likely from candles or fireplaces. A few people came out to look at them, but there were no particular issues. Logan didn't wave. He didn't slow. The headlights swept past them and kept going.

Just before Waynesboro, they passed a man and a woman on the shoulder of the road. The man raised his hand into the headlights, waving them down and yelling that they needed help. Logan caught the look on his face—wild and desperate—and felt his grip tighten. They made a wide arc around them and never slowed down. He understood the new rules now. Stopping was dangerous. People were more dangerous. He wouldn't risk either again.

As they crossed into Wayne County, Logan decided it was time to stop. Based on the map, there was no way to navigate around Waynesboro. There simply wasn't a bypass route.

They had made it at least forty miles, and he didn't have it in him to try to navigate the town, or whatever might lie in it, tonight. That would be a challenge for tomorrow.

When he spotted a stretch of trees set back from the road, he slowed and cut the lights. A fence ran along the edge, broken in one place where the wire sagged and pulled free. Logan guided the cart carefully and eased them into the darkness, pushing back as far as he could without risking noise or exposure.

He shut the cart down and listened.

He scanned the area, looking for signs of people. No lights. No voices. Just the night.

From somewhere beyond the trees, Logan heard the distant moo of cows. The sound drifted through the darkness, steady and familiar. It carried a hint of normalcy, comforting and strange at the same time.

After a few minutes, he nodded to himself. It would have to do.

They unloaded quietly and began pulling out the camping gear once again.

Everything was harder now. Becca would normally find them something to eat while they got the tent ready. Now it was all on him.

He and Tripp set up the tent together, working side by side without speaking. Tripp followed Logan's lead, handing him stakes, holding poles steady, doing exactly what was needed. No questions. No complaints.

When it was done, Logan dug into the food bag. They ate simple snacks, passing them back and forth. Each of them took a small cup of water, careful not to spill a drop. Logan silently watched the level in the jug fall, keeping track of it closely.

After their meal, Logan opened one of the men's bags and found a couple of bottles of water. He opened the first bottle without guilt. He could wash his hands without taking from the boys' supply. He poured some over his hands, scrubbing until the blood loosened and ran into the dirt. For the first time since it happened, he felt like he could breathe.

They crawled into the tent as the night worked toward morning. The boys snuggled close, instinctively bunching together for warmth, or maybe comfort. No nighttime chatter. No funny stories from Tripp. No random why questions from Charlie. Just quiet.

Logan lay awake, staring into the dark, listening to their breathing.

There would be no watch tonight.

The thought settled heavily, but he didn't argue with it. With only him, it wasn't possible. He needed rest. They all did. Whatever risk came with sleep was one he had to accept.

He stared into the dark, willing the night to end. He squeezed his eyes shut, trying to keep his mind from drifting back to the hours before.

He finally faded off, knowing the decisions were his now. Whether they made it home would depend on what he did with them.

CHAPTER 30
OVERCOME

Logan woke Thursday afternoon to the sound of movement behind him.

Luckily, not footsteps. Just fabric shifting around, a quiet rustle inside the tent.

For a moment, he stayed still, listening. His body felt heavy, stiff from the hours of broken sleep. The air inside the tent was warmer now, thick and still. The late afternoon light filtered through the tent fabric.

They slept longer than Logan had anticipated. Becca wasn't there to wake them up.

Thankfully, though, they had made it safely without a watch.

Logan pushed himself upright, trying to figure out what time it was. Unfortunately, it didn't matter now. Everything was measured in miles, water, and gas. The only constant was that once it was dark, they moved.

Tripp was sitting up, rubbing his eyes. He didn't say anything. Just looked around, slow and quiet, like he was trying to orient himself in a new place. Charlie stirred beside him, rolling onto his side and snuggling in closer without waking fully. Logan thought back to Mom. She always called Charlie the snuggle bug.

Logan watched them for a moment instead of the woods.

Tripp noticed Logan's gaze. "When are we going to be there, Lo? I'm tired of being out here. It's scary."

Logan took an extra breath and responded softly, "I'm not sure. I think we are about seventy or eighty miles away now. That should be two days, as long as we don't run into more trouble."

Tripp stared at him. "Two more days? I just want to be there. I don't want to be here anymore."

Tripp sat silent for a second. "When do you think we will see Mom and Dad again?"

Logan closed his eyes. The truth was he didn't know if they were coming at all.

"I don't know that either, bud, but I know they are trying their best to get to us. I know that for sure," Logan said with extra confidence he wasn't sure he actually felt. He hated how easy it was getting to say things he couldn't back up.

He forced himself to move.

Logan pulled the food bag closer and opened it, checking its contents. Two Clif bars left. A small bag of crackers and some of Becca's trail mix. The water jug was lighter than he wanted it to be. The bad guy's water will help, he thought.

Enough for now. His chest tightened. With three of them instead of four, the supplies would stretch a little further.

Logan took some time to check out the camouflage and gray bags he had acquired the night before. He winced, noticing a red handprint on top of the gray bag. His. It instantly transported his mind back to a place he didn't want to be.

In the gray bag, he found a couple of boxes of 9mm ammo. Luckily, it matched his pistol. He also found a big assortment of fine jewelry, watches, and even a lot of cash. He thought how silly it was to have such things now. They had little value since everything stopped working twelve days ago. The world was ending, and those guys wanted watches. They killed for them.

"Stupid," he hissed under his breath. Becca was gone, and this was what they were after.

In the camouflage bag, he was a little more lucky. He found a couple of MREs. He knew what they were because his dad had used them on camping and hiking trips. He found a large knife in a leather sheath, a coat that was way too big, and an odd assortment of tools as well.

Logan and Tripp stepped out of the tent. They were now working together, getting gear stacked, packs tightened, and organized. He laid everything out in the same order it always had been, then paused when he realized why it felt wrong.

Becca wasn't handing him anything. He stood there for an extra second.

Charlie woke, blinking against the open tent door, then crawled toward Logan without a word. Logan hugged him, setting him upright and brushing dirt from his sleeve.

"You good?" Logan asked quietly.

Charlie nodded. Too quiet this morning. No questions. No complaints.

The little boys snacked and sipped some water while Logan continued loading and organizing.

They'd be moving again soon. Night travel meant timing mattered, and daylight was already slipping away.

He laid out the map again. He would have to decide which routes to take now. It was all on him.

Talking it through with Tripp and Charlie, he wanted someone to hear the plan, even if they wouldn't be helpful in the process.

"So, guys, there is a small road south of Waynesboro. We'll take that to stay out of town," Logan said. "Then we'll keep going west on 64. If we get lucky and make it about fifty miles, we'll be in Selmer."

"That's only twenty miles from Grandma and Grandpa's!"

Charlie clapped his hands and yelled, "Yay!"

The boys finished their snacks. Logan decided to forgo his meal this afternoon. He still didn't have much of an appetite.

They sat around quietly, waiting for the sun to set. Logan insisted on moving at night only. Even though Tripp and Charlie complied, it was scary.

Logan took the remainder of the gas from the lighter jug and filled the cart. It wasn't enough. He tossed that to the side and unscrewed the cap of the last jug and topped it off. He thought they would have enough, but couldn't be sure. He pushed the idea away for now. That was a problem for later, he said to himself.

The time came to load up again. Logan had been watching the boys play and keeping a close eye on their surroundings. He hadn't heard anything concerning, nor seen anything. They were safe to move.

As dusk settled in, they rolled out.

The darkness filled their vision. Logan found himself constantly scanning shoulders and treelines, looking behind big trees and watching every intersecting road.

The boys stayed more still now. Their vision locked ahead, taking cues from Logan. The headlights sliced through the darkness as they came out south of Waynesboro and met back up with 64. They cleared the town and were back in open country.

It being late at night, they had only seen a few people. None were threatening, mostly just curious. This reaffirmed Logan's decision to travel at night, even though he hated the night now. He kept expecting someone to step out of the dark at any moment.

He wasn't sure where they were exactly, but they had been moving along nicely. After a few hours, he thought they must have made a good thirty miles or so. Maybe near Savannah, he estimated.

Just ahead, the headlights caught a large patch of broken concrete. Logan lifted off the gas, but it was too late.

They hit the hole at the full pace of the cart. The impact was jarring, almost throwing Tripp off the side. Logan's hand shot out and caught his jacket without thinking. His mind went to Becca before he could stop it. The golf cart creaked and groaned as it absorbed the blow. The engine suddenly spun up loudly as Logan pressed back on the gas. There was no acceleration or thrust produced. Just noise and whirring RPMs. He pressed the gas again, but had the same outcome. It wouldn't go.

They coasted to a stop right in the road, a straight stretch completely open. Logan immediately scanned for people and cut the lights. He waited for several minutes to see if they were alone.

Convinced they were okay for now, he jumped off, asking the boys to do the same.

The little boys were scared. Charlie was quietly crying again, and Tripp was anxiously looking around with his hands deep in his pockets.

Tripp asked quietly, "Are we stranded, Lo? Like, are we stuck here now?"

"I hope not," Logan responded matter-of-factly. "Let me check it out and see what's going on. Let's not worry too much yet. Okay?"

He grabbed his flashlight from the front storage compartment and began inspecting.

He started by looking at the tires. Luckily, all was good. He kneeled down and looked under the front and didn't see any issues. The same with the back. Nothing looked obviously wrong.

Stepping to the middle of the cart, he folded the seat up to look at the engine area. He shined his flashlight around, searching for anything that looked off.

He moved his light over to the clutch and belt area. That was when he saw it. The belt was just hanging on the shaft. The bump must have made it jump off the engine pulley.

"Hey, Tripp, come here and hold my light," Logan said.

Tripp came to him, taking the light.

"Keep it shining right here." Logan pointed at the belt.

He reached in and instantly pulled back with a yelp. The belt and shaft were extremely hot. He yelled and grabbed his fingers as they tingled from the pain.

"Are you okay, Lo?" Tripp asked.

"Yeah, I think so. Man, that hurt!" Logan said, scrunching his face and slinging his hand around. "I guess we'll have to wait for it to cool a little."

The boys sat around in the pitch dark. They didn't want to alert anyone to their presence, and they needed to conserve batteries.

After a short wait, the belt and shaft were now cool enough to work with. Tripp shined the light, and Logan reached back in. He rotated the top of the belt on, but couldn't get the bottom to slip over. He tried starting with the bottom, but now couldn't get the top over. The belt was too tight.

He climbed into the engine area and tried pulling with all of his might. So hard his fingers went numb and started to bleed from small cuts from the belt fibers.

Logan kicked the cart in anger. He yelled out, "How am I supposed to get this stupid thing on?"

He saw Charlie flinch at the outburst and wished he could take it back. Scared, Charlie started crying all over again. He sat on the shoulder of the road, holding his knees.

For the first time, Logan realized Tripp was watching him the way he used to watch Dad. He was quieter now, more focused, doing exactly what Logan asked.

Logan tried to get creative. He put the bottom of the belt on, released the brake, and tried to roll it on. It just kept popping off at the top. After a couple failed attempts, he abandoned that approach.

He took a breath and went to sit down next to Charlie, who was still crying. Charlie complained about the dark and kept saying he was worried about people showing up like last night.

Then an idea hit him. Remembering the camouflage bag from earlier, there were tools in it. Maybe something would help. He pulled the bag off the storage rack and dug through it, holding his flashlight in his mouth. He found something useful, he thought. A long, straight screwdriver. Maybe he could wedge it between the belt and the pulley.

With Tripp holding the light again, Logan slotted the screwdriver between the pulley and under the belt. He carefully slipped the belt on the bottom and used the screwdriver for leverage, pulling up steadily. Suddenly, the screwdriver slipped, scraping metal loudly.

The second time, he pulled the belt tight and steadily applied pressure again. The belt started to slip into place. His arms and hands were shaking from the force. With another hard yank, the belt finally popped into place.

He yelled out, "Yes, that's it!"

Tripp cheered along as Charlie popped up. He had a big smile on his face as he ran up to them. Tripp pulled the seat down into place and they all jumped back aboard.

"Fingers crossed, guys," Logan said as he applied the gas. The engine came to life, and the cart jumped forward under its own power again.

They rolled on. He kept thinking about how close they'd come to being stuck out there.

CHAPTER 31
THE CROSSING

After the close call with the belt, Logan decided they needed to push on. Sure, they could stop and sleep for the night. It might even do them some good to reset, but Logan felt the urge to keep putting distance between them and what was behind them. He thought about the young boys' pleas to just be there, and their constant questioning of when and how long it would take.

If they could push another twenty or so miles, they could make Selmer. That would guarantee they only had one more night in the unknown before the final stretch. He made the decision as the very early part of Friday morning moved in. The moon was bright overhead; they still had four or five hours of darkness to move within.

They could make it. Twenty miles. He pressed on.

For a while, he took it easy on the cart, afraid to push it hard. Eventually, he gained enough confidence to speed up.

As they thumped along, he thought through his planned route. There was only one way through Savannah, and that involved the big bridge going over the Tennessee River. He had been over that bridge a hundred times with his parents when they went to visit his grandparents. That bridge was the only way over the river for miles and miles. He didn't like the idea of being on that bridge under the new rules, but there wasn't a choice. It was a long, four-lane bridge that spanned a good half mile. He decided he'd check it out as best he could before committing to it.

They approached the bigger part of Savannah a little while later. It must have been around one or two in the morning. His chest tightened at the sight of movement. The town was fairly lit up for this time of night. He saw several people walking the streets with packs. There was a man riding a bike along the side of the road. He caught shadows slipping in and out of side streets as the boys drove along the main drag of 64, right through the center of town.

On the route, they passed near the town square and saw an official-looking building, maybe the courthouse, lit up from the inside. There looked to be candles or lamps in many of the windows. Several people mingled near the square, hovering around barrels and makeshift fire pits. He couldn't quite tell, but based on shapes, some may have had rifles. It was too far and too dark to be certain. In the quick glance over, some sort of community had taken root there. Tents and makeshift shelters clustered around the official buildings.

Logan's jaw grew tight at the sights and movement around them. They were the only ones on wheels, and the engine announced their position to everyone nearby. The boys caught stares as they moved by. Nobody seemed threatening. Not yet.

There was a man warming his hands over a barrel at an intersection just past the square. He stared a bit too long. Logan saw him reach into his chest pocket and pull out what looked like a handheld radio. The small green light was overly bright in the darkness. He saw it turn from green to red as the man lifted it toward his mouth.

Just before reaching the bridge, Logan noticed an old grocery store off to the left. All the windows had been shattered and the doors left half open. Trash and debris were scattered throughout the parking lot. It looked like even this small town had seen its share of unrest and desperation.

They made it to the entrance of the bridge. They were certainly noticed, but not bothered.

He was ready to put Savannah behind him. He looked forward to the rural areas between them and Selmer that he knew well.

Logan came to a quick stop beside an old post office.

He waited.

Surveying the entrance to the bridge, he didn't see movement, but he did see a lot of cars stuck in odd directions—doors still open—abandoned quickly. Large orange traffic cones blocked the bridge. It seemed as though it had been shut down. There were also a couple of burn barrels near the front edge of the bridge on each side. Again, no people. No movement. Why would there be traffic cones blocking the bridge when basically no vehicles worked anymore?

Tripp spoke up. "What are you doing, Lo? Why are we just sitting here?"

"I'm just looking around for people and danger," Logan said, staring ahead, scanning.

"Can we go around this bridge?" Tripp asked. "It's too dark, and I don't want to be that high up."

"Me neither," Charlie called out.

Logan realized then that Charlie was awake. He had been in and out during the journey, fatigue taking its toll on his little body.

"Guys, I don't think we have a choice. There's no way around for miles and miles. We don't have enough gas, and all the bridges will be the same as this one."

"It seems okay," Logan added, though even to him the words sounded thin.

The boys went quiet.

Logan's stomach tightened further. He pressed on the gas, jumping forward onto the bridge. His eyes were wide, scanning. He knew there was nowhere to go if they ran into trouble out there. He silently hoped he wasn't making a mistake.

They rumbled along and finally reached the crest of the bridge. Wind coming upriver tore through the cart, threatening to lift loose gear. The smell of water wrapped around them, pulling Logan back to fishing trips with his family when they stayed on the river back home. The last time they went, Becca had joined them. His eyes went watery before he could stop it.

They were now coasting down the other side. So far, so good. They had a couple hundred yards to go before clearing the river and being on their way.

The headlights pushed out just far enough to reveal stalled cars scattered across the bridge, but the smaller cart was able to weave through.

They were almost clear.

Then more burn barrels appeared near the exit. He thought he saw a brief flash of light off to the side. They reached the end and saw more cones stretched across the road. There was no way around them. He slowed to a stop.

Logan jumped out and reached for one of the cones. That was when the flashlight found him—a hard beam from somewhere past the barrels, pinning him in place.

"Step away." The voice came from behind a stalled car up ahead, calm and unhurried, like it had done this before.

CHAPTER 32

COST OF PASSAGE

Logan froze. He opened his hands and held them out in front of him. Behind him, his little brothers squealed, one whimpering his name quietly. He didn't move or turn to look at them. He was trying to assess what was actually happening.

A different voice called out from the right, surprised. "They're just kids."

The first voice, from out front, followed in a firm, calm tone. "Don't reach for that gun on your hip, okay? You're surrounded. No reason to fight."

The headlights lit up the man as he walked around the front end of the car. Then another stepped beside him. At the same time, lights from the left and right shifted closer.

Logan noticed the first guy didn't have a weapon, or at least not one pointed at him. The second man and the ones on the sides did. They eased forward with rifles held low.

The man in front wore a dark shirt, brown pants, and cowboy boots. The others had darker clothing as well, more formal-looking. Possibly military or law enforcement, Logan thought.

"I'm Glen," the first man said in a thick Southern accent. "Can you unclasp that belt and drop it for us? Do it slowly and with one hand."

Logan glanced around, sizing up his situation. He took a deep breath and counted at least six grown men surrounding them. Two stood uncomfortably close to Tripp and Charlie, and their only means of transportation.

He thought a second longer and knew he had no choice. Gently, he reached up with his right hand and squeezed the sides of the belt clip. It came undone. He lowered it carefully to the ground, holding it by the clip end.

He straightened up with empty hands and kept them where they could see them. Six grown men with rifles. His brothers behind him. Nothing he could do but stand still and be careful.

The same firm voice came again. "Good. Now, what are you three young boys doing out here at two in the morning, riding a golf cart with guns?"

Logan looked toward the man, unable to see his face in the shadows. "We're on our way to Mississippi," he said flatly.

Glen let out a short laugh. "You're a long way from Mississippi, son. Why are you going there?"

"That's where my grandparents live," Logan said, then turned back toward his brothers. They were clinging to each other, faces wet.

Logan looked forward again and dropped his head. "We're on our own. Our parents were out of town when it happened. Our Becca, our nanny, died two nights ago when we got attacked."

One of the men behind them bumped the cart with his rifle stock. The clang made Logan jump.

"Who are these two?" he asked.

Logan pointed back. "Those are my two little brothers."

The man in front crossed his arms. "Hmm..." He paused. "That's some story. Well, let's get you boys to Sheriff Bufford. We'll see what we need to do with you. Nobody crosses that bridge without our say." His voice lowered slightly. "Nothing good has come from outsiders."

Glen walked over, climbed into the driver's seat of the golf cart, and motioned for Logan to get in beside his brothers. He called out to the others, "You guys stay and keep watch. I'm taking them to Bufford."

He pressed the gas pedal, and they rolled forward. Glen didn't say a word.

Logan watched the road ahead and kept quiet. The boys had gone still. Tripp had his arm around Charlie, both of them staring at the back of Glen's head.

Logan finally asked, "Who's Bufford? Where are we going?"

"You're fine," Glen said. "Just taking you to Sheriff Bufford so he can figure out what to do with you."

"What do you mean, what to do with us?" Logan shot back.

Glen's voice hardened. "We normally lock up folks who pose a risk to us and the community. We've taken people's things and sent them walking. Some tried to fight." He paused. "That didn't end well."

After a few minutes, Logan saw the sign for Crump, Tennessee. They turned left into an old hotel beside a gas station. It had lights on, the first real lights Logan had seen since leaving the house.

Several armed people stood out front, watching. It looked like a camp. Generators hummed, powering lights. Large tents filled part of the parking lot. Off to one side, people were being served food as they pulled up.

Inside, Logan noticed a large map pinned to the wall with colored lines drawn across highways. Several rifles leaned neatly against one wall. A hand-painted sign near the desk read:

CURFEW – 8PM. NO EXCEPTIONS.

The cart came to a stop. Glen stepped out and told the boys to follow him.

They entered the main office. A dark-haired woman sat at the front desk, clipboards scattered around her as she made notes. She looked at them over her glasses.

Logan noticed she wore a light brown uniform. More law enforcement, he assumed.

"Hi, Vickie," Glen said with a smile. "We found these three boys coming off the bridge from Savannah. We stopped them and brought them in."

"Hey, boys," Vickie said with a small wave.

Glen shot her a look. "We need to talk to Bufford and figure out what to do with them."

Vickie dismissed the look with a smirk, then studied the boys carefully.

"He's at the other end of the hotel dealing with some prisoner issues. You'll find him down there."

"Thanks. Can you keep an eye on them?"

"Sure," Vickie said politely. "You boys come sit over here." She pointed at a row of chairs beside her desk.

When Glen stepped away, she tossed them each a peppermint.

Logan looked at her, confused.

She caught the look. "We all can't be tough guys around here. But don't mistake kindness for weakness," she said quietly. "We lost good people trusting the wrong ones."

Charlie didn't like peppermint because it was too spicy, so he handed his to Tripp. Tripp gladly stuffed both pieces into his mouth. It was the first treat they'd had in almost two weeks.

Logan let the flavor sit on his tongue for a moment before reality settled back in.

"Ma'am, where are we?" he asked.

"You're in Crump, Tennessee," she replied.

"I know that," Logan said carefully. "But what is this place?"

She swiveled in her chair. "This is the new Crump law enforcement office. The old one was burned down during riots about a week ago." She continued, "People thought we had emergency food, medicine, weapons, you name it. We didn't. But we couldn't convince them of that. They tried to take it anyway."

Her voice softened. "We lost good people. The town did too."

She gestured around. "So, we moved here. We use the hotel as a home base. We can lock up troublemakers if we need to. It works, I suppose."

Before Logan could respond, a tall, heavily built man entered, wearing a dark official uniform. His bald head reflected the fluorescent lights above. Logan swore his arms were as big as Charlie.

"I'm Sheriff Bufford," the man said. "Who might you be?"

Logan shrank under his presence. "I'm Logan Hopkins." He pointed toward his brothers. "This is Tripp. And Charlie."

Tripp gave a nervous grin.

Charlie stared at the floor, legs dangling from the chair.

"Why are you three boys out here?" Bufford asked. "Glen said you're headed to Mississippi. That right?"

"Yes, sir."

"What's in Mississippi? And where are you from?"

"Our grandparents," Logan said. "That's all we have. The only place we can go." He shoved his hands into his pockets. "We're from just south of Nashville."

"South of Nashville?" Bufford's voice rose. "You've come all the way from Nashville?"

"Somehow," Logan said quietly. "We lost our nanny along the way. We're just trying to get to our grandparents."

Bufford scratched his chin. "We don't take chances with our people. If we don't know you, you don't stay. Trust got folks killed."

He studied them for a long moment. "You're just kids." His eyes moved from Logan to Tripp to Charlie. "I think we'll talk to each of you separately."

Logan's stomach dropped. "No. They stay with me."

"That's not how this works," Bufford said evenly. "Standard practice. If your stories match, you're fine."

Tripp grabbed Logan's sleeve. Charlie pressed into his side, squeezing him.

What if they forgot something? What if they contradicted him?

"It's okay," Logan said quietly. "Just tell them the truth. Same thing we've been saying."

Two men stepped forward. One guided Tripp down the hallway. Charlie hesitated.

"Logan?"

"I'm right here, bud," Logan said. "I'm not going anywhere." That wasn't entirely true. A hand rested on his shoulder. "Back office," Glen said.

The door shut behind him with a metallic click. The room was small. A folding table, two metal chairs, an old yellow fluorescent light humming overhead.

Bufford stayed standing. "Start from the beginning."

He sat in the metal chair and looked at the table for a second. Twelve days was a long time to explain. He just started.

He told them about Nashville. The outage. The neighborhood. The journey. Becca. The attack. The bridge. Everything.

Bufford interrupted often. "What highway out of Columbia?" "What town before Waynesboro?" "How many men on the ATV?"

Logan answered carefully, replaying every mile in his head. He kept his voice steady.

Through the thin wall, he thought he heard Charlie crying.

He pictured Tripp sitting alone somewhere, trying to be brave. Trying not to mess up.

When he finished, Bufford studied him. "You understand why we don't take chances."

"Yes, sir." Glen left to speak with the other men. Silence stretched.

The door opened. Glen stepped back in. "They line up."

Logan's shoulders sagged.

Back in the lobby, Tripp and Charlie rushed toward him. He wrapped an arm around both of them.

Bufford watched the reunion with unreadable eyes.

"Your stories match," he said. "Doesn't mean we trust you. But it means you're not lying."

The sheriff and Glen stepped outside again.

Logan watched them talk quietly through the glass.

A few minutes later, they returned.

"Here's what we'll do," Bufford said. "If you have resources to trade, I'll let you pass through. If not, I'll keep your things and send you back. The choice is yours."

Logan swallowed. "What do you want? We don't have much."

"Glen's guys went through your stuff," Bufford said.

Logan turned toward the window. The cart was gone.

Bufford raised a hand. "We'll take all the guns and ammo. We'll leave you water, food, and camping gear. The rest is ours. That should get you by. That's the cost of crossing our bridge."

"And...why do you have a bag full of watches and jewelry?" Bufford asked.

"That's from the guys who attacked us. The ones who killed our nanny."

Bufford nodded. "You boys have been through a lot."

"Do we have a deal?" Bufford asked.

Logan forced the lump down. "Sir...one of those rifles is my dad's. It's his favorite. Can I at least keep that one?"

"No," Bufford said without blinking. "We need it here to protect our community."

Logan paused. Something shifted in his chest. That rifle wasn't just steel. It was his dad teaching him to shoot. It was safety. Proof that he could protect his brothers. And now it would belong to someone else.

"Take it or leave it," Bufford said.

"But you don't understand," Logan said, pushing harder than he meant to. "It might be the only thing I have left of him."

"My job is to protect my people," Bufford replied. "That rifle helps me do that."

Logan slumped in his chair. He swallowed and nodded once. "Okay."

Every part of him wanted to argue. To fight. But keeping his brothers and the cart mattered more.

Bufford held his gaze. "If I hear you doubled back this way, the deal's off."

"Glen will get your cart ready," Bufford said.

Glen gave a small nod. "We could use that cart. But you're not getting to your grandparents without it. So it stays with you."

"Good luck," Bufford said. "You're not there yet." He met Logan's eyes. "We've heard Selmer isn't as organized as we are. They've had issues with different groups operating under different rules. Be careful."

Logan understood now. Every place had its own rules.

And they didn't belong to any of them.

CHAPTER 33

THE WEIGHT

Two of Glen's men brought the cart around for the boys. It looked noticeably thinner. Much of the gear had been stripped off, leaving only the sleeping bags and tent. The bug-out bag was gone. The other bags were gone. And most notably, the guns. They would have to make the remainder of the trip with very few resources.

He stared at the storage rack one more time, then over to his brothers. It rolled through his head—another loss stacked on top of a pile of losses. The boys were visibly shaken and exhausted. Logan watched his little brothers climb aboard and couldn't shake the feeling that he'd failed them somehow. The world was so different now. They had no control over any of it—just innocent bystanders.

Glen nodded to the boys as the engine came to life and began pushing the cart west, continuing on 64. Logan hadn't had time to think through the plan. All he had worried about the last couple of hours was their safety.

The few lights of the town faded behind them, along with the sound of the generators powering them. Logan felt mixed about leaving. It was the most normal they had seen in thirteen days. It carried a sense of safety, even though the inhabitants had taken all of their key items and forced them out. It occurred to him that at least they got to keep the cart. They weren't entirely ruthless. He hoped Corinth would have similar resources and help. Somewhere they could belong.

They were riding alone. Three kids, unarmed, unprepared, and unprotected. There was nothing left to trade. No options.

He wondered if Selmer was worse. He remembered the warning from Bufford.

He knew the sun was coming. Sadly, what used to bring light and safety was his enemy now.

They rolled further into Friday morning.

Logan instinctively reached down to adjust his pistol belt that was no longer there. He had gotten used to the weight of it.

As they rode in silence, he ran the numbers through his head. Fifteen miles to Selmer. Then another fifteen to twenty to Grandpa Jake's.

No one discussed the danger they'd just made it through—yet another close call in a string of too many.

They were tired, and with the sun breaking the horizon, he was left with no choice but to stop and rest.

A small glint of ambition pushed into his mind. Maybe he should just press on. Daylight or not. Just get there. He thought better of it as he looked down at Charlie's head lying on his lap, curled up and trying to find rest.

Logan saw the small town of Adamsville coming up. He prayed it wasn't organized like Savannah or Crump.

He didn't want to set up camp that close, so he decided to move through to the other side of town.

They stopped for a moment. Shining his light over the map, he found an alternative route around the small, historic town.

They eased around the south side of town quietly and carefully. They didn't see any signs of structured organization—no lights, guards, or roadblocks, at least on their route.

The bypass had worked. A touch of good luck, maybe. Logan didn't quite believe in that anymore.

A few miles outside of Adamsville, they turned down a small road beside an old repair shop. The road veered left and was surrounded by heavy trees and thick vegetation.

He pulled the cart through a small ditch and up into the greenery. Behind the growth, it opened up just enough under the trees to park. It looked suitable for camp as he climbed off and stretched his stiff limbs.

The sun was now high enough to illuminate the area. That made setting up camp easier. He could use both hands without his flashlight holding him back. By a stroke of luck, the Crump guys had left it in the storage compartment.

Logan noticed that the little boys were still somber and quiet. Probably processing the night's events, but he couldn't be sure.

They snacked on the few items that were left, leaving only a couple remaining. Food, fuel, and water were all in very short supply as they were squarely into day six of their journey—something they had planned to take only three to four days. What a miss—the words flashed into his brain.

After the small meal and sips of water, the three boys removed their socks and shoes and climbed into the tent. They were out of clean clothing, and the smell of the three of them was overbearing in the small quarters. Logan left the front flap of the tent slightly open and removed the vent cover at the top to let some of the smell escape. As he lay there, he hoped his grandparents had extra clothes or at least a way to wash.

He kept an ear out as he rested.

His eyes drifted again and again to the corner of the tent. There was an empty spot where their gear usually sat.

His dad's rifle was noticeably absent. As long as it had been with him, Logan had felt like the protector. Without it, he felt thirteen again.

A new feeling worked its way into his chest and throat. He knew this one. Anger. It built in him as he thought through the last several days. Was he responsible for all of this? Was it his fault that Becca was gone? What could he have done to keep their gear?

Maybe he wasn't leading his brothers to safety. Maybe he was just dragging them through danger and destruction—the new everyday.

He envisioned Becca lying on the ground and her final words.

"Get home."

He whispered them out loud to himself. Emptiness gradually took the place of anger.

"Get home," he whispered again.

He didn't know if he was saying it for her or for himself anymore. But he would. For his brothers. Even if he had to crawl the rest of the way.

He looked at his youngest brother. He was fast asleep, breathing deeply and pulled very close to Logan's side.

Tripp spoke up. Logan hadn't realized he was awake.

"Do you think Grandpa has guns, Lo?"

"Yes, he has lots of guns. Remember when Dad and I used to go hunting and shooting with him all the time?"

"Oh yeah," Tripp responded softly, his mind working behind his eyes. He rolled over, trying to get comfortable.

"I hope he can protect us," he murmured, trailing off.

The words landed harder than Tripp knew.

Logan swallowed. He just wanted his parents.

He didn't respond or question Tripp. He let him drift off, but the words were already chewing at him.

The songs of birds close by were the only comforting thing. For a time, Logan continued rerunning everything through his head, trying to find his way into sleep.

A distant shot punched through the morning air, startling Logan and sending his adrenaline spiking. Thankfully, the two younger boys were already asleep.

He analyzed it quickly. It was distant.

Being around hunting rifles, he knew the sound of a high-powered round.

It was early morning.

He convinced himself it was someone hunting.

The birds remained quiet, like they were thinking too. Everything felt still.

He forced his eyes closed. If it wasn't hunting, there was nothing he could do about it anyway.

CHAPTER 34
LAST OF IT

Logan awoke Friday afternoon to drops of water tapping his face. Rain dripped through the vent he had left open. The rain was steady, the first they'd seen on the journey. The rhythmic tic, tic, tic was almost soothing.

He jumped out to put the cover on. Dark gray clouds moved overhead. Damp air surrounded them, making everything feel heavy.

He pulled their shoes and socks inside, now fully soaked through. With no replacements, that would hurt later.

Thunder echoed in the distance. Logan couldn't tell if it was coming or going, but he didn't love the fact that they were surrounded by trees in a tent. Mom's voice came back to him. If you can hear thunder, you can be struck by lightning.

He longed for that guidance now.

The little boys began to stir, the combination of movement, noise, and thunder waking them.

"Is it storming?" Charlie asked, his eyes still closed.

Logan patted his back. "It is, but it's not a bad one. Luckily, it's just a storm this time."

"I hate storms," Tripp said nervously. Logan knew this about him. Heights and storms were two of his biggest fears.

Logan passed out Becca's remaining trail mix and Rice Krispies treats to share. They talked quietly and sipped water sparingly as the taps of rain kept coming.

We've survived worse than a thunderstorm, Logan thought as Tripp and Charlie argued about which was better, waffles or pancakes. Logan broke the tie with pancakes. Charlie gave him a high-five in agreement, smirking back at Tripp.

The rain finally tapered off, and the boys emerged from their canvas home. The sky was still dark gray but holding back its water. The trees were dripping with the remnants of the storm, and the smell of fresh air lingered.

The air was cool. Logan wished they had the rest of their gear to dry off or warm up, but it was miles behind them, being used for someone else's greater good.

The ground was soft beneath their feet as they trudged around.

It looked to be well into the afternoon or early evening. The clouds were making time estimates difficult.

The boys were rambunctious this afternoon. A decent rest, snacks, and being cooped up in a small tent together for too long seemed to do that.

Logan decided they had waited long enough. He would break his own rule of moving during daylight. They could make up an extra few miles before dark.

Twenty-five miles to Grandpa Jake's. Certainly doable.

Tonight would be the night they completed this insane journey.

The boys slid on their wet shoes with no socks. Charlie got a laugh out of the squishing sound the shoes made as they walked around breaking down camp.

Tripp had stepped up without being asked. He seemed older than eight this morning.

With all the soggy gear packed up and stored, the trio climbed aboard their cart. Logan no longer had his map, but he knew the route by heart. West on 64 until Selmer, then south on Highway 45 until Corinth. One turn. Twenty-five miles to safety and help, he hoped.

They pulled toward the road. The tires spun, trying to find grip. Logan worked the cart through the wet soil and back across the small ditch that now had a stream of water drifting through it.

They eased back onto the road. Steam was still rising from the cooler rain on hot pavement.

Now moving, Bufford's warning replayed in his head. He wasn't sure what they would find, but hoped that, for once, they could just get lucky and slip through. They were so close.

Traveling in daylight was refreshing. It was nice to actually be able to see their surroundings. He liked the sunlight on their faces, even if it was only for a short while.

The little boys seemed to enjoy it too. They were talking among themselves, counting abandoned cars, playing the old license plate state game.

Selmer was a much bigger town than they had been navigating. Not huge, but bigger. Its sprawl became apparent as they hit the outer areas. More and more cars littered the streets. More houses too. They saw a lot of people moving around. Many of them gathered to look at them pass by, like they were a unicorn or something.

That familiar unease returned. This was why they had decided to travel at night now.

There were several people walking along the roads. Some had belongings with them. Some had nothing. All of them looked tired and hungry.

Logan watched everyone's hands closely. Scanning. Looking for threats.

They made their way into the heart of town. Houses were now boarded up. Graffiti littered street signs and buildings.

Driving by the Welcome to Selmer sign, Logan saw it littered with bullet holes.

Commercial buildings were burned out and completely vandalized. As they crossed into the center of town, all the people disappeared. No movement. No activity that he could observe. It seemed the opposite of Savannah and Crump. The people were staying outside the city, not in it. The further in they went, the worse it got.

Logan thought he saw movement in one of the large buildings. Looking back, he couldn't be sure. The sun was beginning to set, and the figure was hidden by shadows.

The orange sky was fading to dark blue. Logan now welcomed the nighttime, realizing he might have made a mistake leaving too early.

They saw the large intersection they were hunting just ahead.

Cars were piled together unnaturally. They didn't seem abandoned but placed. A considerable amount of debris littered the road as well. Logan wasn't going to let up. He picked out a spot to the far left that he could fit through. It was part of the sidewalk, just wide enough for them, but wouldn't have fit a car. He picked his way over the curb and pushed the accelerator down.

His adrenaline was building, but he wasn't sure why. There was no visible threat, but he had learned to trust his gut on these things now.

They raced through the opening, bouncing and jostling around. The little boys squeezed the handles, trying to stay in their seats.

Out of the corner of his right eye, Logan saw a person dart out of the debris pile, then slip back into a group of cars. A faint whistle cut through the engine noise. Three short chirps.

There was no way he was going to stop and investigate further. He wanted to put a gap between them and the alert.

They hopped off the sidewalk near an empty gas station. Logan pressed on with all the cart had. Tripp must have heard the whistle too and looked back.

"I see a man, Logan!" he yelled. "He's running behind us!"

Logan looked back at the man. He wasn't running that hard. More of a fast jog. At that pace, he couldn't catch them.

Logan quickly flipped the lights on. He wanted better visibility as darkness settled around them.

They were just south of town.

It had been a half mile or so from the intersection. Oddly, the man was still trailing behind them. Logan could still barely make out the short chirps from the man's whistle. His stomach tightened. It was like an audible spotlight tracking them through the dark.

Suddenly it all made sense—but Logan was too late.

They had been purposely funneled into a trap.

Sitting across the road in front of them was an old green tractor with a long bale trailer attached. It spanned the entirety of the road. On both sides were commercial buildings. Several fast-food restaurants, a large retail store, and an auto parts shop completed the funnel.

Logan slowed, trying to make sense of it. The man behind them was closing the distance now, no longer pretending to jog.

A figure stepped out from behind the tractor. His rifle was already up, already steady. It pointed straight at Logan.

Two more emerged from the buildings on either side, headlamps cutting through the dim light. Their pistols were raised.

Logan rolled to a stop. Twenty yards from the tractor. Twenty from the men flanking them.

They were boxed in.

The man in front was wiry and filthy. Clothes stiff with grime. Eyes restless and slightly wild.

He walked toward them without hurry.

"Off. Now."

Logan didn't feel that the request was a question.

The boys froze. Charlie gripped Logan's shirt, small fingers digging in. Sniffling. More guns.

Logan's thoughts stalled. If he moved wrong—

The man on the right lunged, yanking Tripp off the cart and slamming him to the pavement. Tripp cried out, clutching his arm.

Logan shifted toward the man to protest. Instantly, the wiry man shifted his rifle to Charlie. The barrel stopped inches from his little chest.

Logan went still.

The man from behind reached them, breathing hard, whistle still dangling from his fingers.

They were now fully surrounded.

Logan looked at the man to his left. He could smell him. He was drenched in dirt, sweat, and smoke. He had the pistol pressed against Logan's ribs, his hand shaking, finger resting on the trigger.

"I said off."

Logan picked up Charlie and stepped off to the side.

"What do we have here, Jody?" the man behind called out between labored breaths to the wiry one in front.

"Looks like we have some new wheels," he said teasingly.

The man on the left was a sturdy individual wearing an old trucker hat and denim overalls. He pulled Logan further away from the cart. Charlie let out a whimper at the jerking motion.

Jody came around to inspect it, looking everything over.

"Nice ride, boys. We appreciate you bringing us some wheels."

Jody ran a hand along the cart's frame.

"Better than that heap," he said, flipping his chin toward the tractor. "And they brought supplies."

Logan found his voice. "That's ours."

The man in overalls let out a laugh. "Not anymore."

Jody swung his rifle back around toward Logan and Charlie. His eyes were more wild now.

"This is ours."

He tilted his head.

"Walk."

Logan looked over to Tripp on the ground. He was still holding Charlie to his chest, which was now soaked with tears.

He had brought them here.

He pushed through town.

He broke his own rule. Don't move in daylight.

That mistake would not happen again.

He paused a moment longer, looking around.

"Okay," he said through clenched teeth.

He stepped around behind the cart over to Tripp. Muzzles followed his movements. He helped him to his feet and brushed him off.

"Come on."

Tripp looked down at the wet pavement and just nodded.

As they stepped past the tractor, one of the men called after them.

"You came down the wrong road, kid."

Logan gave the four men one final glare. Nothing could be done.

They were on foot now.

They started walking. One foot in front of the other—south.

In the distance behind them, Logan heard them congratulating themselves. Then the cart's suspension squeaked, followed by the engine coming to life and fading away into silence.

They took the last of it.

It boiled in his stomach, up into his throat.

He pulled his shoulders back and pushed his chest outward.

Feet moving on pavement.

He reached into his pockets, but his hands felt empty.

Then he found the flashlight he had stuck in his pocket earlier. The discovery pulled him out of his anger just enough. It was something.

"How is your arm, Tripp?" he asked. "Can you move it okay?"

Tripp didn't respond. He just stuck it out in front of them and bent it back and forth a few times, showing that it still worked.

"Lo Lo, how do we get home now?" Charlie asked, walking on his own.

"We walk," Logan said flatly. Then again, quieter, "We walk." He refused to look back. He wouldn't.

The three small silhouettes walked south along the highway, the dim light of the moon shining down on them and reflecting off the damp road.

CHAPTER 35
STRIPPED

They trudged along.

The theft had happened minutes ago. Maybe thirty. Maybe less. Logan couldn't tell. Time felt split clean in two, a before and after—and he was walking in whatever came after.

Highway 45 stretched south in front of them, a narrow strip of pavement cutting through darker trees. The clouds were thinning now. A dull wash of leftover light clung to the horizon.

Logan didn't look back toward Selmer.

If he did, he might stop.

Their shoes were still wet from camp. The rain had soaked them through earlier, and there hadn't been time to dry anything. No socks. Those had been wrung out and left on the cart before everything went sideways.

The cart.

He could still hear the engine cutting off. The scrape of boots on gravel. A man's voice saying, Off. Now. He swallowed it down.

Now each step pressed damp fabric against skin already rubbed thin from days on the road. The back of his heel shifted inside the rubber. A hot spot forming. He felt it and kept walking.

Six miles.

That was the only thought he allowed himself. Six miles south. Almost halfway.

They had planned to ride this stretch. Charlie would've been curled up in the middle by now. Tripp would've been half asleep, leaning against the side rail. Instead, there was only the slap of rubber soles on damp pavement and the steady song of insects rising from the trees.

Tripp walked tight to Logan's left, Charlie glued to his right.

No one complained. Not yet.

The wet shoes began rubbing almost immediately. Logan felt the skin at his heel wrinkle and slide. The heat built, then sharpened. He knew what was coming. He ignored it. Pain meant they were still moving.

The pace was slow, slow enough for Charlie's small legs to keep up. His steps were shorter now, uneven. Tripp kept pace, jaw tight, shoulders rigid.

Logan scanned the road ahead, then the treeline. Every shadow felt closer without the cart. Without the weight of gear. Without the illusion of protection.

They had nothing left. No food. No water. No dry clothes. No weapons.

Just six miles.

"They took everything."

Tripp's voice came flat, aimed at the pavement.

Logan didn't answer right away. He didn't trust his first response.

"They took the stuff," he said. "Not us."

The words sounded steadier than he felt.

Charlie tugged at his hand. "Do Grandma and Grandpa have food? Because I'm really hungry."

The question landed harder than the theft.

"Yeah," Logan said. "They'll have food."

He didn't slow down.

They walked in silence after that. The night air cooled, but the inside of his shoes stayed damp and warm. The blister on his heel gave way with a soft, sickening shift. Raw skin met fabric. He kept walking. He would deal with it later.

A green road sign appeared ahead, reflective in the dim light.

Corinth – 12 miles

At least now they knew.

Tripp let out a low grunt when he read it. Not anger. Not fear. Just tired.

They moved past the sign. A few steps later, Charlie caught the front of his shoe and pitched forward. His hands hit the pavement first. He rolled onto his back, dirt grinding into his palms.

Logan dropped beside him. "You okay?"

Charlie blinked fast, trying not to cry. His hands were scraped and already beading red.

Behind them, Tripp snapped. "Can't you just walk? We have to keep moving." He didn't turn around.

Charlie pushed himself up, shoulders tight. "I'm fine," he said. He hurried forward to catch up.

"Hey," Logan said quietly to Tripp. "Ease up."

Tripp didn't respond. He was limping now, subtle but there. Logan saw it and said nothing. They kept going.

The breaks came closer together after that. The distance between them shrinking. Charlie's steps dragged. Tripp's limp deepened.

Logan bent down without asking and lifted Charlie onto his back. The weight burned immediately through his arms and shoulders. Charlie wrapped his arms around Logan's neck and laid his head against him. Logan adjusted and kept walking.

The trees pressed closer in the dark. Somewhere far off, a dog barked. Then silence.

He tightened his grip. Every sound felt closer.

When Tripp finally stopped, he didn't argue.

"I can't," he said. "I can't go anymore."

His limp wasn't subtle anymore.

Logan nodded once. "Okay. We'll stop."

Up ahead, something caught the faint light, the metal edge and reflective tape of a semi-trailer parked crooked along the shoulder. It would have to do.

They approached it carefully. Abandoned like everything else. Logan checked the cab. It was locked.

"Under," he said. "We'll stay under it."

"This is where we're sleeping?" Tripp asked.

"It's shelter."

They crawled under the trailer. The asphalt still held warmth from the day. The air smelled of diesel and old grease. Logan leaned back against the rear tires. Tripp sat beside him. Charlie curled up across his lap. It was good to be off their feet.

They pulled off their shoes. The skin on Logan's heel was peeled raw, white and red. Tripp's sockless ankle was rubbed open. Charlie's small feet were blistered along the sides.

Charlie looked up at him. “How far now?”

Logan hesitated.

“Not far.”

Charlie studied him a moment. “Can we walk in the daytime?”

That would break the rules. They moved at night.

But what were they hiding now?

They had nothing left to lose.

“Yeah,” Logan said. “We’ll go in the morning.”

Charlie nodded and settled against him.

When his breathing slowed, Logan stared out past the edge of the trailer into the dark road.

He thought about Becca. About the roadblock. The guns. The cart disappearing into the night.

He had been proud when they left home. Proud of the plan. Proud of himself.

There had been four of them then. Now there were three boys under a trailer with blistered feet and empty hands.

He didn’t feel scared anymore. He felt something else.

Harder. Quieter. Angrier.

There wasn’t a plan anymore. There was just eight miles.

CHAPTER 36

EIGHT MILES

Logan opened his eyes.

Day fourteen since the event. Day seven of the trip. Saturday.

It was early.

The sky was dull, gray, and bland. His back was stiff against the asphalt. Little rocks pressed into his skin. His neck kinked from sleeping crooked.

For a moment, he lay still, taking stock.

Mouth dry. Lips cracked at the corners. No saliva came when he tried to work some up. When he swallowed, there was almost nothing there.

Logan rolled out from under the trailer and stood. His left heel screamed when it hit the ground. He grabbed the trailer frame to steady himself. The raw skin from the night before had stiffened while he slept, and every step would break it open again.

Down the highway south, it was the same road. Same trees. Same gray sky.

Eight miles.

Beside Charlie, Logan crouched and put a hand on his back. "Hey. Let's go."

Charlie blinked and rolled toward him but said nothing.

Tripp was already half awake, staring at the underside of the trailer like he'd been watching it for a while. He sat up without being asked and reached for his shoes.

The same grunts came from all three of them as they tried to slip their shoes on. Frustration and pain worked over their faces. A necessary evil.

Then a slow exhale when it was time to move.

Logan said, "Let's go," and they went.

The first mile was the worst.

Their bodies hadn't warmed up yet. Tripp's limp was bad from the start this morning, worse than last night. Without saying anything about it, he compensated with his stride, weighting his left side. Logan watched it and let it go.

For the first mile or so, Charlie kept pace. Walking quietly. Eyes forward.

The road was empty for now. Just the three of them on the four-lane highway cutting south through Tennessee pines and overgrown roadsides. Somewhere a crow called out and went silent. Morning birds started up. The world sounded almost normal if you didn't think about it too hard.

He was thirsty in a way that was starting to feel like something other than thirst. A pressure behind his eyes. A dullness at the back of his head. He'd read somewhere once that by the time you felt really thirsty, you were already behind. He believed that now. It had been almost twenty-four hours since their last sip of water.

Two miles in, Charlie reached up and took Logan's hand. He didn't say anything. Just took it and held on.

Logan let him.

A farmhouse sat back off the road, up a gravel drive. An old mailbox at the end of it with an American flag sticker half peeling off.

Logan stopped and looked at it for a moment. A curtain moved in the front window. He caught it. Just a shift, like someone stepping back from the glass.

Someone was home.

Logan passed Charlie's hand to Tripp. "Stay here."

"What are you doing?" Tripp asked.

"I'm gonna ask for water," Logan said.

Both hands out at his sides, Logan walked slowly up the gravel drive. About halfway to the porch, a screen door pushed open and a man appeared. Older and thin. A shotgun rested across his forearm, the barrel pointed down.

Logan stopped. Raised both hands chest high.

"I'm not—I'm not here for trouble," he said. His voice came out rougher than he expected. Dry. "We've been walking all night. We just need water."

The man looked past him toward the road and saw Tripp and Charlie, then looked back at Logan again. Something moved across his face.

"I've got a family in here," the man said. "Four kids of my own."

"Yes, sir." Logan nodded.

The man paused.

"I can't." His voice dropped. "I got barely enough."

Logan lowered his hands. "I understand."

He understood. He didn't want to, but he did.

"Thank you anyway," he said.

Logan turned and walked back down the gravel drive. The screen door shut behind him. The curtain moved again.

They got back to the road and didn't say anything.

Neither did his brothers. Just questions flashing across their faces.

They walked.

His dad would've known what to do.

That thought had been showing up more lately with the absence of Becca. It came slipping in when he wasn't guarding against it.

He could picture his dad at the farmhouse. It might have been a different outcome. His dad had a way with strangers. Easy, unhurried, making them feel like they'd known him for years. He would have already had Plan B by now, and Plan C, and he'd probably be cracking some dumb joke about it.

Logan missed that so much. He felt the pressure growing in his sternum.

Then Mom came to mind. She'd have kept spirits up the whole way down here, singing something stupid to make Charlie laugh. Counting down the miles with them. She'd have driven through the night herself if it meant getting her boys somewhere safe.

They were just out there somewhere. Stranded. Trying to get home the same as them, maybe. Logan hoped they were together at least. He hoped they had water.

He hadn't let himself think about worst-case in a few days because it didn't help anything.

He just had to get there.

By mid-morning, his headache had settled in behind his eyes and wasn't moving. A dull, steady throb.

Tripp's limp had gone from subtle to obvious. He was dropping his right shoulder with each step to compensate, his whole stride lopsided. Logan had watched him try to hide it, stop trying to hide it, and now just push through it.

Charlie had stopped talking completely. He wasn't crying. Just moving. Small feet working the pavement, arms hanging at his sides.

Logan studied him. Something cold turned over in his chest.

"You okay, Char?"

"I'm thirsty," Charlie said.

"I know."

"Really thirsty, Lo."

"I know, bud. I know."

There was nothing else to say about it. He just left it.

Tripp was the first one to cramp.

It hit him in the left calf, and he made a short, sharp sound, stopped walking, and grabbed at his leg. He tried to straighten it and couldn't. His face went tight and pale.

Logan grabbed his arm. "Come here. Sit down."

They got him to the shoulder of the road. Logan bent the foot back, stretching the calf. Tripp let out a yell through clenched teeth.

"Hold still."

"It hurts."

"I know. Hold still."

He worked it for a minute. The muscle finally released. Tripp exhaled hard.

When Tripp could stand, Logan pulled Charlie up.

"I can't carry you yet," he told him quietly. "Save that for later, okay?"

Charlie nodded. Logan thought he understood more than he let on sometimes.

They started walking again. Slower.

Logan's mouth had gone past dry. It was something else now, a thick, cottony feeling that made his tongue feel wrong. He kept swallowing at nothing.

Charlie had stopped asking about it, which was worse than when he was asking.

He heard it before he saw it. A thin sound, water moving somewhere off the road to the right. He slowed.

Through the treeline, maybe thirty yards off the shoulder, a drainage ditch ran alongside an old fence row. It looked shallow.

Logan stared at it.

He knew what ran into ditches like that. Road runoff, fertilizer, animal waste, rust from old culverts.

He stood there another moment.

Charlie sat down on the shoulder without being asked.

Logan looked down at his little brother. Then back at the ditch.

He pushed through the weeds.

Up close, it was gross. The bottom was silted and dark. A rusted culvert fed into it from a nearby ditch. The smell was earthy and faintly sour. A plastic bag had snagged on a root near the bank, moving with the stream.

He crouched down.

Behind him, Tripp watched without saying anything.

Logan cupped his hands and drank the brown water before he could change his mind.

It tasted like dirt and metal. He drank again. His stomach turned slightly, and he breathed through it and drank a third time.

He waved the boys over.

Tripp crouched beside him without a word and drank. Made a face, then drank again.

Charlie looked at it. "It's dirty."

"I know," Logan said.

"Like really dirty, Logan."

"I know, bud. Drink anyway."

Charlie looked at it for another long moment. Then he cupped his small hands and drank a little. He gagged once, then kept going.

They drank until they couldn't anymore. Logan didn't know if it would help or hurt them later. He pushed that thought down to where he was keeping everything else he couldn't do anything about.

They climbed back up to the road.

Tripp wiped his mouth on his sleeve and looked at Logan.

Logan looked back at him.

They turned south and kept pushing on.

There was another man walking toward them farther up the road. He was coming from the south. The opposite direction.

As they got closer, Logan called out.

"Hey—hey, sir."

The man straightened. He was broad, middle-aged. His shirt hung loose and damp with sweat. He looked like he hadn't slept.

He watched them carefully.

"Do you have any water you could spare?" Logan asked. "Anything."

"No, son, I don't," the man said. "They took everything I had."

Logan frowned. "Who—what do you mean?"

"The folks up the road here," he said. "I was trying to get through Corinth and work my way to my son's house in Iuka. They took my stuff and sent me this way."

"Are you heading to Corinth?" the man asked.

"We are," Logan said. "We're trying to get to our grandparents."

The man nodded. "They've got checkpoints set up outside of town." He pointed in the direction the boys were heading. "They're organized. Better than most places I've seen."

The man turned away from them and started walking again. He called out, "Good luck to you guys."

Logan watched him go.

Checkpoints and organized. He knew what those words meant now. He'd learned them in Selmer when the cart drove away without him.

He looked down at his brothers. They had nothing left to trade. Nothing left to take. Just three kids on a road with blistered feet and a flashlight.

Grandpa Jake was only two miles past it.

He turned his brothers south and kept moving.

The stream water helped for a while. An hour, maybe. Then the sun got higher, and the headache crept back in, and Charlie's feet gave out.

He didn't fall this time. He just stopped.

"Lo," he said. "I can't."

Logan bent down without arguing. Charlie climbed onto his back. Skinny arms around his neck. His weight dropped onto Logan's shoulders and burned through his arms immediately.

He stood up and kept walking.

Tripp walked quietly beside them.

A few minutes passed.

"Lo," Tripp said.

"What."

"We left home a week ago today."

Logan hadn't thought about it. A week ago. A week ago today they were sitting in the house planning their escape from Richard and Carol. Was it the right decision?

A week felt like a year.

"I know," Logan said.

"Do you think Mom and Dad know where we are?"

"No," Logan said. There wasn't a point in lying about it. "But they're trying to get to us. Same as we're trying to get to Grandpa Jake's."

Tripp didn't respond.

Charlie's chin was resting on Logan's shoulder. After a moment, his small voice came, close to Logan's ear.

"Are they okay?"

Logan swallowed. His throat was still dry even after the water. "Yeah," he said. "They're okay."

He said it like he believed it.

He kept saying it in his head after, like if he said it enough times it might stay true.

They stopped under a tree when Tripp refused to go another step.

Logan didn't fight him on it. He put Charlie down, and they all sat. Shoes came off.

It was bad.

Tripp's heel was split open at the back, skin ragged and red, the blisters long since burst and the raw patches beneath it worn further. Charlie's right pinky toe had a blister the size of a grape, the skin gone translucent.

Logan didn't take his off at first. When he finally did, his own left heel was worse than he'd realized. He'd been walking on it for hours without fully acknowledging what it was. The skin had rolled back at the edge like a page corner.

He stared at it.

Then he pulled the bottom hem of his shirt and tore a strip off. Then another. He handed Tripp a strip without explaining and wrapped his own heel and tied it off above his ankle.

Charlie watched him and wordlessly held out his foot.

Logan wrapped it.

When they put their shoes back on, they all did it slow and deliberately. Logan stood and took one step, and the strip shifted immediately. He adjusted and took another.

They moved ahead.

They crested a long, gradual rise in the road about an hour later.

At the top, Logan stopped.

On the horizon, maybe a few miles out, smoke rose from multiple points. He counted three distinct columns, maybe four. Dark against the pale sky.

Logan stood there and watched it.

Tripp stopped beside him, catching his breath, hands on his knees.

"Is that good?" Tripp asked.

Logan didn't answer. Smoke could mean cooking fires. Burning debris. People. He wasn't sure.

Probably people.

Probably a lot of people.

He watched another moment.

"Let's go," he said.

The last several miles were grinding.

Logan's headache had moved from behind his eyes to the top of his skull. A steady pulse that flared in the direct sun. His vision didn't exactly blur, but there was a slight shimmer at the edges when he looked into the light, like heat rising off asphalt.

Charlie was on his back again. His weight felt like twice what it was. Logan's arms ached up into his shoulders. He shifted him higher and kept walking.

Tripp's limp had become a stagger. He was putting almost no weight on the right foot now. But he was still moving. He hadn't asked to stop.

They finally crossed into Mississippi.

The sound came first. A generator, distant, unmistakable once you knew what to listen for. A voice carrying, though too far to make out words. Then the smell of wood smoke.

People.

Something moved through him, quiet and exhausted. Not quite relief. More like a signal. Something in him saying they were there.

Signs of people ahead.

Then they came around the bend.

And Logan slowed to a stop.

Vehicles had been positioned across the road, three of them angled intentionally. A weathered pickup, an old SUV, and a flatbed trailer forming a staggered line. Plywood panels filled the gaps.

Orange safety cones and striped barricades ran along either side where the road met the ditch.

Men stood at intervals. Five that he could count. Maybe more behind the vehicles. Armed but not erratic, rifles slung across backs or held low. Some wore reflective vests over civilian clothes. They moved like they'd been doing this for a while.

Logan stood there.

Charlie still on Logan's back. Tripp breathing hard at his side.

He was too tired to be properly afraid. His body had spent the last of that currency somewhere around mile five.

One of the men at the barrier stepped forward. Thin build. Vest. He walked with purpose but not aggression, hands visible, watching them approach.

He stopped them about twenty yards out.

"Where are you coming from?"

Tripp's voice came from beside him. Low. Exhausted.

"Logan..."

Charlie tightened his arms around his neck.

Logan stared at the man across from him.

He shifted Charlie higher on his back. Then he looked the man in the eye and stepped forward.

CHAPTER 37

NAMES MATTER

The guard's question hung in the air.

Logan was still holding Charlie on his back. His arms had gone past aching into something duller—a numbness that started at the shoulders and ran down to his wrists. His fingers tingled where they locked under Charlie's legs. He had to flex them once to keep from losing his grip. Charlie's weight hadn't changed, but Logan's ability to carry it had.

Tripp stood just off his left hip, breathing heavily.

"Where are you coming from?"

Logan looked at the man. He had a thin build and wore a reflective vest over a dark shirt. He was older—maybe his dad's age. He had a rifle slung across his chest, his hands loose but close to it. His eyes scanned constantly.

"Tennessee," Logan said. His throat felt dry. He swallowed. "Up near Nashville. We've been walking ever since Selmer."

The man didn't react. He just looked them over—Charlie on Logan's back, Tripp's uneven stance, the cloth wrapping above Logan's shoe where his heel had been bandaged.

"How long have you been walking?"

"Since this morning."

A second man stepped out from behind the flatbed. He was stockier. Older still. Maybe sixty. He wore a canvas work shirt with the sleeves rolled up. He walked up and stopped a few feet behind the first guard.

There was more movement near the pickup. A third man stood there with a notebook, writing something down. The first guard shifted his weight, still studying them.

"You got anything on you? Any knives or weapons?"

Logan hesitated. Not because he did, but because he knew what it meant if they didn't believe him.

"No, sir."

The guard held his eyes a second longer than necessary. Then he looked at Tripp.

"You?"

Tripp shook his head.

"Hands where I can see them," the second man said firmly.

Logan adjusted Charlie slightly and lifted one hand as much as he could without dropping his brother. The movement threw his balance more than he had expected. His heel slipped against the inside of his shoe, and for a split second the world tilted.

He caught himself, and Charlie tightened his arms around Logan's neck.

The first guard stepped forward half a pace. Close enough now that Logan could see the wrinkles around his eyes.

"Are you boys traveling alone?"

"Yes, sir."

"Nobody behind you? Nobody coming this way?"

"No, sir."

The man studied him. Logan forced himself not to look away.

"Where are your parents?"

"Dallas," Logan said. His voice almost caught on the word. He cleared his throat. "They were there when everything happened."

Silence settled between them. The first guard looked back at the older man. Something quiet passed between them. The morning air sat heavy and warm.

"So, who are you traveling with?" the older man asked.

"Just us," Logan said. "Me and my two brothers."

"Nobody else?" the first guard followed up.

Logan took a step, gravel crunching under him. "We had someone." His voice dipped without meaning to. "We lost her on the road."

The older man's jaw tightened slightly. He didn't ask.

"What are your names?" the first guard asked.

"Logan Hopkins." He shifted Charlie's weight again. His grip slipped for a second before he reset it. "This is Charlie," he said, shifting his brother higher. "That's Tripp." He nodded toward Tripp.

The man with the notebook looked up.

"How old are you?"

"Thirteen."

A flicker crossed the older man's face at that. Surprise, maybe.

The older man's eyes moved over him carefully. The road was quiet except for the low idle of something mechanical farther back behind the barricade.

"What's your business in Corinth?" he asked.

"We're trying to get to our grandparents," Logan said.

"Where?"

Logan hesitated for just half a second.

Saying the name felt like using something he didn't fully understand. Like spending money he wasn't sure he had.

"Jake Cookson," he said, flat and clear. Just as his dad had taught him. "He's our grandfather. We're headed to his place."

The first guard went still. The older man uncrossed his arms.

"Jake Cookson?" the first guard said.

The older man stepped forward. "The place off County Road 412?"

"Yes, sir."

The man with the notebook stopped writing.

Nobody spoke.

Logan felt sweat slide down his back under Charlie's weight.

The older man scratched the back of his neck and exhaled slowly. "You're Jake's grandson?"

"Yes, sir."

Another pause. Past the men, Logan saw a handheld radio clipped to the flatbed rail. Another man stood farther down the road near stacked barricades, watching closely.

This wasn't just three guys and a truck.

"We don't let strangers through anymore," the first guard said. "Haven't in about a week." He let that sit.

"You understand why."

"Yes, sir," Logan said. Unfortunately, he did.

The older man nodded once.

"You go straight there. No stops. No turning around. No detours. You're on 45. Go west on 72. County Road 412 cuts off to the right about a mile past the water tower. You'll see it."

"Yes, sir."

The first guard held his gaze.

"We'll know if you don't."

It wasn't a threat. It was information.

Logan believed him.

"We're not here for anything else," Logan said. His voice was steadier now. "We just want to get there."

The older man tilted his chin, and the guard stepped aside.

The barricade opened for them. They stepped forward and moved through.

His knee almost buckled on the first step through. He locked it in time and kept moving.

He didn't realize how tight his chest had been until it loosened all at once. No one said anything else.

After thirty yards, Logan glanced back once.

The barricade was already closed. The older man stood where he'd been, arms crossed again. The man with the notebook had gone back to writing.

They were keeping records.

Logan faced forward and moved along with his brothers in tow.

If he hadn't said the name, they would've been turned back or told to sit and wait. Or separated. Maybe worse.

Three kids on foot with bloody heels and ditch water sitting wrong in their stomachs.

The name had moved something. He didn't fully understand why yet, but he knew it mattered.

Tripp spoke without looking up. "Are we okay, Lo?"

"Yeah," Logan said. "I think we're good."

Charlie lifted his head slightly.

"Where are we going now, Lo?"

"Grandpa Jake's," Logan said. "We're almost there."

Charlie dropped his head back down.

They kept walking.

The road west of the checkpoint felt different. It was quieter. Tire tracks lined the shoulder. Wood smoke lingered faintly in the air. Another barricade stood far behind them. This place wasn't chaos.

It was organized. They were inside.

His headache was still there. His heel still burned with every step. His arms trembled under Charlie's weight.

But something had shifted. The road felt shorter.

In the distance, a water tower stretched above the trees.

"Tripp," Logan said.

"What," Tripp responded.

"You see that?"

Tripp nodded.

A mile. Maybe a mile and a half.

Logan didn't say anything else. He just walked.

One foot. Then the other.

A mile and a half.

CHAPTER 38
JUST KEPT GOING

They continued on, using the water tower as a beacon. The blisters still burned, but something else was pushing through them. He walked a little straighter now.

He hoped his grandparents were there. He hoped they were safe. That the dangers and evil hadn't found them—worse yet, taken them like they took Becca.

"They're tough," he told himself. They were older, and they had resources.

Which also made them a good target.

As his feet kept hitting pavement, moving toward that water tower, he could feel all of it pushing and pulling him at the same time.

"We're almost there, guys," Logan said.

Charlie straightened a little. Tripp's limp eased without him even noticing. It was strange what the mind could do when it believed there was a finish line.

The air changed as they moved farther off the main stretch of highway. Fewer abandoned cars. More open fields. The smell shifted too. Cut grass, damp soil, and livestock close by.

On the right, they passed two muddy ponds Dad and Grandpa had taken them fishing at many times. Logan could almost see himself standing there with a pole, acting like he knew what he was doing.

Just past that was where Logan killed his first deer. He remembered how loud the gun was when it went off, how Grandpa had slapped him on the back, congratulating him like he'd won something. They walked a little faster after that.

They closed in on the small regional airport near where his dad had grown up. Logan felt the familiarity of it, layered with the stories that had been shared over the years. This wasn't their home. But it was home.

They passed Mr. Bank's farm. Logan told the boys how he used to sneak ears of corn off the edge of the field and try to cook them over a fire behind the barn until Grandpa caught him and pretended to be mad about it.

He pointed out the memories as they came. The little boys didn't remember most of it, but they got a kick out of hearing the stories.

The closer they got, the less they felt the miles behind them.

They saw County Road 412 before they saw the house. The sign was still there, tilted a little to the left, like always. Something steady settled in Logan's chest when he saw it. The edge of his grandparents' property ran along that road before cutting back toward the house. Farther up the road were patches of large oak trees Mom used to play in when she was a little girl, sitting at the front of the property, slightly shielding the house and barn from the road.

The boys turned right onto 412, only a couple hundred yards from the front door now. The little boys were giddy and restless.

Just an hour ago, all three could have passed out from pain and exhaustion. All of that was gone.

The pavement was rougher here. Gravel collected along the edges. A mailbox with their mom's maiden name leaned toward the ditch but still stood. The fence line stretched ahead, weathered wood posts, wire pulled tight and patched in places. Beyond it, pastureland. Cows clustered near the far corner, flicking their tails.

Everything looked...normal.

They crested the final rise in the road at the entrance to the long gravel driveway. The magnolia tree near the front door was blooming with large white flowers against dark green leaves. Logan hadn't thought about that tree in years, but seeing it there tightened something in his throat.

Logan stopped at the mouth of the driveway and stood there, breathing slowly, taking it in.

The house.

The barn.

The fence.

The trees.

If he stepped forward, it would be real. His legs had gone heavy. Not from exhaustion. Something else. Like they didn't know how to do the last part.

There were no signs of danger. No signs of trouble. A thin stream of dark smoke rose from the chimney. He could hear cows lowing behind the house.

The house looked like it always had. White metal siding, a few dents near the bottom from years of use. Grandpa Jake had built it by hand with help from church friends and neighbors. The barn sat to the left, darkened by weather, the roof patched in a few different shades of tin.

The air felt heavy. The sight, surreal.

"Is that it?" Tripp asked.

Logan nodded, but couldn't move.

Then the dogs came.

Maggie, the big white lab mix, barked first, sharp and unsure. Her tail was low, hair raised along her back. Scooter trailed behind her, short legs pumping, trying to sound tougher than he was. Logan flinched at the noise before he recognized it.

The dogs ran at them cautiously at first. Tripp called Maggie's name.

Her ears twitched. Her tail started to move. Then she ran the rest of the way and nearly knocked them over, whining, circling, jumping up on their legs. Scooter followed, barking before understanding this was family.

Logan saw the front door open.

An older shape stepped out in jeans, boots, and a pocketed flannel shirt. Rifle already in his hands.

Grandpa Jake.

The dogs danced around the boys as they worked their way toward the house. Gravel crunched under their injured feet. Jake's stance hadn't changed.

He was squinting toward them. The rifle hadn't moved.

They got closer. They were most of the way there before Jake stopped squinting.

His eyes widened just slightly.

The rifle lowered. "Logan?" Jake said.

Grandma Annie appeared behind him. Her hands went to her mouth. She just stared.

Logan bent and picked Charlie back up for the final stretch. His arms were shaking again under the strain. The fatigue still there.

The grandparents came down off the porch faster than Logan had seen them move in years.

Grandpa grabbed Logan while steadying Charlie at the same time. He squeezed his shoulders hard and looked straight at him, eyes wet and searching, like he needed confirmation.

"Boys," he said, voice thin. "You made it."

Logan tried to answer, but nothing came out. Jake looked all three of them over closely. Checking faces. Checking hands. Taking inventory.

Grandma kneeled in front of Tripp and Charlie and pulled them into her. She smelled like soap and something fried at the same time. Logan stood a step back and watched. No one else had held them since Becca.

"Where are your parents?" Grandma asked, already knowing the answer. "They were in Dallas, weren't they?"

"I had hoped somehow they made it home," she whispered. "Or they never left for their trip."

She looked back toward Jake with heavy eyes, saying everything without words.

They moved toward the house together. Logan stepped over the threshold and noticed it without meaning to. The small lip of metal between outside and inside. He had crossed it a hundred times growing up. It felt different now.

Inside, everything looked mostly the same. The same couch. The same lamp in the corner. A few extra supplies were stacked neatly along one wall.

Logan stood there, unsure what to do with his hands. He had been the one deciding where to sleep, when to move, what to ration for two weeks. The space felt unfamiliar. Grandpa Jake pulled him in again, and Logan let himself lean into it.

"Guess who's here with us?" Annie asked the boys.

"Mom?" Charlie asked.

She smiled softly. "I wish. Grandpa Wayne made it in about a week ago. He's been helping out."

Tripp lit up. "Where is he?" he asked.

"He's out at the greenhouse. I'm sure he'll be in soon, after all the commotion," Annie said.

They sat around the kitchen table under working lights. Logan noticed that the windows were covered with blankets. He didn't remember that being a thing before.

The boys drank water like they hadn't seen it before. Logan tried to pace himself and failed.

Jake looked at him. "Where's Becca?"

The room went still. Tripp looked at Logan.

"She didn't make it," Logan said. It was the first time he'd said it plainly. Out loud. To someone who loved her too.

Annie sat down, her shoulders sagging. Jake removed his hat and set it on the table.

No one spoke for a long moment. The only sound was the hum of the refrigerator and the generator rumbling out back.

Jake cleared his throat. "I'm sorry," he said quietly.

The back door opened a few minutes later, and Grandpa Wayne stepped inside, wiping his hands on a rag. He stopped when he saw them. His face shifted from confusion to recognition.

He crossed the room and wrapped his arms around them one at a time. He felt lighter than Logan remembered. But solid.

They asked practical questions after that. Where had they come from? How long had they been walking? How did they cover that distance? Had they seen anyone organized on the way?

The kind of questions adults ask when they're trying to understand.

Annie stood. "You boys look hungry."

They all nodded at once. She moved around the kitchen with ease, pulling out flour, oil, and a box of macaroni. The smell of chicken hitting hot oil filled the room. Logan hadn't realized how much he missed that smell.

Annie worked up a typical grandma meal.

They ate fried chicken tenders, macaroni, and mashed potatoes. Real food. Hot food. Tripp and Charlie didn't complain about anything on their plates. Even the potatoes.

When Annie set a plate in front of Logan, he stared at it longer than he meant to.

He took one bite. The salt burned his tongue. His hands started to shake.

He pressed them flat against his thighs. It didn't help.

He blinked hard. Then again. A tear slipped out. Then more.

"I just kept going," he said.

Jake slid around the table and kneeled beside him, one firm hand on the back of his neck.

"You brought them here."

He didn't say anything else.

Logan's shoulders dropped. His chest hitched once, then again. He let the tears fall without wiping them away, dripping onto the plate.

For the first time since the power went out, he wasn't responsible for the next decision.

He ate slowly after that.

The grandparents watched them closely as they ate. Almost like they were still taking inventory.

Near the end of the meal, Logan noticed Charlie sitting very still.

Too still.

Charlie's hands trembled against the table. His face had gone pale. He slid off his chair and walked to the trashcan without saying anything.

He vomited hard.

For half a second, Logan thought, Not here. Not now.

He jumped up to help.

Jake caught his arm. "We've got him."

Logan hesitated, then stepped back, letting his grandparents take care of him.

Annie pressed her hand to Charlie's forehead. "He's warm." She grabbed the thermometer from the drawer like she'd done it a hundred times before.

Wayne was already filling a bowl with water.

"My belly feels funny too," Tripp said, rubbing it.

"It's the water," Logan said. "We didn't have any, so we had to drink from a stream."

"We were so thirsty."

Jake nodded once. "We'll get them through it."

They laid the boys down on the couch with cool rags. Annie moved quietly between the kitchen and the living room. Wayne adjusted the fan so it pushed air across them.

"Logan, how do you feel?" Jake asked.

"I'm okay," Logan said, surprised that it was true.

With the boys resting inside, Logan and the grandparents stepped out onto the front porch to watch the sun fade behind the oak trees. A breeze carried the smell of grass and distant manure from the pasture.

It was the same sky as in Nashville. Same color. It just felt farther from everything.

Crickets chirped in the background as they sat.

Grandpa Jake sat beside him in silence for a long time. He was looking at the road beyond the fence when he spoke up. "You're safe now," he said.

Logan nodded.

He'd brought them here. Both of them. That was real.

But his parents were still out there. And Becca was still gone. And the world was still whatever it had become.

He looked over the treeline, tracing the fence in his head, still scanning, still calculating. He wasn't sure how to stop.

CHAPTER 39

INSIDE THE FENCE

Jake was watching Logan's gaze.

"You don't have to be on watch right now, Logan," he said confidently.

Logan turned to look at him. Blankly at first. The words took a second to land. He wouldn't have to be the protector now.

Grandpa Wayne and Annie were talking nearby about the little boys. They seemed to be doing all right. Resting and getting much-needed sleep. She mentioned that they were still filthy, but that would be a problem for tomorrow.

Logan listened to the crickets a little longer, sitting in silence. They had made it, and part of him still didn't believe it.

"Can I go to sleep?" he asked Annie.

"Of course." She smiled. "You can have the pullout in the living room."

She got up to guide him inside. She gave him another big hug and looked him over one more time.

She went to the linen closet and took out some clean sheets, a blanket, and a pillow. She laid them out neatly and made the bed while he stood there looking at the clean white sheets. The smell of fresh linen. And how dirty he was.

Annie noticed and laughed. "Don't worry about it. We can clean you and the sheets tomorrow. You need rest." She reached up and brushed his cheek. "Get some sleep. You've carried enough."

Then she returned to the porch with both grandfathers.

Logan sat on the edge of the mattress, realizing how soft it was. It had been a week or more since he'd felt anything comfortable to sit or lie on, for that matter. He gently untied his shoes and pulled the laces out farther than normal, trying to get them as loose as possible. He knew the pain that was about to follow and dreaded the thought of it.

Gingerly, Logan pulled each foot free, biting down hard, his muscles tense. The pain from the blisters and miles came back all at once. Torture almost.

After pulling off his dirty jeans and hoodie, he slid under the covers and lay flat and still. The journey turned over in his mind again and again. He was wired when he should have been exhausted.

From the porch, his grandparents talked and laughed in hushed tones. They sounded happy. Excited. It was reassuring to be there with them. Tonight, he didn't have to be on watch. He could be a teenager.

The hum of the generator was soothing, a quiet reminder that things might be different now.

For a while, he listened closely. Looking for footsteps. Mapping the house in his head.

Checking the locks crossed his mind, but he stayed in bed.

Then he finally drifted off.

Logan awoke late Sunday morning to the front door shutting a little too hard. The clank of metal triggered something in his mind. For a second, he wasn't sure where he was.

Ceiling fan.

Clean air.

No damp tent smell.

He had been out for a while. That deep, restorative sleep you can only get when you truly need it.

He sat up and took stock of the room. His brothers were moving around, still resting on the couch. They appeared to be feeling better, talking together and tickling each other's toes.

"Hey, guys," he said. "How are you feeling?"

"Good," they responded, then went back to their game.

Grandma Annie was in the kitchen with Grandpa Jake. They were already working on breakfast for the boys. A skillet popped softly on the stove, and Logan caught the smell of sausage, eggs, and maybe pancakes.

He slid over to the side of the bed and tested his feet. They touched the cold hardwood floor. Shots of pain ran through them into his legs. He tested again, then stood up, taking on the pain. He made his way over to the table and got off his feet as quickly as possible.

Jake noticed him limping and came over to look at the sores.

"Those look rough, son," he said, scratching his chin. "We'll have to get them cleaned up. Your grandmother already took care of your brothers' feet after they got a warm bath." Jake looked over at them. "That was the first bath I've seen them actually want to get."

Logan laughed at the joke. "Well, I'm right behind them after breakfast."

"Good, you need it!" Grandpa Wayne said as he appeared from the pantry.

Everyone sat down to eat the warm meal Annie had put together for them.

"It's nice sitting at a table again," Logan said. He hadn't realized how much he'd taken it for granted.

"Go get cleaned up, and we'll catch you up on what's going on," Jake told him.

"Does the water work?" Logan asked.

"It does," Annie told him. "The well has plenty of water for us, and the generator keeps the pump running."

She pointed to the pantry where the hot water heater was. "Just be quick. It puts a strain on the generator."

Logan nodded and walked toward the bathroom and shower.

Logan tried to be quick in the shower, but it was hard. He wanted to stay in it forever.

Bracing his hands on the wall, he let the water run. It was washing away more than grime.

His feet took the longest. Skin peeled from several of the raw areas. It was painful, but necessary.

After turning off the water, he dried off with a clean towel that smelled like Grandma. The bathroom mirror was fogged around the edges, and a neat stack of clothes waited for him outside the bathroom. Some were old ones he had left one time or another. He gladly slid into them, feeling new again.

In the kitchen, the boys were carrying on and nibbling at their food. A welcome sight, given their condition last night. They slinked over, limping too, giving him a hug and commenting on how his pants were too small.

Grandpa Jake helped him put some cream on his feet and wrapped them with gauze around the heel and big toe area. He then slipped them into some socks that fit loosely and slid back into his shoes.

"Can you walk okay, Logan?" Jake asked.

"I think so," he said, testing the pressure.

"Let's go take a walk with Wayne and catch up on everything."

The three of them stepped out the back door to a beautiful day.

"It's May first," Wayne said, looking out over the pasture. "Can you believe we're on day fifteen of this thing?"

The other two just shook their heads. It was surreal. The world had essentially ended fifteen days ago.

School would have been almost over. Everyone would have been excited about summer. Now he would actually like to go back to school. That was no longer an option.

They made their way around the property.

"What's it been like here, Jake?"

"Mostly quiet, actually. We've been making it okay. As you know, your dad and I had always talked about something like this." Jake thought briefly. "We had a lot of stuff ready. We have about six months of food, maybe more. Plus, we have the animals. We get milk, eggs, and have meat if we get to that point."

"We're stable. For now."

Logan followed along, curious about the logistics. The grass was wet against his shoes as they walked.

Jake continued. "A lot of folks weren't prepared. They burned through everything quicker than they thought. That's why you see people moving around. They are looking for resources. Food. Water." He slowed a bit. "In some cases, they are taking it." He let that sit for a second.

"Has it been dangerous around here?" Logan asked.

"Not too bad. The first week was the worst for us. Everyone panicked, just like you guys saw. We had our share of looting and even small riots, but everyone sort of banded together. Downtown emptied fast."

Wayne added, "That's the great thing about small communities like this. We all live and work together. We know one another."

"They put together security teams and checkpoints. That helped keep a lot of outsiders from coming in and causing trouble, although we still have to be vigilant."

"Yeah. It didn't feel like that in Nashville. Everyone just looked out for themselves."

Jake was quiet for a second. "Yeah, it's been calm here for the last week. Either that's a good sign, or something or someone out there is coordinating." He didn't elaborate.

Logan changed the subject. "How about gas?"

"We've been running the generator eight to twelve hours a day. Luckily, we had around two hundred fifty gallons of fuel in the big metal tank out there." Jake tilted his head toward the tank on the metal frame.

"Should last us another few weeks if we're smart about it. When that runs out, we step backward."

They walked farther, checking some fence posts and wire. Wayne found a spot that had been cut or broken recently. They weren't sure. He pulled it tight and wrapped a new strand around it.

They looked over the chicken coops, where chickens scratched and clucked in the dirt, and checked on a calf that was a few days old. A new surprise, and much more valuable now than just a few weeks ago.

Wayne pointed out the perimeter and some access points.

"We've had a few people test the fence. We set up rotating watches to be safe. Mostly it was singles or harmless families passing through."

"We try to help where we can, but have to be careful with resources."

"Has anyone tried to band together and set up community sharing? You know, for the greater good type thing?"

Jake laughed. "No, not around here. That wouldn't fly. All of us worked hard for what we've got."

He took a few more steps. "We'll all help where we can. They don't have to gather or combine it."

They made their way over to the old barn and looked down toward the highway. Back toward Memphis.

"Have you seen a lot of folks coming out of Memphis?"

"We have. They are bleeding this way. It's a long walk, as you guys can attest. Some of the ones we talked to said it was really bad there. They just wanted out. To get their families to safety."

Logan paused his stride and looked over at both grandpas.

"This isn't being fixed, is it?"

"No," Jake said without hesitation.

Logan nodded once. He knew.

Something inside him settled. Not despair. Just finality.

"From everything we've learned, all the microchips and newer electronics are dead. Nothing survived unless it was hardened or protected somehow. Those are few and far between."

He stuck his thumb toward the house. "I've been on the ham radio most days, and that seems to be the consensus for our region and likely beyond."

Wayne let Jake finish. "Without chips, most of what we built in the last forty years won't work." He paused longer. "It's going to take a very long time to fix this. Especially around here in rural America."

"What you see is what we get now," Jake said distantly. "For as long as we can hold it."

They stood there looking down the road toward Memphis.

The field was green. The sky was clear. The farm was running like it always had.

But beyond the fence, the world was still breaking.

CHAPTER 40
ROUTINE

Logan was awake before anyone called him.

He lay still for a moment, the way he'd been doing since arriving at his grandparents'. Assessing. The generator was already running out back with a low hum.

The chickens were making noise outside. He could hear the cows shifting in the pasture. Beside him, one of his brothers rolled over, and the sofa creaked.

He sat up and reached for his shoes.

His feet were better than they'd been on the road. The wrapping Jake put on them yesterday had helped, and he'd had two nights of actual sleep, which had done more than he expected. Still, he snugged the laces carefully, trying to keep pressure off the sores. He was dressed and moving before everyone else noticed.

Grandpa Jake was in the kitchen doorway when Logan came down the hall, already in his boots and flannel, coffee mug in hand. He looked at Logan steadily.

"You coming?" he said.

Logan nodded and followed him out the back door.

He'd gotten a general walk-through of the generator the day before. Where it was. That it ran in the mornings and evenings. That the fuel supply was finite. And that was that. This morning

Jake went deeper into the details. Logan paid attention with a different kind of focus than he had yesterday. Yesterday he'd been absorbing. This morning, he was trying to learn.

Jake showed him the fuel gauge on the side of the tank, a simple float indicator with a handwritten scale in Sharpie next to it. Then he walked him through how to read it. He showed him the runtime log they kept on a clipboard hanging just inside the generator enclosure, a plain chart with dates, hours, and fuel used. He explained that Logan would be the one filling it in on his shifts going forward.

"You said yesterday you've got about a hundred gallons left," Logan said.

"Give or take. That's why the log matters. If you're not tracking it precisely, you don't actually know what you have."

Logan looked at the chart. The entries were neat and consistent. Jake had been keeping it since the first day. He thought back to the food inventory Becca had kept at the house, her running list of what they had and what they'd used, always updated without being asked.

He picked up the pencil on the clipboard and looked at the last entry.

"What time did you start it this morning?"

"Six-ten," Jake said.

Logan wrote it down.

Jake ran through the rest: the freezer staying shut, the water heater schedule, a few rules Logan had already started to piece together on his own.

"What's the backup if the generator fails?" Logan asked.

"It depends on what fails. If it's mechanical, Wayne can usually sort it. If it's fuel, we don't have a backup," Jake said plainly. "Worst case, we trade for more or pull it from abandoned cars."

Logan nodded.

Wayne was out behind the barn when they found him, working the west fence line. He moved deliberately, checking wire tension as he went, tugging at the posts. He'd shown Logan the general layout of the property the day before, the blind spot behind the barn, the low spot near the oak trees.

Cans were strung in the brush along the front and west edges.

"There's always Maggie for backup," Wayne said, pointing down at the panting lab.

"Walk with me."

They went north first, then cut toward the back treeline. Wayne wasn't narrating this time. Logan followed, watching what he checked and why. A post that rocked more than it should. Wire sagging where it shouldn't. Ground disturbed near the fence line. Tracks.

At the back corner of the property, Wayne crouched and studied one of the low wires near the brush.

"Anything disturb these?" Logan asked.

"Not recently."

"You said people cut through."

"Yeah, sometimes people cut through," Wayne confirmed. He looked past the wire into the neighbor's tree break. "And when they do, they don't come along the fence line. They come at an angle from the road."

Logan looked at the dip near the oak trees Wayne had shown him yesterday. From here, he could see how someone coming down from the highway at night would naturally find that low ground. The path of least resistance. It led straight to the driveway, then up to the house.

He filed that away.

They finished the west and south lines and came back around to the barn. Wayne checked the cans in the brush along the front again, working each one gently to confirm they were still set right, then straightened and looked at Logan.

"Morning check takes about twenty minutes if you know what you're doing," he said. "You'll do it alone starting tomorrow."

"Yes, sir."

Wayne nodded and headed toward the house.

The middle of the morning settled into the regular rhythm of the farm, which Logan was trying to understand.

He fed the chickens while Tripp hauled water buckets from the spigot to the greenhouse, two at a time, sloshing more with every trip. By the third run, his pants were wet at the knees, but he didn't complain. Logan watched him adjust his grip and keep going.

Charlie played in the dirt near the garden fence with a stick and an arrangement of rocks. Grandma Annie sat on the porch swing nearby, the rusty chain creaking softly while Charlie narrated his game under his breath.

Somewhere down the road, a small engine passed. Charlie looked up. Just a glance. Then he went back to his rocks.

Logan heard it too, but kept working.

He spent the late morning in the barn, straightening tools, stacking hay, cleaning up after the chickens.

The cuts on his hands from the golf cart belt repair were still there, thin and sore when he flexed his fingers. His feet were slower to forgive him.

It was quiet in the barn, and he didn't mind the quiet the way he used to. Before, he would have filled it with a game or a phone.

Now quiet meant something else.

It meant safety—at least for now.

Dust drifted through the light coming in between the boards. The smell of hay and diesel hung in the air. For a minute, standing there with his hands in his pockets, Logan let himself believe that if he kept working, kept watching, and kept learning, their world might stay contained to this farm.

He stayed busy.

In the early afternoon, Jake came around the side of the barn and found him near the old tractor.

He held out a rifle.

Nothing fancy. Not like his dad's, which had been taken away. Just a tool handed to someone who needed it.

"Check the west fence line," he said. "Keep an eye out."

Logan took it. He slid the action back. Checked the chamber. Confirmed it. Closed it. Then let it settle across his forearm. Grandpa Jake watched him do it without saying anything, then turned and walked back toward the house.

With the rifle, the world felt less random. Less unpredictable. He didn't like that, how it made him feel calmer.

Logan stood at the west line.

The pasture opened wide in front of him, high grass bending in slow waves as the wind moved across it. Beyond that, the road cut through in a straight line, pale and empty in the afternoon light. The oak trees near the driveway cast long shadows toward the fence, and the tree break beyond looked darker than it had that morning. He let his eyes travel the distance again, from corner post to treeline to road shoulder, memorizing it.

If something stepped out, he wouldn't just be reacting.

Not anymore.

Time passed slowly. Eventually, he walked back to the barn and handed the rifle to Jake.

Jake winked. "Good man."

After dinner, when the generator had been off for a while and Annie had lanterns going in the kitchen, Logan sat with Jake and Wayne at the table. His brothers were down the hall, already asleep. The house had gone to that particular quiet it got after dark, out here.

He'd been thinking about how to ask since the day before.

"Do you think they could make it?" he said. "From Dallas."

Jake and Wayne looked at him. Wayne answered first.

"Dallas is a long way."

"I know it is," Logan said. "We made it from Nashville. I'm asking if it's possible."

Jake filled in the gaps. "If they're alive, they're moving. That's the most honest answer I can give you. Your parents are strong. They're smart."

Logan looked at the table. Since yesterday, the question had changed. This wasn't about rescue anymore. It was about whether they were still out there.

"Have you heard anything on the radio? Any call signs near Dallas or out that way?"

"Not specific ones," Jake said. "I've got contact with someone near Shreveport and someone in Alabama. Nothing out of Texas yet." He paused. "The bands are opening up more each week. That could change, though a lot of equipment probably got fried in the event."

"That's probably why it's been so quiet," Wayne said.

Logan nodded. He looked toward the dark window over the sink for a moment.

They talked a while longer about the week's schedule: the garden, the fence post on the south line, whether to run the generator an extra hour in the morning to get the water heater fully hot with three additional people. Small things. Adult things.

Before Logan turned in, Jake stopped him in the hallway.

"Tomorrow, you take the full second shift," he said. "Both fence lines, the greenhouse, and the fuel tank."

"Tonight, Wayne and I've got it."

"Yes, sir," Logan said.

"You know where everything is. Good night," Jake said, then went down the hall.

Logan stood in the doorway of the living room where his brothers were sleeping for a moment, listening. Then he went out to the front porch and stood in the dark, looking at the big oak trees and the road beyond.

The property was still. Cans hung untouched in the brush. Limbs barely shifted. The road beyond the fence was empty as far as he could see.

The night air came in off the pasture, cooler again tonight.

Maggie barked once from somewhere near the west pasture.

It sounded sharp. Alert.

Logan stood still, listening.

She didn't follow up. No second bark. No movement from the cans.

His instinct was to step off the porch and check on her.

Instead, he stayed where he was.

Wayne was on watch tonight.

Logan stood there another minute, forcing himself to let it go.

The yard stayed still.

He turned and went back inside. After pulling the door shut behind him, he checked the lock out of habit.

CHAPTER 41

A TEST

Six days passed.

Not quickly and not easily, but they passed. The farm ran on a schedule now, and Logan ran with it. Fence check at first light. Fuel log after breakfast. Second watch. Afternoon shift on the west line. Resource count at night, which Jake had started doing quietly and Logan had started doing with him without being asked. Firewood stacked in rows along the south wall of the barn. Hay moved and re-stacked to get at the older bales first. The generator cycled on and off at the same times each day.

Maggie had figured out his schedule before he had. She fell in beside him at the fence line every morning without being called, moving ahead and circling back, nose working the ground along the wire. Scooter did whatever Maggie did, more or less, though his legs were short enough that the tall grass near the lower fence was a real obstacle. He pushed through it anyway.

Logan knew where the blind spots were now. He knew the dip near the oaks and what it concealed. The back corner of the barn blocked the porch's view of the southwest fence. There was a stretch of lower pasture a person could cross without being seen until they were almost on the house. He thought about these things the way he used to think about game strategy. Angles. High ground.

Jake had stopped explaining things and just started nodding when Logan showed up where he was supposed to be. That was its own kind of acknowledgment, and Logan had begun to look for it.

The evening of the sixth day was the quietest they'd had.

Annie made soup from the garden and what was left of a canned ham, and it was better than it had any right to be. His taste buds were shifting along with his brothers'. Weeks ago they wouldn't have touched the stuff.

They ate at the table with the lanterns going, and Tripp told a long story about something that had happened with the calf that afternoon. It was mostly made up but funny enough that Wayne laughed out loud a couple of times. Charlie had finished his bowl and most of Tripp's before anyone noticed. He sat with his chin in his hand, eyes glazed, not quite asleep but headed that direction.

Jake got up once during the meal to look out the side window. He lingered a while, then came back without saying anything.

Maggie was stretched out on the porch. Scooter was a brown lump near the steps.

The wind moved through the pasture in long, slow gusts.

Wayne leaned back in his chair and looked out the screen door. "The cows are quiet tonight," he said.

Jake set his spoon down and listened for a second before picking it back up. They all finished eating.

The next morning, near midday, Logan heard the engine before he saw it.

He was near the barn when the sound came up the driveway, not fast, not loud, just the particular pitch of a small utility engine working its way over gravel. He moved to where he could see the driveway and watched a dusty side-by-side Gator roll up, an older model, faded green, carrying one person. The man behind the wheel wore a hat pulled low and didn't kill the engine right away when he stopped. He just sat there for a second, like he was deciding something.

Jake came off the porch. Logan followed from the barn.

The man's name was Jonathan. Logan had heard it but hadn't met him. A neighbor from a couple of miles south, someone Jake had known for years. He climbed out of the Gator, shook Jake's hand, and nodded to Logan. The look on his face said whatever he was here for wasn't good.

"Sammy Morgan's place got hit," he said.

Jake went still.

Jonathan's eyes stayed on the ground. He gave the facts the way people do when it hasn't gotten easier to say it out loud. There was an organized group. Four or more, based on the tracks.

They came at night and knew where to go, which was the part that mattered most, the way Jonathan said it. They didn't wander around looking. They went straight to the barn. Straight to the fuel storage. Straight to where the guns were kept.

"They took the food," Jonathan said. "Took the fuel. And they took his guns." He paused. "Sammy and his wife." He paused again. "They didn't make it."

No one said anything for a moment. The rest of the family had gathered around.

Logan knew the name the way you know the names of people your grandparents mention. He was gruff. Didn't talk much. His kids had moved off years ago, and he'd remarried late in life. A good man. He loaned feed to neighbors when they needed it and once shared medicine for a sick cow with Jake without being asked twice. The kind of man who showed up when it mattered and didn't require credit for it.

It felt strange how a person could go from someone your grandparents talk about to gone in one sentence.

Jonathan said he'd ride the rest of the road before dark and check back in by radio if he heard anything else. He climbed back into the Gator and headed down the drive.

Jake stood and watched the Gator until it reached the road. Then he stood there a little longer.

Logan waited.

"That isn't desperate," Jake said. His voice was level. Unshaken. Just working through it out loud. "Desperate people take what they find. They don't know where the fuel is stored. They don't know where the guns are."

He turned toward the barn.

"That was planned."

"They'll move outward," he added. "That's how this works. They hit one place, take what they need, then find the next one."

Logan understood the geometry of it immediately. Sammy Morgan's farm was southwest of here. That direction meant towns. More people. More empty shelves.

They hadn't wandered onto his land by accident. They'd gone where the food was. Where the resources were.

That meant they'd either been told...or they'd been watching.

He didn't say any of that out loud. Jake already knew it.

There was no panic. Just a tightening.

That afternoon, Jake and Wayne walked the lower fence line and added cans along the section nearest the road, stringing them lower than the others, closer to the ground where a boot would catch them in the dark. Logan helped run the wire while Wayne worked the posts and cans.

Logan got rotated into a later watch shift, eleven to two, overlapping with Wayne's window so they doubled up in the late hours of night and early morning. He didn't love being awake at that hour, but he didn't argue with the reasoning. Over the next two days, he reinforced the habit of checking every section of fence twice instead of once, and he started paying attention to the road from the upper pasture in the evenings, watching for headlights or movement that didn't belong. Listening.

Maggie and Scooter were restless at night. Not barking. Just awake. Logan would hear Maggie shift on the porch and lift her head, and he'd lie still and listen. Usually, it was nothing, a possum moving through the brush or the wind picking up. Scooter operated mostly off of Maggie's reaction, which meant that when she relaxed, he did too. When she didn't, neither did he.

Jonathan checked in once by radio the day after his visit. He used the two-meter band. Nothing new from his end. The group hadn't been seen moving farther east yet, as far as he knew.

Jake thanked him, signed off, and spread his hand-drawn map of the property out on the kitchen table. He marked something near the south fence with a pencil. Logan looked at it, but didn't ask. He'd learned that Jake would explain what he wanted explained, and pushing for more usually got him less.

He did notice the mark was near the dip by the oak trees.

Two quiet days passed after the strike on the Morgans.

It wasn't completely quiet. There was still the regular noise of the farm, the work, the meals, his brothers bouncing off each other the way they always had. Tripp had taken to following Wayne around in the mornings, asking questions about everything he did with the patience of someone who had decided to learn a trade. Charlie had started helping Annie in the garden, which mostly consisted of him pulling up things that weren't weeds and bringing them to her apologetically. But he was out there and focused, and that was something. And cute.

The days passed and nothing happened. By the end of the second day, Logan started to breathe a little easier. Not entirely trusting it. There were people out there who wanted what they had.

He was already half awake when Maggie reacted.

It was before first light, that heavy part of early morning when the dark feels thicker than it does at midnight. He'd been lying still, not quite asleep, just coming off his watch, listening to the house. Then Maggie made a sound from the porch, not a bark. A low growl, short and controlled. The kind that meant she had something specific.

Logan was up before he realized why.

He had his shoes on and the familiar rifle in his hands before his brain had fully caught up, moving on the habit of the last eight days. He got to the back door and stopped to listen.

Then the cans.

One. A single metallic tap, thin and brief.

Then another a few seconds later, slightly different in pitch. A different section of fence.

Scooter scrambled up and pressed himself against the door. Maggie was already off the steps, moving toward the lower fence in a straight line, locked in.

Jake appeared in the hallway behind Logan, rifle up, moving fast and quiet. He put a hand briefly on Logan's shoulder, not to stop him, just to announce he was there, and went to the side window. Wayne was already outside somewhere.

Logan moved to the corner of the porch where he had a sight line to the lower fence without being exposed from the roadside. He could see Maggie near the wire, rigid, nose forward, not barking.

Nothing visible. No engine. No voices. No lights.

He held position, watching, and the silence came back slowly.

They stayed that way for a long time. Long enough that Logan's legs ached from crouching. Long enough that the dark began softening at the edges, black turning to deep blue, shapes forming in the pasture.

Wayne came up to meet them. He came from the northeast side.

Nothing came.

When there was enough light to see clearly, Jake said to walk it.

They went to the lower fence first, the section Maggie had moved toward. Logan followed Jake along the wire, looking at the cans and the ground, moving deliberately. Maggie stayed with them, still alert but quieter now. Scooter was more worried about the grass.

Most of the cans were undisturbed.

Near the second post from the corner, one was twisted slightly, not swinging. Just different. Logan had checked it himself. He knew.

Jake crouched at the base of the post.

The ground there was soft from the rain two nights ago, still holding impressions. Logan crouched beside him and looked at what Jake was seeing.

A shoe print. Single. Clear. Deep at the heel. Heavy tread, not like anything they wore on the farm. It came from the direction of the road and stopped at the fence.

Just the one.

No other prints near it. Not a crossing. Not someone who had come through. Someone who had walked to the fence, stopped, and then gone back the way they came.

Jake stayed crouched for a long moment. Then he looked out toward the treeline, toward the low ground Logan had been worried about.

"There was only one," Jake said.

He stood slowly.

"They were testing us."

Logan looked at the print, then at the fence, then at the road beyond the treeline. It wasn't the print that bothered him. It was the idea of someone standing there, measuring what they had.

He thought about Sammy Morgan's place.

Organized people didn't hit a place blind.

They learned it first.

Jake turned and walked back toward the house without saying anything else. Logan stayed at the fence a moment longer, looking at the shoe print in the soft ground.

Then he followed.

CHAPTER 42
OFF GUARD

Back at the house, Jake said what all three of them were thinking.

"They were checking our response."

Wayne nodded. "I think they came from the front corner. Maybe the road. I was on the other side of the house when Maggie went off."

Logan's stomach tightened. "Do you think they will come again? Tonight?" he asked.

The word tonight sat heavier than he expected. He hadn't been thinking that far ahead. Now he was.

"I'm not sure, but we need to be ready now," Wayne said.

"Let's get back to work. Wayne, get some rest. You're going to need it, I'm afraid," Jake said as he walked back outside.

The feeling stayed with him as he followed Jake out and made his way toward the barn. Maggie moved ahead of him like normal, but she kept stopping and looking toward the road. Once she gave a low growl at nothing Logan could see. The wind was pushing from the north. If someone came from the road again, she might not catch them until they were close.

The rest of the day worked as usual. The same rhythm. The same duties.

Logan found himself checking corners. Listening longer than he needed to. The generator hummed steadily behind the house. He had grown used to that sound. It meant water. It meant lights if they needed them. A semblance of normal.

Now it also meant noise.

Annie worked in the greenhouse, Charlie hot on her heels, asking question after question and never caring much about the answers.

Wayne returned to the lineup after resting. He had the early morning shift now and needed the recharge. Tripp joined him immediately. They fed the cows and played with the new calf.

Evening came and went.

Wayne cooked the usual simple dinner that night. The boys played and joked. UNO turned dramatic, and Clue somehow got worse.

Logan laughed at something Charlie said and then caught himself. His focus was still tuned outward. Every now and then he thought he heard something beyond the generator's low hum. He would pause and listen.

Nothing.

Night fell. He needed rest before his watch, but he couldn't bring himself to close his eyes. Each noise or ruffling of covers set his imagination moving. He knew Jake was out there, but was that enough? What did the watchers know? What did they have planned?

It was time for him to join Jake on the double watch. Midnight to early morning. The darkest hours.

He squeezed his rifle as he walked the porch, down the steps, then around the house and back. Every sound mattered. He was on high alert. His eyes scanned the night, using the moon and stars to illuminate the low spot and the far fence line.

If they hit, it'll be at night. The words rolled over in his head.

Halfway through his loop, something shifted in the grass near the south fence. He stopped and brought the rifle up. Maggie lifted her head but didn't bark. Just wind pushing through tall grass.

He exhaled, but it didn't settle him.

He didn't like not knowing.

Jake worked his way around near the barn, back over to the greenhouse, then looped around the fuel and generator areas. They had good coverage, he thought.

The night was dark but quiet. The shift dragged on. It felt slow and heavy. No pings from the metal cans. No alerts from Maggie.

Suddenly, it was over. Still quiet—no intruders.

Logan finally turned in for the night as Wayne took over the last stretch before dawn. By now he was dead tired and suspected he wouldn't have much trouble falling asleep. He lay for just a moment, listening, then looked over to Maggie. She was calm and still, Scooter curled up near her head.

Logan would have to put his faith and safety in Wayne, some metal cans, and an old mixed lab.

He closed his eyes anyway.

The little boys started stirring before everyone else this time. As usual, they were wrestling and asking the grandparents for breakfast. Biscuits were decided on. Annie and Jake worked together, kneading dough and cutting circles. They cooked them on Jake's woodstove to conserve energy.

They used a heavy black Dutch oven with butter layered over the top. Jake kept rotating the pan to keep them even.

The generator hummed faintly outside while the stove popped and cracked.

Two systems keeping them alive.

The biscuits came out moist, fluffy, and delicious. Tripp smothered his with honey. They disappeared quickly to cheers and approval.

Annie cleaned her plate in the kitchen. "We made it through the night, I suppose," she said to the room.

"Yeah, we got lucky. If they come, it'll be dark, you can bet on that," Jake replied.

Logan glanced toward the window without meaning to.

The farm moved through the morning routine as usual. Logan didn't have to look for Jake anymore. He knew what needed doing and just did it. No one redirected him. No one corrected him. He relished the routine and the patterns.

He noticed Jake studying the generator and walked over.

"What's up, Grandpa?"

"The fuel. We're getting critically low now," Jake said.

"How low?" Logan asked, not wanting the answer.

"Maybe only a few days. We'll have to start working on a plan to find more or trade for some." Jake wiped his brow with his flannel sleeve. "Maybe Jonathan has some extra. Or maybe from the cars on the highway."

Logan nodded and added the new problem to his mental list.

No fuel meant no well. No well meant no water.

Tripp ran up to them. "Grandma asked me to get some water for the greenhouse. She and Charlie are in there working."

"You go help them, Lo. I'll work on this problem," Jake said, turning toward the big fuel tank.

Logan and Tripp went over to the spigot near the front of the house. It came directly off the well, a well powered by the generator that was almost out of fuel.

He raised the handle, and water filled the buckets. Sloshing.

Out of the corner of his eye, Logan caught movement near the greenhouse.

Grandma, it flashed in his brain.

Instantly it registered.

The movement was too low. Too controlled.

He looked again as two figures slipped behind the back corner, working up toward the front of the greenhouse. They wore camouflage clothing, dark masks, and had rifles ready in hand.

They weren't wandering.

They were stacking up on the corner.

"Go inside now," Logan told Tripp, shoving him toward the door.

His voice came out sharper than he intended.

Logan covered the short distance quickly to the front porch, where his rifle was sitting against the wall. He picked it up, eyes locked on the front corner of the greenhouse and the door where Charlie and Annie were. He slid the charge handle back and let it go with a metal clack. Safety on.

The greenhouse was angled toward the back of the house and out to the side. There was a blind spot in the back left corner.

He could hear the generator humming near him.

He waited just long enough to confirm, then picked up movement again along the far wall. Two grown figures moving slowly and deliberately toward his family. He had a clear sightline now as they crouched at the front corner, waiting on something or someone.

They hadn't seen him yet.

They thought they had the surprise.

Logan pulled his rifle up and braced against the corner of the house. He checked the greenhouse door one more time before working his dot left, settling it on the first man's chest.

Still crouched. Still waiting.

His breathing felt too loud.

No time.

He made the decision and flicked off the safety.

His finger found the trigger. His breathing went flat.

The gun fired with a roar. The recoil hit harder than he expected from this angle. The first man dropped instantly, folding where he crouched.

Logan followed him down and rechecked the greenhouse door.

Annie hadn't opened it.

He pulled back around to the second man, who had turned and was running back the way he came. Logan fired two or three more times. He couldn't be sure. The rifle bucked against his shoulder. His ears rang sharp and high. The smell of burned powder clouded his nose and eyes.

As he scanned, something hissed past him, followed by a loud metallic impact on the siding just beside his face.

Inches away.

Metal shards and paint sprayed across his cheek.

For half a second, he didn't understand what had happened.

Just behind him, Jake opened up with a barrage of rounds.

Logan spun toward the low spot on his left. Two figures near the trees. He rushed a couple of unaimed shots toward them with no success. Dirt kicked up short. He forced himself to slow down, but Jake was already steady. Measured and firing in two-round bursts.

One person crawled back toward the road and started running once he cleared the trees.

The other lay still.

Silence fell back over the farm.

The generator was still running behind them.

Logan turned back to the siding.

That was where his head had been.

He stared at it for an extra second.

What if it had been a couple inches to the right?

Annie and Charlie peeked around the greenhouse door. Instantly, Annie began screaming and Charlie started crying. The man lay just feet from them. He was armed. Intimidating. Now he was still.

Logan and Jake made their way to the greenhouse, rifles still ready.

"Annie, take Charlie inside, okay?" Jake said.

Without a word, she led Charlie toward the back of the house and inside.

They reached the man and took his weapon, sliding it away in the gravel.

Logan looked down at him, frustrated at the decision he'd been forced to make.

The man was older than he had expected. Not young. Not a teenager playing soldier. His hands were rough. There was a ring on his finger. Dirt under his nails and a scruffy face.

Jake put an arm around his shoulder, sensing what Logan was thinking.

"You protected your family, son."

Logan felt a flicker.

Not guilt.

Not pride.

Something else.

He had not hesitated. He had seen the threat and stopped it.

He'd said he wouldn't let it happen again.

He didn't.

CHAPTER 43
AFTERMATH

The generator was still running.

That was the first thing Logan noticed. Through everything, the shots, the yelling, the ringing in his ears, it had just kept humming behind the house like nothing had happened.

"Let's clear everything, and then we'll come back and figure this out," Jake said, watching in the direction of the road.

Logan nodded and moved.

Wayne came around the barn in a low crouch, rifle up, eyes working along the treeline. He didn't stop or look at anyone. He just kept moving south along the fence, then held at the corner post and watched the road.

Logan covered the greenhouse side.

There was no additional movement. No engines.

Maggie stayed keyed up, pacing the fence with her nose down, circling back every few minutes. Scooter kept close to the porch steps and didn't move from them. He clearly hadn't liked the shots.

Eventually, Maggie settled down.

Jake picked up the weapons from both downed men and carried them to the porch without a word. Logan watched him check each one and set them against the wall with the others in a neat row.

Logan went back to the corner of the house where the bullet had hit the siding.

The gouge was minimal, but it would have been enough. There was a small hole where the metal had curled in on itself. White paint chips and flecks of gray primer were scattered across the concrete below it. He measured the distance from the ground with his eyes, then measured it against where his head had been.

He stood there with his hand flat against the siding beside the hole, not touching it. Just looking.

He waited to feel shaken, but it didn't come. That bothered him more than the hole did.

Inside, Annie was at the kitchen table with both hands wrapped around a cup she wasn't drinking from. The water was cold. It had been cold for a while. Tripp sat across from her with his elbows on the table, watching her face.

Charlie was at the window.

"Is the guy still sleeping out there?" Charlie asked.

Nobody answered right away.

"Why don't you come away from the window, bud," Logan said.

Charlie stepped away and came over to join them at the table.

Annie looked up at Logan. Her eyes moved over him quickly, checking for injuries. When she didn't find any, she looked back down at the cup.

Logan noticed her hands. They weren't shaking badly. Just enough to notice.

He didn't say anything to her. He didn't know what to say. He knew that she had been in the greenhouse when it happened. That she had heard the shots, and that when she opened that door and came around the corner, she had seen what Logan had done.

What he had to do.

He didn't know what that meant to her. He wasn't sure if he wanted to know yet.

So he went back outside.

The burial took most of the afternoon.

Jake chose a spot along the north fence, past the garden, where the soil was softer. Away from the animals. Away from the house.

They worked the ground manually. Two shovels going at the same time. Wayne and Logan traded off while Jake managed the depth and shape. The dirt was manageable on top, but harder underneath. It fought them.

They didn't talk much.

At one point, Wayne said, "Nobody wins in something like this."

Not to anyone in particular. Just out loud.

Logan kept digging.

They lowered the first man in, then the second. No formal words. Jake stood still for a moment with his hat in his hands, head down, then put it back on and shook his head slightly.

Logan stood at the edge and looked at the ring on the man's finger as they covered him. A plain band, gold or something close to it, dulled with wear. It caught the light one more time before the dirt covered it.

Someone had been waiting on him somewhere. Or maybe they had been taken, like Becca.

The thought should have made him feel worse. Instead, it just made his grip tighten around the shovel.

He put the shovel back in the ground and scooped.

By the time they were done, his hands had blistered. Aching, he pressed them against his dirty jeans and headed back toward the house.

He waited the whole walk back to feel something heavier than the weight of the shovel.

It still didn't come.

Dinner was quiet.

Annie heated soup from the garden and set it out without saying much. The little boys ate. Tripp glanced at Logan every few minutes like he was trying to read something. Charlie stayed close to Annie all evening, following her between the kitchen and the table, not letting her get too far.

Logan ate and kept his focus on the outside. It was easier than looking at the faces around the table.

The generator went off earlier than usual. Jake turned it off to conserve fuel and said as much.

They used the double watch again that night. Wayne took the first half, Logan the second, and Jake mixed in the middle.

Logan sat in the dark near the back corner of the porch, where he could see the south fence and the low spot at the same time. Every sound came through clear. A distant dog somewhere northeast. Wind in the pasture. The settling noise the siding made around two in the morning when the temperature dropped.

Maggie lifted her head a couple of times. Both times, Logan went still and sharpened his focus. Both times, she lay back down.

No second wave came.

He ran the fence check at first light before anyone was up. Everything was where it should be. The security cans were undisturbed. The soft ground still held their prints near the corner post.

He came back inside and made coffee.

As morning came, Jake reviewed the fuel situation.

He stood at the tank with his clipboard, tapping his pencil against the float indicator. Logan stood beside him and looked at the Sharpie scale on the side.

It wasn't good.

Logan looked at the numbers Jake had written in the log. He understood what it meant without needing it explained further.

"We need to go find more," Logan said.

Jake looked at him.

"We'll go together."

They left early the next morning with rifles slung over their chests. Just the two of them, on foot, with a hand siphon and four empty jugs. Logan carried two, and Jake carried two, and they walked down to the highway where the abandoned vehicles had been sitting since day one.

Logan looked around at all of it. "It's been over a month now," he said toward the road.

Jake paused at the thought of it, but didn't respond.

The road was mostly empty in both directions. The cars just sat there like they had for the last thirty-something days. Doors still open on some, trunks up on others. Morning fog lay low across the fields beyond the shoulder.

Logan worked the hand siphon while Jake watched the road. Then they switched. It was slow work. The first two cars had almost nothing in their tanks. The third and fourth gave them something measurable. By the time they finished, they had enough to matter. Not a surplus. Just enough to push the timeline out.

Logan carried his two jugs back. He didn't think too much about being outside the fence now.

That was new.

A couple of weeks ago, even a short trip off the property would have pulled everything tight in his chest. Now he just scanned the road, calculated cover, and kept moving.

He noticed it on the walk back. The way his eyes moved without being told to. The way he automatically kept himself on the side of the road that had the better sightline. The way he looked at angles and access to cover. He tracked potential concealment spaces for threats.

He didn't decide to do any of that. It just happened now.

A couple more days passed without incident. Just a quiet routine.

No tracks at the fence. No sounds in the night beyond the usual. Maggie settled back into her normal rhythm. Even Scooter seemed less jumpy.

They heard Jonathan's Gator come up the driveway in the afternoon, dust trailing behind it. He climbed out and shook Jake's hand, then noticed the patched siding near the corner of the porch.

He looked at it for a second.

Jake gave him a brief, even answer. Jonathan nodded along, his eyes narrowed, but didn't ask more.

They stood in the shade of the porch while he talked through what he'd heard on the road. No new incidents reported nearby. The group that had been moving east hadn't been tracked recently. Either they'd pulled back or shifted direction entirely.

"I don't think they're gone," Logan said.

Jonathan and Jake both looked at him.

"They tried to hit us. It went sideways. And now they're quiet," Logan said. "I bet they're regrouping."

Jonathan looked at Jake.

Jake didn't disagree.

Jonathan shifted his weight and reached into his vest pocket. He pulled out a folded piece of paper with handwritten notes.

"There's something else." He looked at them. "Have you been monitoring the two-meter repeaters?"

"Not recently," Jake said. "Nobody's really been using two meters. Plus, we've been busy since the attack."

"There was a CQ call yesterday afternoon. Someone was asking for you by call sign." Jonathan looked down at his notes. "They asked if you were okay. They wouldn't give names or a location." He paused. "They said they were heading this way."

Jonathan folded the paper once in his hands.

"Whoever it was, they knew enough to be careful."

The porch went quiet.

Logan felt something shift in his chest.

He tried to keep his face steady.

Jonathan glanced toward the door, where Annie had gone, still in the kitchen. She was holding a dish towel with both hands, not moving. She stared back at them.

"The guy said it twice," Jonathan added. "Same call, same message. It was a strong signal on the repeater. I'm not sure which part of the net they were on, though."

Logan looked at Jake.

Jake had gone still, the way he did when his mind was working through something, quietly, behind serious eyes.

He didn't say it was them.

But he didn't say it wasn't.

The radio on the shelf inside the kitchen had been quiet for a week. Now Logan thought about it differently.

Someone with a good signal who knew the repeaters. Someone who knew Jake's call sign. Someone who wouldn't give a name or a location and still said they were heading this way.

He didn't let himself finish the thought all the way. Just held the weight of it.

Jonathan tucked the paper back into his pocket and said he'd keep listening. He climbed back into the Gator and headed down the driveway.

Logan watched him go.

When he looked back, Jake was still standing where he'd been. Hat in his hand now. Turning it over by the bill.

Annie had set the dish towel down on the counter. Her hands rested flat on top of it.

Neither of them spoke.

Charlie came through the back door at a run, already asking about something that had nothing to do with any of it. His voice filled the porch, loud and ordinary.

Logan looked out past the fence line toward the road west.

He thought about the distance.

He thought about the things he knew could happen on a road that long. He'd seen it.

But he also thought about someone calling for Jake by call sign. Keeping names quiet. Still moving this way.

And for the first time in weeks, he let himself think about the possibility that they might make it. That they were still out there trying to get to them.

He didn't let himself stay there long.

But it was there.

CHAPTER 44
AT THE GATE

Logan woke before the sun broke.

For a moment, he didn't move. He lay still, listening to the wind in the pasture. The chickens shifted in the coop, soft clucks and the occasional complaint from one of the hens. A loose birdhouse rattled on its pole near the garden. The generator was still off at this time of morning.

Each sound registered without effort.

Then he reached for the rifle.

Not because he heard anything wrong. Just because that's what he did now.

The kitchen was dim when he came down the hall. The coffee supplies were already laid out from the night before. His doing. He finished prepping it without much effort.

The radio sat on the counter now. Its new home. At some point in the last week, Logan had moved it without asking, and nobody had moved it back or argued.

He flipped the rocker switch on the side and scrolled through the repeater channels, then switched to the upper sideband frequencies, scrolling carefully and listening.

It was mostly static. Occasionally, a faint structured tone somewhere in the noise that turned out to be nothing.

After adjusting the squelch slightly, he waited.

Still nothing.

A few minutes later, he finally turned it off.

Jake came in from the back door and poured himself a cup. He watched Logan work the knobs, then turn the radio off without saying a word. He just sipped his coffee and leaned against the counter.

Tripp wandered in a little while later, still wobbly from sleep.

Logan looked at him. "Good morning. Can you go check on the chickens and feed them for us? Come back and tell me how many you count."

Tripp looked up and smiled.

He pulled on his little boots at the door and went out.

Logan drank his coffee. He needed it now.

When Tripp came back, he reported it like a soldier might. "The chickens are fed. We have eleven hens and three roosters."

"So we have all of them?" Logan asked.

"Yep."

Logan nodded and clapped his shoulder. He didn't praise him or make a thing of it.

Annie was at the sink. She had been watching the whole exchange. Logan only caught it when she moved to dry her hands.

Jake smiled at Annie, then stepped out the back door with his cup.

Mid-morning, Jake came back inside and turned the radio on again. He moved through the same channels Logan had checked earlier, slower and more deliberately, adjusting knobs and clicking switches like he was looking for something specific.

Still nothing.

Tripp was sitting at the table playing with army men. He looked between Jake and the radio, then said it.

"That thing Mr. Jonathan was talking about. The call on the radio." He paused. "Do you think it was Mom and Dad?"

Jake looked at him. He hadn't expected that.

He took a breath. "I don't know, bud. It could be a lot of people. The message wasn't very specific."

Tripp looked at Logan.

Logan was watching the radio. He didn't offer anything. The hope was there. It had been there since Jonathan's visit, sitting just under his chest. He wasn't going to say it out loud or encourage his brothers. That wouldn't be fair.

Jake clicked the radio off.

The kitchen settled back into quiet.

The afternoon moved forward. The usual routines. Just survival now. Moving along the same way it had for the last few weeks.

Logan ran the west line with Maggie just before four. She moved ahead of him with her powerful nose working the ground and air around them. Logan's eyes scanned the normal spots. He stayed vigilant. Intrusion could come at any time now.

There was nothing disturbed or out of place this time. Too quiet. Like it had been since the last attack.

He stood for a minute and looked out toward the road. His rifle rested across his forearm. He tracked the wind direction automatically, southeast, light, maybe five miles an hour. He noted the treeline and the shadows it would throw in another hour when the sun dropped lower. He thought about the low spot by the oaks and what it looked like from the road.

Dusk settled in fast.

Jake had shut the generator off twenty minutes earlier. He was right on schedule. The shadows came. The property went quiet the way it did every evening, that drop in ambient noise when the rumble stopped and everything else filled back in. The cows at the far end of the fence. A loose tin can tapping.

The family had drifted to the front porch. No particular reason. Just the end of the day pulling everyone together.

Logan was on the steps. Tripp beside him. Charlie was on the floor behind them, pushing rocks around in some game only he understood.

Then the engine.

Not a tractor. Not Jonathan. It was different, somewhere down the road. It was coming toward them from the west, getting louder at a steady pace.

Nobody spoke.

Logan tilted his head.

Tripp looked up and said, "Do you think—"

He didn't finish.

Charlie looked up from his rocks with a bright look. "Is it them?"

Annie took a step forward from where she was standing near the door. Just one step.

Jake said nothing. He was already listening in the same way Logan was, working the pitch and rhythm, trying to place it.

Logan didn't move toward the road. Didn't step off the porch. He listened to the engine and tried to read it. It was moving slowly, but it was moving toward them.

He waited.

The vehicle came into view on the road.

They didn't recognize it. It was a large SUV of some sort. Faded red with big, knobby tires.

More than one shape moved behind the glass. It slowed at the edge of the property line.

It didn't turn in. No headlights flashed. No horn. No friendly wave or acknowledgment.

It just sat there at the road, idling roughly.

Hope faded.

Three figures stepped out. Intentional spacing between each of them. They moved like they knew what they were doing. Two of them were armed. They were dressed the same way the last guys had been.

Logan already had the rifle up when the doors opened.

One of the men raised binoculars toward the house.

The engine kept running.

Logan's thumb found the safety. Click.

Jake stepped up beside him. "Not yet."

Logan flicked it back on and lowered the barrel slightly. He understood. They were at the road. Outside effective range. Nothing to shoot at yet and every reason to wait.

He calculated instead.

If the one on the left moved toward the fence, that was the blind low spot. If the vehicle started forward, he had seconds before they reached the gate. He didn't know how many were still inside the vehicle either.

His finger rested on the receiver above the trigger. His breathing stayed even.

The man with the binoculars held them on the house for a long moment. Logan could see the glass catch the last of the sun. A brief hard glint. Then the man lowered them and said something to the others.

One of them turned and walked toward the gate, his eyes on the family.

He didn't move fast. He reached the gate and stopped.

He just stood there and looked at it. Looked toward the chain, then focused on the posts on either side. His eyes moved along the fence line in both directions. He was studying it.

Then he turned around and walked back to the vehicle.

They climbed back in one at a time, doors closing without hurry. The SUV idled another moment. Then it rolled backward, straightened in the road, and turned back west.

It didn't race away. Just moved away at the same methodical pace it had arrived.

Logan kept the rifle up until the engine faded completely, and the road was empty again.

Then the quiet followed.

Charlie said it softly, almost to himself. "It wasn't them."

No one answered.

The words sat there on the porch with all of them.

Logan lowered the rifle.

He knew his parents. They wouldn't have stopped. They would have come through the gate and up to the house, because that's what you do when you've been trying to get somewhere for a month.

You don't sit at the road and measure.

It wasn't them.

But they were out there somewhere. And he believed they were still coming.

He would be here when they did.

What stayed with him wasn't the SUV. It was the man at the gate.

The way he watched them. The way he studied the chain. The posts. The fence line.

Like he was deciding whether it was worth it.

Jake stood beside him. The family was behind them both.

Logan looked out at the dark empty stretch of road where the SUV had been long after it was gone.

He understood now.

The world wasn't done testing them.

And he would be ready.

EPILOGUE

David set the handheld ham radio on the cracked vinyl seat between them and listened as the static settled in again.

The old Ford rattled underneath them.

It had been blue once. Now it was mostly rust and sun-faded paint from years of sitting out in the open.

But it ran. That was all that mattered.

"Well," David said, keeping his eyes on the road. "At least we got someone."

Nicole looked over at him. "What was his name? Jonathan?"

"I think so," David said. "I'm glad the repeaters are still working."

"Me too," Nicole responded.

David glanced down at the little radio. "I just wish we had something with more range than this handheld. Two meters only gets you so far. I'm not sure your dad even monitors two meters."

Nicole stared through the windshield at the road ahead. "I hope Dad gets the message somehow."

She was quiet for a second.

"You should've used actual names," she said. "We should have told them we were okay and that we were coming."

David nodded but didn't answer right away.

They passed another dead car on the shoulder, a gray sedan sitting crooked with both driver-side doors open. Someone had already torn through it. The glove box was open. Trunk up. There were clothes scattered across the road.

Nicole watched it move past her window.

"You can't do that now," David said.

"Why not?" Nicole asked.

"Because we don't know who's listening."

Nicole's mouth tightened.

"If we use names, we put them at risk," David said. "We put ourselves at risk. Names, places, directions, family. All of it matters now. We have to be careful."

Nicole didn't argue. She just looked back out her window.

The road rolled on ahead of them, two gray lanes with grass pushing up through the cracks. Pine trees crowded them on both sides. Every so often, the smell of honeysuckles drifted in through the open windows, thick and sweet.

It should have felt peaceful. Like home.

It didn't.

"I wonder how bad it is there," Nicole said quietly. "Lord, I hope the kids made it."

David tightened his hands on the wheel.

"If it was at all possible, Becca got them moving," he said. "She knows the plan."

"She's never had to do anything like this," Nicole said.

"None of us have."

Nicole looked over at him then, and he could see everything she was trying not to let out. The fear. The exhaustion. The part of her that had been running on nothing for weeks and still refused to break.

"Do you think Logan remembered enough to help her?" she asked.

David looked back at the road.

He pictured Logan half-listening at the kitchen island, pretending he didn't care whenever David talked through the plan. If everything goes down, we go south and get to the farm. Above all, protect your brothers.

He had listened.

David knew he had.

"Yeah," David said. "I think he did."

Nicole blinked hard and looked away.

"He's only thirteen, and the other boys are so little."

"I know."

David swallowed. "But he has it in him."

The truck vibrated on.

They had come through Memphis. They didn't want to talk about it, and hadn't slept right since.

A city wasn't supposed to look like that. He had understood things could fall apart. He had talked about it plenty, even planned for it. Maybe too much. Power, supply chains, fuel, communications, food. All of it held together by thinner strings than most people wanted to admit.

But understanding it and standing in the middle of it were different things.

Memphis had looked like a warzone. Only worse, somehow.

In a war, at least you were supposed to know who the enemy was.

Now there was no front line. No clear side. No uniforms. No one to point to and say they were the problem. Just people who were scared turning on people who were also scared, and no way to know from a distance who was desperate, who was dangerous, and who still had enough in them to be decent.

Those memories would haunt his sleep for a long time.

That night, they found a place to stop off a county road in north Mississippi. An old equipment shed tucked behind a tree line where the truck was hidden from the road.

They didn't build a fire or talk much. The journey sat heavy on them.

They ate what they had and split a bottle of warm water that tasted like plastic.

Nicole took first watch. David woke around midnight and took the rest until sunrise.

As daylight broke, he tried the radio again.

He only heard static. They tried reaching Jonathan again, but no one responded.

David left the radio on, listening as they packed up what little they had and prepared to leave.

Before setting out, he tried one more time while Nicole watched and listened closely, leaning over the rusted hood of the old Ford.

"CQ, CQ, this is—" David stopped himself before saying his call sign. Old habits were hard to kill.

He keyed the mic on the small handheld again.

"CQ, CQ. Looking for any station near Corinth or Walnut. Any station near Corinth or Walnut, come back."

Just static.

He waited.

Nothing.

He lowered the radio.

Nicole looked at him.

"We keep going," he said.

She nodded and climbed into the old truck.

They rumbled back out onto the highway and kept pushing toward Corinth.

The truck was a '72 Ford F-100, and it ran about as well as it looked. They had discovered it abandoned outside Hot Springs, Arkansas.

The truck would turn over but wouldn't fire. David found the problem under the hood. One of the ignition wires had worked loose from the coil. Once he tightened it back down, the old Ford stuttered back to life.

Since then, they had siphoned gas from dead cars they passed along the way.

Analog was the way to go. He had always known that.

No screens. No sensors. No computer telling the engine what it could and couldn't do. Just steel, fuel, spark, and air.

Nicole had made fun of him for talking like that more than once.

She wasn't making fun of him anymore.

By the time they pushed deeper into Mississippi, the land started to feel familiar.

The roads seemed narrower. The fields opened up. Old barns sat back from the pavement with faded tin roofs. Kudzu vines swallowed everything that had stopped being looked after.

David caught himself checking the odometer every few minutes even though he already knew the distance. They were getting close.

Nicole leaned forward slightly, watching the road signs as they passed.

"There it is," she said as a green sign stood ahead on the right shoulder, half-faded and dirty.

WALNUT

David felt something loosen in his chest and tighten again almost immediately.

Fifteen miles from Jake's.

Fifteen miles from answers.

Fifteen miles from whatever was left.

Nicole's hand reached toward the dash, like she needed to steady herself.

They passed a wide intersection at the edge of town. An old gas station sat dark on one corner, windows busted out, the pumps stripped down. David slowed without meaning to. This place had been ransacked just like everything else.

They pushed through the intersection, weaving between stalled cars long abandoned.

That was when he saw it.

An old Bronco came toward them from the direction of Corinth. It was faded red and, like the F-100, had seen better days.

David sat a little straighter. Nicole did too.

It was one of the only vehicles they had seen running in days. Maybe weeks. They had seen a tractor, an old motorcycle, and a few four-wheelers. But not much else.

The Bronco rolled closer, engine low and rough. As it passed, David looked over without turning his head too much.

Three men sat inside. They were middle-aged and hard-looking. Capable.

That was the word that came to him.

He didn't like it.

All three of them looked straight into the truck as they passed.

David kept his speed.

Nicole's voice dropped. "David."

"I see it," he responded.

He looked into the rearview mirror. The Bronco kept going for a few seconds.

Then the brake lights came on.

His stomach went cold.

The Bronco slowed near the intersection behind them. For a second, it just sat there in the road.

Then it turned left, looping around back behind them.

Nicole looked at him. Her eyes were wide.

David reached down between the seat and the door and wrapped his hand around the 1911 he'd traded for in Dallas.

Thank You

Thank you for reading. If you enjoyed this book, please consider leaving a review on Amazon. Reviews help other readers discover the story.

You can also visit: Https://kevinhawkinson.com

About the Author

Kevin Hawkinson writes grounded survival fiction focused on family, resilience, and the quiet discipline required to endure uncertain times. His stories explore how ordinary people adapt when the world shifts beneath their feet.

By day, he works as a commercial insurance professional, where risk, preparation, and worst-case scenarios are part of the job. By night and on weekends, he writes stories shaped by the same questions that often follow him home: What would happen if the systems we count on suddenly failed? Who would we become? And how far would we go to protect the people we love?

Preparedness-minded, an outdoors enthusiast, and a licensed ham radio operator, Kevin spends more time thinking about contingency plans, communication systems, training, and gear than most people probably should.

He lives in the American South with his family.

The Ones We Protect is his debut novel.

www.kevinhawkinson.com

www.ingramcontent.com/pod-product-compliance
Lightning Source LLC
LaVergne TN
LVHW040213110826
845155LV00031B/719

* 9 7 9 8 2 3 4 1 0 4 8 2 3 *